The Nearly Dearly Departed Club

ANTHONY GRACE

THE END

CHAPTER ONE

Lucas Thorne was about to crash.

He could see it on his dashboard. The flickering dial on the speedometer. Forty … fifty … sixty miles per hour in a residential area. Throw in the winding roads that refused to straighten. The angry horns as he cut up fellow drivers or swerved to avoid them. The cheers and jeers from boozy revellers enjoying a Saturday night out in North London. It wasn't their fault; it was an inbuilt reaction. An unavoidable habit. Who didn't look and then look again when a police car flew past at over twice the legal speed limit?

And then there was the rain. The constant bloody rain. Lashing down on the windscreen. Obscuring his vision.

Thanks for that. You're welcome.

Yes, Lucas was well aware that he could crash at any moment. And yet he also knew that slowing down just wasn't an option. Not until he had done his job. What he was paid to do. No, it was more than that. His duty.

You can't just let them get away with it.

The *them* in question was a burnt orange Ford Focus that

had shot three red lights in quick succession before accelerating hard when the driver had clocked the flashing lights in his rear-view mirror. A swift check back at base had revealed that the car's owner was a Mr Percy Sharman, aged seventy-eight, retired Headteacher, no points on his record.

Percy Sharman wasn't driving now, though.

The kid that had raced past Lucas was closer to seventeen than seventy-eight. Up until a few minutes ago the car hadn't been reported stolen, but it would be. Probably first thing tomorrow morning when Mr Sharman climbed out of bed and opened his curtains. By then the Focus would be written off or sold on. Either way, it wouldn't be heading back to its owner.

Unless …

Lucas touched the accelerator and the Skoda sped up. The police had used a Skoda as their patrol car of choice ever since the turn of the Millennium, give or take the odd year or three. It was safe and reliable and, perhaps most important of all, good value for money. Whatever their reasons, Lucas couldn't have cared less. He could drive anything. Like the Skoda, he was safe and reliable. Always in control. He hadn't had a crash in over ten years and, despite what his head told him, he had no wish to start now. Especially not for some spotty little teen in fake gold and poor imitation knock offs.

You can't just let them get away with it.

Sixty-five miles per hour …

The Focus took a sharp left, barely slowing as it swung around the corner. Lucas followed accordingly. The Skoda juddered slightly, but that was all. Nothing to fret about.

Lucas wiped the sweat from his forehead before it dripped into his eyes. The kid in the stolen car knew the roads well. A local then. Born and raised on the streets of Edmonton. Lucas could call on some knowledge, but it clearly wasn't enough. Whilst the kid let the steering wheel run freely through his fingers, Lucas had to hold on tight and concentrate. Take in his surroundings.

Focus on the Focus.

The kid had edged away from him. Not by much, but enough to get Lucas thinking. Dare he go any faster?

The decision was taken out of his hands when he spotted something in the middle of the road. It had appeared from nowhere, wandering into the traffic without care or consideration. Hood up, head down, hunched over, Lucas had no idea if it was a man or a woman. Not that it mattered. His first response was instinctive. Protect the public. Without missing a beat, he veered out of his lane and tried to mount the pavement. It was a heavy collision. Hitting the kerb at an awkward angle, the tyres screeched and the car shuddered and shook as it skidded on the wet concrete.

Lucas tensed up, fearing the worst.

The impact was powerful enough to tip the Skoda onto its side. It began to roll. Once … twice … three times across the pavement before it smashed into a lamppost. When it finally ground to a halt it was on its roof.

The Focus, meanwhile, raced off into the distance. For the time being at least, the kid had escaped. He would live to fight another day.

Unlike Lucas.

Upside down, his body straining against his seat belt, he felt nothing. No pain. No panic. All he knew for sure was that this was it. He was drifting away. He couldn't move, but he no longer cared. His eyes were closed, but he could still see a darkness falling over him. The kind of darkness that takes hold and refuses to let go. That suffocates the life out of you. That swallows you whole.

Was any of it worth dying for? The chases? The fights? The abuse? The job?

No, probably not.

Still, you can't just let them get away with it, can you?

CHAPTER TWO

Chin up, chest puffed out, Tommy O'Strife strolled casually between the mounds of rubble, discarded scaffolding poles and murky, brown puddles that made up much of the abandoned building site in Hackney.

Midnight was fast approaching. As Tommy had expected, the site was deserted. Sombre and subdued. And dirty. Absolutely filthy, in fact. Whose idea was it to meet in a shithole like this?

Fearful of where he was about to tread next, Tommy slowed his step so he could take a look around. He spied the three goons immediately. They were stood beside a black Land Rover. The car of choice for prosperous farmers, minor royalty and your bog standard local gangster.

The difference being that prosperous farmers and minor royalty didn't tend to meet on abandoned building sites at midnight.

Tommy battled to control his breathing as he ambled towards the car. In … out … in … out. No need to shake it all about. He was jumpy enough already, thank you kindly. Naturally, much of the blame lay at the invisible feet of his nefarious partner in crime. His best friend in the whole wide world.

Cocaine.

Also known as that evening's stimulant of choice.

Tommy struggled to remember how much he had snorted before he left the bar. Grams. Plural. More than usual if truth be told. Like it or not, he would have to rein it in from now on. Ease off it a little. Too much of a good thing always seemed to end in disaster. Everybody knew that.

And yet today wasn't tomorrow. The night was still young and so was Tommy. No need to put a dampener on things if he could help it.

To a man, the three goons by the Land Rover were all small and stocky with black bomber jackets, stonewashed jeans and scuffed biker boots. Skinheads and snarls mixed with cheap steroids and florescent energy drinks. Given the chance, they'd rip out your tongue and swallow it right in front of you.

The solution? Don't give them the chance. Obvious really.

Tommy tried to conceal a smirk as he edged closer to the goons. Why did all Eastern European gangsters look and dress exactly the same way? Maybe they had to sign an agreement before they were allowed to start. Thou shalt not break the mould. Stick to stereotype. Admittedly, it had always worked in the past and would, undoubtedly, work in the future.

Just not tonight.

Rewind a few years, months even, and Tommy would have felt intimidated by such a show of strength. Not anymore, though. These days he was familiar with the *facade*. The boiling rage and bulging veins were just a substitute for a lack of intelligence. Anybody could punch someone in the face. Kick them in the balls. But not many people could duck and dive and, ultimately, stay alive when the odds were stacked so heavily against them.

Not like Tommy.

He stopped when he drew level with the Land Rover. Smiled. 'Good evening, boys. You with Kamil?'

The oldest of the men stepped forward. He had greying stubble and a squint in one eye. 'I *am* Kamil.'

Tommy didn't attempt to conceal his surprise. 'Wow! I'm … erm … honoured. Truly. I wasn't expecting the big man himself to grace me with his presence.'

That was greeted with silence.

'I'm Tommy. Tommy O'Strife. I work for … *with* the Marquis brothers.'

Kamil grunted. 'Is that supposed to scare me?'

'Not in the slightest,' said Tommy, shaking his head. 'Just making small talk, that's all. Still, I guess we could always get straight down to business if you prefer.'

'I prefer,' said Kamil. 'You have the money, yes?'

Tommy lifted a black holdall. 'It's all here. One hundred and fifty grand in used notes. If you don't trust me—'

'I don't trust you,' Kamil echoed.

Tommy nodded. 'Fair enough. You can count it if you like. Lay it all out in the back of your car and try not to let it blow away. It won't take long for your boys to run out of fingers, though. One … two … err …'

The goon to Kamil's right lashed out suddenly, catching Tommy in the chest with the palm of his hand.

'Relax, brother,' Tommy grinned. 'That was a joke. I was just trying to lighten the mood.'

'I am not your brother,' spat the goon.

'It was a term of endearment. I'm well aware that we're not actually related. You're nowhere near as handsome as me for a start.' Tommy stopped talking. Shook the holdall. 'There's your money, Kamil. We're good, right?'

'It is late.' Kamil passed the holdall to the third man, who placed it in the Land Rover. 'I only work with people who deliver on time.'

'You'll have to take that up with the Marquis brothers,' said Tommy. He peered over his shoulder. He had heard something, a shuffling sound, but there was nothing there. 'This has been nice, but I've really got to shift,' he said, edging away. 'I'm a young man and young men have their needs. I'm sure you understand. Until we meet again …'

With that, Tommy turned back the way he had just come. Repeated the mantra. *Walk, don't run.* His mind was racing, though. So, that was the famous Kamil Milik. Not that impressive up close. Quite unremarkable, in fact. Still, you could probably say the same about Hitler or Mussolini at first glance. Short man syndrome at its most extreme. Angry from the toenails up.

Tommy had almost left the building site behind when the Land Rover pulled up beside him. The passenger side window dropped to reveal Kamil, stony-eyed and deadly serious.

'I'd like to send a message to the Marquis brothers,' he began sullenly. 'A personal message. From me to them.'

Tommy hesitated. 'Sure. I can pass it on later.'

'You can pass it on *now*.' With that, Kamil Milik poked a Glock 19 out the gap in the window. It was a gun Tommy had seen on many occasions. That he had used from time to time, mostly for bravado. Now there was one pointing straight at him.

Kamil didn't wait to pull the trigger. The bullet hit Tommy in the chest, just above his heart. He staggered forward, unsteady on his feet, before slumping to the ground a moment later.

'Go!' ordered Kamil. Settling back in his seat, he passed the gun to the man behind him as the Land Rover accelerated out of the building site. Workmen would find the body eventually. It would come as a shock, of course, but they would soon get over it. As would the police. One less scumbag on the streets of East London was nothing to stress about. If anything, Kamil had done them a favour. Just another sad casualty of the warring drug gangs.

Rest in peace, Tommy O'Strife. You won't be missed.

CHAPTER THREE

Mercy Mee climbed into the ring as the cheers of the crowd reverberated around the old barn.

She felt good. Pumped up. In the shape of her life.

She was a damn fine boxer. People told her that every day, on repeat, but she knew it anyway. Yes, she trained hard – seven days a week without fail – but it was much, much more than that. Any joker could train hard. Put the hours in. *I want it. I need it. It means everything to me.* But not many boxers had her natural talents. Her power. Her reflexes. Her speed of thought and foot. Quite simply, Mercy knew how to win.

But then she also knew how to lose.

That evening she had travelled to a remote farm on the outskirts of Gloucester. It was a long way from her home in Stevenage, but it was worth it for the pay packet. Cash in hand, straight in the back pocket. No questions asked because nobody cared what you had to say anyway.

Despite her best efforts, Mercy couldn't help but recall the exact moment she had given up on her ambition to be a professional boxer and switched, instead, to the somewhat shady, always volatile underground bare-knuckle scene. It was Asif, Mercy's trainer, manager and all-round dogsbody, who had first broached the possibility. Small and slightly built, Asif dressed like a bus driver who had lost a ridiculous amount of weight in an incredibly short space of time. He spoke softly with the merest hint of a lisp and always shook everybody – men, women and children – by the hand. Promoters respected him, though. He had studied economics at university which always seemed to impress them. He was also honest and dependable and fiercely loyal when it came to Mercy. Okay, so he could barely rip open a bag of crisps when his hands were cold, but that didn't mean he couldn't talk his way out of almost any situation with just the right amount of charisma. He was the brains to Mercy's brawn. Her safety blanket in a brutal world where hitting strangers as hard as you possibly can is considered perfectly normal behaviour.

Asif laid it out like so. 'We can either live for today and make money ... and good money at that, way more than you would ever make in a factory or call centre ... or we can go for broke and aim for the stars, albeit with the kick in the teeth of maybe ... probably ... falling short? It's your choice, Mercy, because I'm buggered if I know. You're the best I've ever worked with, but talent only gets you so far. After that, it's in the lap of the Gods. So, what do you reckon? Are you feeling lucky? Or shall we start living in the real world?'

Mercy didn't need to think about it for long. Luck had largely deserted her, even from a young age. She'd had nothing then and still had nothing now. Only her fists. It would be nice to have a little bit of something for a change.

Asif had got the ball rolling immediately. He had rung around, spread the word. Promoters were interested. And they were willing to pay. At least five hundred quid a fight. Three or four fights a week. Mercy and Asif had agreed to split the money equally, fifty-fifty, no arguments.

That wasn't the only way to boost the coffers, though.

Cue a chain-smoking, cider-swigging promoter called Buster Blow. Asif doubted that was his real name, but chose not to bring it up for fear of upsetting him. Besides, it was what Buster had to say that really intrigued him, not what he chose to call himself.

'May I ask you a question, Asif, me old mucker? Something to get the cogs turning. Do you know the difference between doing a good thing and doing the right thing?' Buster took a wheezy breath before answering himself. 'If Miss Mee does a *good* thing tonight, she wins her fight and goes home happy. If she does the *right* thing, she goes down in the fourth round and we *all* go home happy. Do you catch my drift?'

Asif caught it alright. With both hands. And then wished he could drop it like a hot potato.

Buster wanted Mercy to throw the fight. Lose on purpose. Well, that wasn't going to happen. Not on your life. It was morally wrong. She was better than that. They were *both* better than that.

And yet …

That evening, Mercy had gone down in the fourth. She had lost the fight, the first in twenty-two bare-knuckle bouts. She had also headed for home completely unscathed with double the money. Buster had paid her a grand. A grand in cash for fifteen minutes work. It was a no-brainer.

Tonight, she was going to do the *right* thing again. Her instructions were simple. Go down in the third and don't get up.

Mercy skipped around the ring as the bell sounded to signal the start of round one. Her opponent was a chunky German girl with a sour face and swinging pigtails. Heidi something or other. She was the underdog. A complete unknown. Nobody had bet a penny on her. And that was why she had to win. That was the deal. Like Mercy, she knew that the fight was going to end in the third.

Round one passed without incident. Mercy boxed clever, dodging Heidi's bigger blows whilst offering up some of her own. It was a tight, even contest. No one watching would ever have suspected a thing.

'You're doing great.' Leaning over Mercy, Asif dabbed her forehead with a sponge before letting the water run down the back of her vest. 'Very convincing. Keep going, yeah?'

The bell rang for the second round. Jumping up off the stool, Mercy made her way confidently to the centre of the ring. The German looked angrier than ever. What was her problem? She was going to win regardless. There was no need to ruin things now by overacting.

The next three minutes posed no problems for Mercy. Jab ... block ... jab ... block. It was a well-worn formula. The German was strong, but under normal circumstances Mercy would've finished her off with ease. Four or five rounds at a push. The big ones always tired early.

Mercy lowered her fists as the bell rang for the end of the second round. She was about to turn back towards her corner when something caught her eye. She tried to block it, but she was too late to stop Heidi's fist from colliding with the side of her temple. Not only was it a cheap shot, but it was also hard enough to send Mercy staggering to one side. She had been punched before, but this felt different. Heidi had put all her weight behind it. Twelve stone of solid German aggression. Mercy's head had been a soft target. Unprotected. Impossible to miss.

The barn fell oddly silent as Mercy rocked back and forth on the spot. Everything suddenly felt off-centre. Slightly twisted. As if her brain had been dislodged from its resting place.

She collapsed a moment later.

One by one, people began to gather around, the worry evident on their blurry faces.

Something was wrong. Seriously wrong.

There was blood. It was all over someone's hands, dripping from their fingertips. Was it hers? Mercy looked away as both the barn and her stomach started to spin.

'I'm here.' Asif rested a hand on her shoulder. 'Don't try and sit up.'

Mercy ignored him. She didn't get far, however, before the strength deserted her and she fell back down again. Her head flopped onto the canvas. The last thing she saw was the crowd quickly dispersing through the barn doors. Everyone was leaving. Even Asif.

'It'll be okay,' he said, edging away, ready to flee. 'I promise.'
But it wouldn't be. Not now. Not ever. Mercy knew that.
And she was right.

CHAPTER FOUR

A Fine City.

That was what it said on the sign on the way into Norwich. And it *was*. For most people who lived there at least.

Just not for Rose Carrington-Finch.

It wasn't that she hated the city itself, more what it represented. The soul-sucking demands of being a junior data analyst. The ridiculously early starts and chronic late nights. The claustrophobia of the office. The whirring monitors, endless telephone calls and lagging internet connection. The way some people – colleagues, not friends – called her Rosie, whilst her boss seemed to have settled on Roxanne. Days off, though few and far between, were no better. Twenty-four hours spent in a dreary one-bed apartment. Hollow walls and squeaky floorboards. Eating chocolate in her pyjamas whilst staring blankly at whatever happened to flash up on the TV. Soap operas, reality shows, documentaries about animals she had never even heard of. She was all alone, but that wasn't the worst of it. It was the emptiness of her existence that really weighed her down. The monotony. The constant, never-ending, mind-numbing drudgery of life.

It was shit. All of it. So shit, in fact, that at some point things would have to come to a head.

That point was today.

With nothing left to live for, Rose took what she considered to be her last breath before she kicked the stool out from under her. The rope tightened around her neck. The shock was real. The pain immediate.

This was it. There was no turning back now.

A pounding on the door ruined the serenity of the moment.

'Rosemary.'

The voice was instantly recognisable as Mrs Blanchard, her elderly neighbour.

Just ignore her …

'I know you're in there. I can see you through the keyhole.'

No. This wasn't supposed to happen.

Straining with her foot, Rose dragged the stool back towards her until it was close enough to stand on.

'What are you doing in there, Rosemary?'

Rose caught her breath before she spoke. 'It's Rose – not Rosemary. It's never been Rosemary.'

'What's that, dear? Something bothering you?'

'Oh, nice of you to notice,' Rose sighed.

'No, it's just a mumble. Can you speak up a bit?'

Rose loosened the knot around her neck, stopping it from pressing against her throat. 'It's almost midnight, Mrs Blanchard. Bit late for a social call, don't you think?'

'Midnight? Is it really? Oh, maybe it can keep until tomorrow.'

'Maybe it can.' Rose waited for the old lady to trudge back to her apartment.

She didn't.

'I am quite busy, Mrs Blanchard. I'm … erm … changing a light bulb. What is it that you actually want?'

'Want?' Mrs Blanchard took more than a moment. 'Nothing. Not really. I'm busy myself as it happens. I'm off to visit my brother first thing in the morning. Just for a day or two. You remember Colin, don't you? He's got one eye bigger than the other and hair sprouting out of every available orifice. Anyway, let's not waste our time worrying about him. Not when there are more urgent matters at hand. Namely my Prunella.'

Rose shook her head with so much force it made the stool wobble beneath her feet. Prunella was Mrs Blanchard's narcissistic cat. Rose guessed that the old lady wanted her to feed it. Maybe even house it. Both, however, were completely out of the question if she was going to hang herself.

No, not *if* – *when*. Now. This minute. Or the next. Yes, that was it. Definitely the next minute.

'Like I said before, I'm quite busy,' insisted Rose. 'I might not be here—'

Mrs Blanchard interrupted her with a snort. 'Really? Where else will you be? You don't go anywhere except to work.'

'I do. I mean, I will … I think—'

'Is there something I don't know? Got yourself a boyfriend, have we?'

Rose replied too quickly. 'No.'

'Ooh, girlfriend then, is it? Doesn't bother me either way. As long as you keep the noise down and don't flaunt it in my face—'

'I haven't got a girlfriend,' Rose snapped. 'I haven't got anyone.'

'No, thought not. Don't know why. You can be quite pretty when you make an effort and put your best face on. You must have a few friends at least—'

'I've got friends. I've *always* had friends,' added Rose unnecessarily.

'If you say so.' There was a slight hesitation whilst Mrs Blanchard's brain shifted into gear. 'Well, if you're not doing anything with all these friends of yours you can look after my Prunella, can't you? I mean, don't put yourself out on my account. I could always take her to a cattery. I've probably got enough in my savings account to pay for—'

'Fine,' muttered Rose.

'What's that?' asked Mrs Blanchard, perking up.

'I said fine,' shouted Rose. 'I'll take care of Prunella.'

'Good girl. I knew you'd see sense. You've got a key, haven't you? There's cat food in the bottom cupboard, but I don't mind if you'd rather take Prunella back to yours. You'll enjoy the company. Right, see you when I get back, Rosemary. Three or four days at most.'

'I thought you said one or two ...' Rose let the sentence fade. At a guess, Mrs Blanchard had already gone. She had got what she wanted, after all. A cat sitter. A *free* cat sitter.

This changed things considerably. Hanging herself was

no longer an option. Not whilst she had responsibilities. Someone – okay, a cat – was reliant on her for one or two (or three or four) days. She couldn't just let it fend for itself.

Lifting her arms, Rose began to fiddle with the knot around her neck. Funnily enough, the video she had found online hadn't told her how to undo it. She figured that wasn't something that cropped up that often. Unable to see what she was doing, Rose tugged frantically at both ends of the rope. She was getting desperate. What if she couldn't free herself? What if she was stuck up there forever?

Rose was still panicking when the stool slipped out from under her.

The rope strained against her neck as she dropped, stopping her from landing on the carpet. Instead, she just hung there, about a foot off the ground. Her first reaction was to wriggle about, but it only made things worse. The knot was tightening with every movement, cutting off her air supply, strangling the life out of her.

Rose didn't want to die. Not now. Not like this. She could change. She had things to live for. She could *find* things to live for.

Too late for that now.

She was losing consciousness. This was it. No comebacks. No salvation. No escape.

Her last thought was about Prunella. If nothing else, she hoped the poor cat didn't starve.

One death in the apartment block was quite enough for anybody.

THE SITUATION

CHAPTER FIVE

Agatha Pleasant drew a weary breath before striding confidently into Shakermakers cocktail bar.

Hidden away in a grimy Soho back street, it was a tacky little place with bright neon lights, a sticky floor and ridiculously overpriced drinks with far too much ice and not enough alcohol. It was a Sunday evening in November. Gone seven. Agatha didn't want to be there, but you would never have guessed. Bright eyes and an even brighter smile were a mask she wore regularly. Warm and friendly and all of it fake. Truth is, she'd had a tough few days. Next week it would only get tougher, though.

Next week she would meet the new recruits for the very first time.

Agatha looked around. The bar was practically empty so he was easy to spot. *He* being Roger Hammerton. They had worked together several lifetimes ago. Things were different then, of course. You could bend the rules to breaking point and then sweep any complaints under the carpet before those up above got wind of it. These days it was all paperwork without the paper. Health and safety gone hysterical. Enough to slow you down until you ground to a complete halt. Or just died on the job. Whichever came first.

Roger, meanwhile, had done everything he could to slow *himself* down. He hadn't just put on a bit of weight in the intervening years; he had almost doubled in size. Thinning hair accentuated a bloated face, several chins and a swollen neck that strained against the collar of his shirt. His jumper was tight, but his trousers were baggy. Both were beige. That's what retirement did to you, thought Agatha. You lost your edge. Took your eye off the ball. She tried to recall when Roger had finally called it a day, settling on ten years ago, but that was just a stab in the dark. If she remembered correctly he had jumped before he was pushed, bowing out early with a nondescript clock, a half decent pension and a limp pat on the back from his superiors.

Run along now, my good man. We've already found your replacement. Younger. Stronger. Faster. Cheaper.

Roger clambered down from his stool when he noticed Agatha approaching. For one awful moment, she thought he was going to hug her. Thankfully, he saw sense and switched it to an uncomfortably moist handshake instead. 'It's lovely to see you, boss,' he barked. 'What's it been? Eight? Nine years? Maybe more if I'm being honest.'

Agatha nodded affably. 'Time flies—'

'—when you're having fun,' finished Roger.

'Not much fun to be had in our line of work.' Agatha checked herself. '*My* line of work.'

'Sit down, sit down,' said Roger, gesturing towards one

of the high-backed stools. 'Would you like a drink? Glass of wine perhaps? Or one of those fancy cocktails? Sex in the Vicarage or something? You used to drink brandy back in the day if my memory serves me right. Lots of it, too. Then again, we all did.'

'I'm good, thanks,' replied Agatha, climbing up onto the stool. It started to wobble so she rested a hand on the table.

'You look well,' said Roger, studying her with intent. 'You've hardly aged. I don't know how you do it. Must be all that fresh air you don't get—' A harsh cough interrupted him mid-sentence. It was coming from the woman sat beside him. 'Oh, how rude of me,' said Roger, cringing slightly. 'You two have met before, haven't you?'

Agatha smiled at Roger's wife. She was tall and thin. Well dressed, albeit in an old fashioned kind of way. Yes, they had met before, more than once, but Agatha couldn't quite recall the woman's name. Margaret. Maureen. Martha. Take your pick and hope for the best. 'Hello, Martha.'

'Cynthia,' said the woman coldly.

Agatha winced. 'Of course. Sorry. I've got a terrible memory for names.'

Not true. Roger didn't pull her up on it, though.

'Wow, it's been a long time,' he said again. 'A long, long time. I wasn't sure you'd come, Agatha. What is it that you do these days?'

'This and that and everything in between,' replied Agatha sheepishly. 'You know I can't tell you. It'd be more than my life's worth.'

'Ain't that the truth.' Roger sipped his pint. Wiped his

mouth across the back of his hand. 'Do you remember when we worked down in the Cellar? Happy days, they were. Nick 'em in the morning, bang 'em up by lunch. We were a good team. The best in the business. You, me, Brian, Big Al …'

Agatha forced a smile. What was this? Some kind of reunion? And what was the wife doing here? Except for the constant steely glare she had fixed on Agatha's forehead ever since she had got her name wrong, she hadn't done or said anything of any merit.

'I saw Brian the other week,' Roger continued, his eyes widening. 'He's just got back from Ibiza. Been there about five years. Not clubbing it. He's far too old for that sort of nonsense. Besides, his heart wouldn't let him even if he wanted to. No, as far as I can tell he's just been taking it easy. Enjoying the sun. Big Al was still working the doors the last I heard—'

'Roger.' Agatha stopped him mid-sentence. 'I don't mean to be rude, but it's been one hell of a week. Is this just a cosy catch-up, or is there something else you'd like to discuss with me?' She paused. 'Something serious?'

'Oh, this is serious alright.' Roger glanced at his wife as if seeking her approval. 'We've got a problem, Agatha,' he began. 'And you're the only person who can help us.'

CHAPTER SIX

Resting his elbows on the table, Roger waited for a casual drinker to pass before he spoke again.

'Do you remember my son Benjamin?' he asked quietly.

Agatha pretended to think. She didn't. Not in the slightest. 'Vaguely. It was a long time ago …'

'I won't hold it against you,' said Roger, seeing through her lie. 'You only met him once or twice. He was tiny back then. Just a child. He's not tiny now, though. He's bigger than me.'

'You had him later in life, didn't you?' said Agatha. 'What is he now? Eighteen? Nineteen?'

'Twenty,' said Roger.

'Twenty-one next week,' added Cynthia. 'And it's Benji. Nobody calls him Benjamin.'

Agatha nodded. She had an uncomfortable feeling she knew where this was heading. Still, let's not make things any easier for them. 'You don't want me to organise his birthday party, do you?'

'If only it was that simple,' sighed Roger. 'Benji's a good lad, Agatha, but he's got in with the wrong crowd.'

And there it was. *The wrong crowd.* Agatha could've laughed out loud. How many times had she heard that from a worried parent? Children went off the rails. That was a fact. Sometimes a little, sometimes a lot. And yet it was always somebody else's fault.

'Go on,' said Agatha.

Roger took another sip. 'Benji left home, and London with it, over a year ago now. He met a girl. Gina. Followed her when she moved away. They went to Stainmouth of all places.'

'Stainmouth?' Agatha shivered as she spoke. She had never been there before, but all she could picture was a cold, bleak northern town. 'What's Stainmouth got to offer?'

'Bugger all as far as I can tell,' snorted Roger. 'Except for this Gina. Benji quit uni for her and everything. He said it was love, the bloody fool—'

'Gina's not the problem,' snapped Cynthia.

'No, Gina's not the problem,' Roger echoed. 'But that's where it all started. Benji wanted to provide for the pair of them. He needed money. And that's how he got mixed up with a lowlife scumbag called Vernon Gold. I've done a little bit of digging, Agatha, and it's not good. Gold's your modern day businessman-cum-gangster. On the face of it, he's perfectly legit. A nightclub … a few bars … a massage parlour. Then there's the other stuff. The *shady* stuff. Sex and drugs and whatever else takes your fancy. If there's a demand for it than Gold is only too happy to supply.'

'He's a parasite,' Cynthia blurted out. 'He preys on the weak and desperate.'

'That's as maybe, but he's nothing out of the ordinary,' Roger shrugged. 'You'll find a Vernon Gold or ten in every town and city across the UK. Benji's been ... *working* for him for about eighteen months now. The money's decent by the sound of things. The problem is, you have to do everything that Gold asks of you.'

'Which is fine when you're working the bars,' said Agatha, thinking out loud as the pieces of the puzzle began to slot together. 'But not so great when you're peddling pills to teenagers on the streets.'

Cynthia visibly shook. 'Benji's not a drug dealer.'

'Isn't he?' shot back Roger. 'Because he could be – or worse – and we would never know.' Leaning over the table, he locked eyes with Agatha. 'You know me. Back in the day I would've sorted this out myself. I would've stormed up there, thrown a few threats around and wideboys like Gold would've listened. These days, however ...' Roger glanced down at his ever-expanding gut. 'These days I'm not quite the man I was. I've got more ailments than you've got fingers. Angina. High cholesterol. Diabetes. Asthma. The list is endless. If I tried to throw my weight around now I'd be laughed at—'

'And I won't be?' said Agatha.

Roger screwed up his face. 'I'm not stupid. You're still in the game. You know people. You've *always* known people. People who can make the likes of Vernon Gold disappear as if by magic—'

'Let me stop you there!' said Agatha abruptly. 'Times have changed. I'm a different person now in a different line

27

of work. Yes, you're an old colleague ... a friend even ... but that still doesn't make me babysitter for your errant son who just wants to play bad boy until he decides to grow up.'

Agatha regretted her words instantly. Too fierce. Too harsh. Too honest.

'Tell her,' urged Cynthia, nudging her husband. 'Maybe she'll change her mind.'

'There's something else,' said Roger hastily. 'Benji's got a daughter. Our granddaughter. We think.'

Agatha frowned. 'You think?'

'We've never met her,' Roger admitted. 'The last time we spoke to Benji was about a year ago. It was also a week before Gina's due date. He told us they were going to have a girl and call her Amelia. And that's that. We don't know anything else about her. Not even her birthday.'

'We've got a rough idea,' said Cynthia. 'She should be one next week.'

'A double celebration.' Agatha drew a breath. She had to get out of there. 'I'm sorry – honestly, I am – but there's nothing I can do. This isn't my line of work. You should find yourselves a private detective. There's plenty about.'

Cynthia nudged her husband again. Once ... twice ... three times before he looked at her and scowled.

'I know ... I'm going to,' he mumbled. He turned back towards Agatha. Swallowed. 'I wouldn't ask for your help, you know that. Not normally. The thing is ... you owe me.'

'I owe you?' Agatha tensed up. 'I ... owe ... you?'

'I did stuff,' said Roger, lowering his tone. 'Back in the day. Things I should never have done. Horrible things. And it was you who told me to do them.' Roger was rambling now, his tongue moving faster than his brain. 'What happened to the bodies, Agatha? Yes, they were bad people ... evil ... wicked ... but they were still people. I don't know how you covered it up. The tabloids would have a field day if they ever—'

Agatha raised a hand. 'Wrong approach, Roger,' she said, trying to keep her composure as she climbed down from the stool. 'I'm leaving now, and I'd prefer it if you never contacted me again—'

'Are you a mother?' asked Cynthia out of the blue.

Agatha turned to look at her. She was surprised to see that the steely glare had vanished, only to be replaced by tears. A steady stream. Rolling down her cheeks. Smudging her make-up. 'Yes, I'm a mother. Not that it—'

'And a grandmother?' pressed Cynthia, her voice choked up.

Agatha nodded.

'Then you'll know,' Cynthia breathed. 'You'll know how desperate we are. We just want to see our Benji back home, safe and sound, with his daughter. We're terrified what will happen otherwise. Where this could end. It might scar them for life. Or worse ...'

Roger put an arm around his wife's shoulder and pulled her in close. They were both crying now. Agatha looked away. Despite the low numbers in the bar, the Hammertons were making a scene. Agatha didn't like scenes. Scenes drew attention. Attention got you noticed. Recognised. And that only led to trouble.

The sobbing grew louder. Agatha was all set to leave

when a thought held her back. Next week she would meet the new recruits. They were raw and unproven. Untapped potential, yes, but they still needed moulding into shape and fast. The best way to do that was out in the field. On the job. Work experience for the not so wise and worldly.

Agatha put two and two together and came up with a solution. A solution that killed two birds with one stone.

'You're right, Roger, I *do* know people,' she confessed, sitting back down at the table. 'Now, wipe your eyes and tell me everything you can about this Vernon Gold character. If I'm going to find your son then I'd like to know exactly what I'm letting myself in for.'

CHAPTER SEVEN

'Get your fuckin' hands off me!'

Tommy O'Strife exploded into life, lashing out in anger at the man stood over him. His swing was ponderous, though. Too slow, too clumsy, too predictable. Too easy for the man to avoid.

'Calm down. You'll do yourself some damage if you're not careful.'

Sure enough, a sharp, stabbing pain hit Tommy in the chest, forcing him back onto the bed.

'Take a deep breath,' said the man. 'In … and out … in … and out … in …'

'I know how to breathe,' Tommy muttered. 'I've been doing it for long enough.'

The man held up his hands. Took a step away from the bed. He had short, dark hair, greying at the tips. Clean shaven with a strong jaw and chiselled features. Dressed head to toe in black (trench coat, pin-striped trousers, suede gloves, leather shoes), he was more than just smartly turned out. Closer to immaculate, in fact. Like a catalogue model for a funeral directors.

Tommy looked beyond the man, focussing on his surroundings. White walls. White floor. White ceiling. Nothing of any colour. He shifted his gaze onto himself. He was wearing some kind of gown. There were patches of blood down one side of it. 'Where am I? Hospital?'

'You could say that,' nodded the man.

Tommy screwed up his face. 'So, what does that make you? My doctor?'

'Afraid not.' The man fought hard to hide a smile. 'I'm just here to help.'

'What? Like a therapist or something?'

The smile switched to a frown. 'Is this a game you play with everyone you meet? Guess the occupation? I bet you're a thrill a minute at parties.'

'At least *I* get invited to parties,' shot back Tommy.

'You *used* to get invited to parties.' The man held out a hand. 'I'm not here to be insulted. I can either help you out of bed, or I can leave you be. It's as simple as that. The choice is yours.'

'Hmm, tricky decision.' Tommy pretended to weigh it up. 'What did you say your name was again?'

The man faltered. 'Miles.'

'Well, Miles, thank you for your kind offer … and please don't take offence … but get the fuck away from me!' To Tommy's surprise, the man in black turned towards the exit. 'Whoa! Where do you think you're going? I've not finished with you yet.'

Miles stopped. Oddly enough, he showed no signs of irritation.

'Okay, I get it,' sighed Tommy. 'I'm acting like a dick and now you're teaching me a lesson. That makes sense I suppose. But this doesn't. None of it. My head's in bits, mate. I just want to know where I am.'

Miles ran his tongue over his teeth. 'It's not for me to say.'

'Why not?'

'Above my pay grade. Strictly classified.'

Tommy lifted his head, ready to blurt out something highly inappropriate, when the same sharp pain stabbed him in the chest. 'What … happened to me?' he asked between breaths.

'You were shot,' explained Miles. 'The bullet missed your heart by a fraction of an inch. Any lower and we wouldn't be having this conversation. But then *you* wouldn't be having *any* conversation. With anybody. Ever again.'

Tommy let the words soak into his frazzled brain. It was followed by a memory that made him wince. He had a mental image of himself, leaving the building site … the Land Rover as it pulled up beside him … the gun … the *crack* … then … then nothing. Kamil, you sneaky bastard. There was no need for that. Tommy had done everything that had been asked of him. Okay, so the money was a day or two late, but that was all down to the Marquis brothers. He was just the middleman.

'You look a little vacant,' said Miles. 'You're not going to be sick, are you?'

'No, just thinking,' Tommy scowled. 'There's some scores I need to settle when I get out of here.'

Miles raised an eyebrow. 'Good luck with that.'

Tommy let that go, largely because he couldn't figure out if the man in black was taking the piss or not. 'What day is it?' he asked instead.

'Wednesday. Wednesday evening.'

'Wednesday?' It took Tommy a moment to work backwards. 'But I got shot on—'

'Saturday night,' said Miles. 'Slash Sunday morning. We got the call and picked you up on the stroke of midnight. Brought you straight here. You've been in and out of consciousness ever since. This is the first time you've been fully awake, though. And that's why I was trying to help you when I saw you stirring. I didn't want you to fall out of bed and panic.'

'Panic? I wasn't panicking! I was trying to leave—'

'Leaving is not an option.'

Tommy bit down on his lip. He was getting nowhere with this prick. 'Listen,' he hissed under his breath. 'The day I need anything from you will be the day I die. Do you get that?'

'Yes, I do.' Turning on his heels, Miles walked swiftly towards the exit. 'I'll see you tomorrow. Hopefully, you'll be feeling a little more appreciative by then. Not quite so ... frosty.'

'I'll give you fuckin' frosty!' Tommy waved a fist in Miles's direction, but it was all to no avail. The man in black, the hired help, had already left the room.

Now it was Tommy's turn to do the same.

Sitting up in bed, he swung his legs over the side and

tried to stand. He realised the moment his feet touched the floor that it was too much, too soon. His knees buckled under the weight and he crumpled to the ground. That was when the pain came again. It was unbearable. He had to do something – anything – to get rid of it.

Fortunately for Tommy, that particular problem was taken out of his hands when he passed out.

The pain, for the time being at least, was no longer an issue.

CHAPTER EIGHT

Miles felt the vibration the moment he left the room.

Removing his phone from his pocket, he answered immediately. He didn't look at who was calling, largely because he didn't need to. As far as he was aware, only one person had that number.

'Boss.'

A sigh. 'Miles, how many times have I told you? Please don't call me boss. I am not an ogre. I have a name. Agatha.'

'Agatha,' repeated Miles stiffly.

'See. That wasn't so hard now, was it? So, how are things?'

Miles glanced back at the closed door he had only just exited. He thought he could hear O'Strife shuffling about in there. It was followed by a dull *thud* as if he had fallen out of bed. 'Things are … progressing.'

'Progressing?' Agatha took a moment. 'And that's a good thing, yes?'

'Yes.' Miles frowned. Just the one word, and yet the way he had spoken was bound to draw attention.

'You don't sound convinced,' pressed Agatha. 'How are

the new arrivals settling in?'

'Physically, they're getting better all the time,' replied Miles honestly. 'Of the four, O'Strife has suffered the worst of the injuries, but even he'll be back to full strength before long. He's a gobby little shit, though.' Miles pulled a face. 'Sorry. I didn't mean to—'

'There's no need to apologise,' insisted Agatha. 'I may be a bit ... a *lot* older than you, Miles, but that doesn't mean I'm easily offended. In all seriousness, I value your opinion, even the foul-mouthed version. So, what has O'Strife been saying?'

'Too much,' moaned Miles. 'He doesn't shut up. It's just a constant stream of nonsense and abuse. I'm worried he might rub the others up the wrong way.'

'Perhaps,' said Agatha, 'but they'll soon get used to it. They'll have no choice. Remember, Miles, they don't have to be the best of friends; they just need to learn to work together. So, physically they're fine. What about mentally?'

'Mentally they're all over the place. I get it. Of course I do. It's only been four days since their ... accidents. Then they wake up and ...' Miles broke off. Looked along the length of the empty corridor. At the bare walls and closed doors. 'Sometimes I barely know what I'm doing here myself, so what chance do they have?'

Agatha nodded. He had a point. 'Have they been asking questions?'

'Whenever they're awake, yes. I haven't told them anything, though, in case you're wondering.' Miles walked back towards O'Strife's room and pressed an ear to the door.

It had gone worryingly quiet in there. 'I thought you'd want to drop the bombshell yourself,' he added.

'It's not a bombshell; it's a resurrection,' said Agatha, correcting him. 'I've given them a second chance at life. If all goes to plan, it may even be better than the first one they had.'

'I just hope they don't let you down.' Miles pulled open the door and froze. O'Strife was sprawled out on the floor. Unconscious perhaps. Hopefully, nothing more. 'Something's come up,' he said calmly. 'Something unavoidable. It's probably for the best if I sort it—'

'One last thing,' said Agatha, interrupting him. 'Transport will be coming to collect you and the four new recruits early tomorrow morning. I told the driver to get there at six. I hope that's okay. You can move them from their beds, but try not to wake them. Fingers crossed, they might still be asleep by the time they arrive.'

Miles hesitated. 'That sounds … interesting.'

'Interesting is one way to put it,' said Agatha. 'There's a little job that needs sorting. Nothing too strenuous. It'll be the perfect opportunity for our new recruits to prove their worth.'

Miles crouched down by Tommy's side and felt his pulse. Still alive. That was a start. 'And where is this little job?'

'Stainmouth,' revealed Agatha. 'Pack a bag, Miles. We might be there a few days.'

DAY ONE

CHAPTER NINE

Lucas Thorne couldn't understand why nobody would tell
him anything.

He guessed he had been awake, on and off, for about four
days now. Dazed, yes. Confused, definitely. But not
completely out of it. In all that time he had only seen two
people. The man in the white lab coat and mask who had
seen to his wounds; Doctor Cheung it said on his name
badge. And the other man. The man in black.

Neither of them had answered his questions.

Where was he?

What was going on?

And when could he go home?

Earlier that morning, Doctor Cheung had come into his
room and given Lucas an injection in his arm. The last thing
he remembered was his bed being wheeled out into a long
corridor. When he finally awoke he was sat up in a chair. It
was the kind you'd find in a school. Hideously
uncomfortable and as cold as ice, especially when you were
wearing nothing but a thin gown. It wasn't the chair,

however, that made Lucas ache so much.

No, that was the crash.

Lucas could still see the figure in the road. He had spotted them late, but that was no excuse. He shouldn't have lost control of the car as he swerved to avoid them. The noise that followed as the tyres struck the kerb would live with him forever. As would the sickening feeling in the pit of his stomach as the Skoda began to roll.

After that it was all blank.

Lucas tried to put the memory to the back of his mind as he studied his surroundings. It was a rectangular-shaped room, high ceiling, bare brick walls and a distressed wooden floor. One look through the window straight ahead told him it was dark outside, but the fact he couldn't see much else beyond that suggested they were high up. An empty office block perhaps. Or deserted warehouse.

Not *that* deserted.

There were three more chairs to his right. Two of them were occupied by women, both of whom were dressed in the same white gown as he was.

They say never judge a book by its cover, but Lucas chose to ignore that particular cliche with everybody he met. Today was no exception to the rule. Within seconds of noticing the women he had already come up with an instant assessment of them both. Maybe it was a police thing. Or maybe it wasn't. Maybe he was just an awkward sod.

The woman sat next to him had black skin with cropped hair and soft features. She was a nice colour. Slightly lighter than him, it suited her well. Curiously, she had a number of marks and scars around her face. A cut above one eye. A split lip. Various bruises of different shapes and shades. Had she been attacked recently? Mugged? It was a possibility, but Lucas doubted it. Okay, so she wasn't the biggest physically, but there was something about her, an air, a presence, which suggested she wouldn't let herself be pushed around easily. So, what did she do then? She was too rough around the edges to be a teacher. A youth worker perhaps. Generous with her time, but ever ready to knock a few mischievous heads together if the need arose. Lucas had known women like that all his life. He had grown up with them. And that was why he couldn't help but like the one sat next to him, even at first glance.

The woman sat furthest away, however, couldn't have been more different. Perched on the edge of her chair, she was rocking back and forth whilst gazing intently at her feet. She had long, straight hair, brown in colour, which hung limply over a pale face. She was the kind of thin you only ever saw on super-models. Under fed and under nourished. The way she kept on blinking made Lucas wonder if she had recently swapped glasses for contacts. Or maybe it was a nervous thing. He took a stab in the dark and settled upon librarian. No, too obvious. He could do better than that. A charity worker then. Yes, that was more like it. Charity work involving cats. Lucas even went as far as to check if she had any scratches on her hands. She didn't.

There was one other person in the room. The man in black. He was stood with his back to them, facing the window. He must've sensed that someone was staring at him because he turned around a moment later. Lucas refused to look away. The man had a tough demeanour, but not in a cruel way. Ex-military perhaps. Or police. Or, more likely, something clandestine. MI5 or MI6. Public schoolboy, fast-tracked to the top. Lucky swine. He hadn't had to drag himself up by his bootlaces. Ignore the abuse. The racist slurs. Spitting. Swearing. Scum.

Too much ...

Lucas blew out in frustration. At the same time he felt a flash of pain shoot up and down his arm. He instinctively winced, a reaction that the man in black couldn't fail to notice.

'You okay?'

Lucas nodded. He was in no mood to give anything more away. Not yet anyway. Not until he had found out what was going on. For all he knew this guy could be the enemy.

'Why are we here?' Lucas asked. The Youth Worker turned to him when he spoke, whilst Cat Charity practically trembled.

The man in black, however, barely bat an eyelid. 'Patience.'

Brilliant.

Lucas was ready to press the matter further when his attention switched to the exit. The door had opened and somebody else had entered the room.

'Good evening.'

The new arrival was an elegant-looking lady, completely at odds with their dark, dank surroundings. Medium height, medium build. Early sixties maybe, it was hard to call. Short grey hair paired perfectly with a sharp grey suit. Cheekbones and chin. Friendly though, not fierce.

'Sorry I'm late. I've had a frightful day. Completely unavoidable, of course.'

Closing the door behind her, the lady walked over to the man in black. She smiled once before turning towards the four chairs.

'My name is Agatha Pleasant,' she said brightly. 'From this day forth, you all work for me.'

CHAPTER TEN

Agatha waited a moment to see how they reacted.

The policeman seemed confused. The boxer looked fit to explode. The data analyst appeared to have drifted off to somewhere else entirely. And the criminal … where was the criminal?

'Oh, I seem to have jumped the gun,' said Agatha, gesturing towards the empty chair. 'Why didn't anybody tell me we were one down? He's not … dead, is he?'

The man in black, Miles, shook his head. 'Regrettably not. He's just … erm … relieving himself. He has been quite a long time, though.'

'He can't escape, can he?' asked Agatha warily.

'He can try,' replied Miles. In other words, no. 'Maybe I should go and … maybe not … I'll just stay here … with you.'

'I'll be fine.' Agatha waved him away. 'The sooner you find him, the sooner we can get down to business.'

Miles hesitated before striding purposefully towards the door.

'Are you going to tell us what's going on?' asked Lucas.

He was about to stand when Agatha raised a hand.

'Sit down please,' she said calmly. 'You've had a fatal accident. One which you've not quite fully recovered from yet. As for your question, all will be revealed in due course. If it's okay with you – with *all* of you – I'd rather wait for our final new recruit so I don't have to repeat myself.'

Lucas leant back in his chair, sighed. *A fatal accident.* It couldn't have been that fatal. He was still alive, after all. And what did she mean by new recruit?

'You said I work for you,' scowled the woman beside Lucas, almost as if she could read his mind. 'I don't work for no one, lady. You got that. Not today. Not tomorrow. Not ever.'

'There's a first time for everything, Miss Mee,' smiled Agatha.

Mercy was all set to object when the door swung open and in marched Miles. Several paces behind him, strutting confidently into the room, was another man.

Tommy O'Strife.

Lucas gave him a quick once over. Medium height. Slim build. Fashionable haircut. Shaven at the back and sides, scruffy on top. Stubble. Wild eyes darting this way and that. Like the rest of them, he was dressed in a gown.

'Greetings one and all,' laughed Tommy, slumping down onto the fourth chair. 'This is nice, isn't it? Four weirdos in hospital dresses and some stuck-up suit and his mum. Still, I've had worse night's out ...'

He was a wrong 'un; Lucas could see that a mile off. It was in his mannerisms. The way he walked and talked. Even the way he breathed. He literally reeked of dishonesty. Lucas tried to figure out how he made his money. Burglar? Unlikely. Too much hard work for limited gains. Nothing online either. He wasn't smart enough for that. Drug dealer then. Yes, that made sense. All cocksure swagger and bullshit bravado. More mouth than muscle. To Lucas, he was the sworn enemy. And yet here they were, sat together in the room.

Not for much longer, though.

'I'm leaving.' This time Lucas did stand up. 'I know my rights. You can't keep me here against my will.'

'Sit down!' said Miles sternly.

Lucas tensed up. 'Make me!'

'Yeah, make him,' said Mercy, jumping to her feet. 'And me whilst you're at it. Because I'm leaving too. And there's nothing you can do to stop me!'

'Don't test me,' warned Miles.

'Dream on. There are four of us.' Mercy glanced at the other woman sat beside her and had a change of heart. 'Okay, *three* of us. We'll easily overpower you.'

'Yeah, you go, girl,' cheered Tommy, clapping his hands together.

'Please,' said Agatha, struggling to make herself heard above the noise in the room. 'There's something I need to tell you. It'll help you see things a little more clearly.'

Lucas held his ground. 'This better be good …'

'I don't think any of you quite understand the nature of your situation,' began Agatha. 'You can't leave because you've nowhere to go. And you've nowhere to go because you no longer exist. Your lives have ceased to be. There's no easy way to tell you this … but you're all dead!'

CHAPTER ELEVEN

'Dead?' That was Lucas. 'I'm not dead. None of us are.'

'Well spotted, bruv,' smirked Tommy. 'It's a good job you're here to set us straight.'

Lucas spun around in anger. 'Don't you dare call me that! We're not brothers. I'm nothing like you—'

'Please, Mr Thorne,' said Agatha, gesturing for him to settle. 'I understand that tensions are running a little high at present, but fighting and squabbling amongst yourselves won't do anybody any good. Yes, things might seem a trifle peculiar—'

'A trifle peculiar?' cried Tommy, throwing his arms up. 'Seriously …'

'But I can explain,' continued Agatha. 'I'll tell you everything. If you'll let me.'

Lucas finally sat down, Mercy following his lead shortly after. The four chairs were silent now. They were waiting for answers.

The truth.

Positioning herself in front of Lucas, Agatha took a moment to choose her words.

'Mr Thorne,' she began, 'you were pronounced dead at the scene of an RTA on Saturday evening—'

'You've lost me already,' frowned Tommy.

'Road traffic accident,' revealed Agatha, before turning back to Lucas. 'You lost control of the patrol car you were driving during a high chase pursuit. You hit an obstacle and rolled over several times. The coroner said you didn't stand a chance.'

'Patrol car?' Tommy leant forward. Glanced along the line. 'I knew you were the law. It's obvious. I can spot a little piggy with my eyes closed—'

'Shut it, dickhead!' yelled Mercy. 'How are we ever supposed to know what's going on if you keep butting-in?'

Tommy slumped back in his chair, deflated.

'Are you alright, Mr Thorne?' asked Agatha. 'You look a little … vacant.'

Lucas blinked. She was right. He had been lost in his thoughts. 'I've done every driving course under the sun,' he muttered to himself. 'I never lose control of the car. Something must've happened.'

'Yeah, you crashed,' grinned Tommy.

Lucas gripped hold of the chair beneath him. *Don't let him get to you.*

'Miss Mee,' said Agatha, shifting her gaze to Mercy. 'You were found in an old cowshed—'

'No comment,' sniggered Tommy.

'You had been involved in a bare-knuckle boxing contest,' Agatha continued. 'You were struck on the temple. When the paramedics found you, you were all alone. You had been left for dead.'

Mercy rubbed the huge bruise that had formed on the side of her head. 'They'll regret that.'

'That may be true,' nodded Agatha, 'but it won't be at your hands I'm afraid.' She side-stepped to her right. 'Mr O'Strife,' she said, looking Tommy up and down. 'As far as I can tell, you've spent you're entire life fulfilling the role of a petty criminal—'

'Petty?' Tommy feigned outrage. 'There's nothing petty about me, sweetheart. *Pretty* perhaps …'

'Pretty dumb,' remarked Mercy under her breath.

Tommy rolled his eyes at her. 'I don't know why, but I get the feeling you don't like me.'

'That makes two of us,' said Lucas.

'Ah, you don't count, policeman plod. You were born to dislike me. It's in your genes. The boxing babe, however …' Tommy reached over and ran a hand down Mercy's thigh. 'I think she's just pretending.'

Mercy pulled away. 'Touch me again and I'll break your teeth.'

'Interesting foreplay,' smirked Tommy. 'I think I'd rather just kiss and cuddle in all honesty.'

That was the cue for Mercy to leap up off her chair and let fly with a flurry of furious punches.

Two struck Tommy around the head before he could properly defend himself. They weren't hard enough to do any damage, but that's not to say they didn't hurt. Mercy was about to land a third when Lucas grabbed her by the arms. He felt the power in her biceps and vowed never to get on her wrong side. Not like the scruffy-haired idiot at the end of the line.

'What you doing, you mad bitch?' Tommy stood up, unsteady on his feet. 'I don't make a point of punching women, but I'm prepared to make an exception.'

Lucas felt the boxer strain against his grip. If he wasn't careful she would break free. Then what? Given half a chance she'd probably rip the mouthy one's head clean off.

Which, all things considered, might not be such a bad outcome.

Agatha, meanwhile, had seen enough. Without a single word being passed between them, Miles removed a Sig Sauer P365 handgun from the inside pocket of his jacket and aimed it at the ceiling.

Lucas, Mercy and Tommy stopped what they were doing when he pulled the trigger.

'That's your first and only warning,' said Agatha, her voice calm and composed. 'Any more after that and Miles won't be firing for fun. Do I make myself clear?'

CHAPTER TWELVE

Tommy was the first to sit back down again.

'Crystal.' He lifted a hand as if he was about to rub his head before deciding against it.

'Miss Mee, you have a ferocious temper,' remarked Agatha, gesturing for Mercy to take a seat. 'In our line of work that's both a good *and* bad thing. In my presence, however, you will learn to control it.'

Mercy took a long breath before she finally did as she was asked.

'Our line of work?' repeated Lucas, massaging his fingers as he perched on the edge of the seat. Damn, that woman beside him was strong. 'So, what is *our line of work* exactly?'

'I'll come to that in due course,' said Agatha. 'All these unplanned interruptions seem to have set us back a little. Now, where was I?'

Miles waved the gun at Tommy. 'The petty criminal.'

Tommy flinched, but this time held his tongue.

'Ah, yes, Mr O'Strife,' nodded Agatha. 'You were found on a building site in East London. You had been shot once in the chest. Just above the heart. A passer-by saw everything and called an ambulance. You were rushed to hospital, but it was too late. You had lost too much blood.'

Tommy sighed, frustrated. 'Call me stupid, but I'm not getting this. How can it have been too late? I'm still here. Ask her if you don't believe me,' he said, jabbing a finger at Mercy. 'She'll tell you how hard my head is.'

'I don't need to ask anybody, Mr O'Strife,' said Agatha. 'I can see for myself that you're still here. And I, for one, am extremely grateful. You're more than just a person of interest to me – you're a key component of all I hope to achieve.'

'And what is that exactly?' pressed Lucas.

Agatha shook her head. 'Mr Thorne, your line of questioning is really quite intense at times. As I've already said, I will get to that in due course. There is, however, one other person present in the room …' All eyes turned to the final chair in the line. 'Miss Carrington-Finch,' began Agatha. 'You hung yourself in your apartment—'

'I didn't.' For the first time since they had all been in the room together, Rose lifted her head. 'That's not true.'

'Oh. Our intelligence seemed to suggest you had …' Agatha let her words peter out, half expecting Rose to fill in the gaps. She didn't. 'All the signs pointed to suicide,' Agatha said eventually.

'I wouldn't … I couldn't,' mumbled Rose. 'It was an accident.'

'Bit clumsy if you ask me,' said Tommy. 'You don't accidentally find a noose around your neck—'

'Mr O'Strife.' Agatha pulled the kind of face that suggested she didn't care for his interruption. That wasn't what bugged her the most, though. No, it was the inaccuracies in her own information. 'Thank you for correcting me, Miss Carrington-Finch,' she said, through gritted teeth. 'I will personally see to it that your records are modified. Still, whatever happened before you ... erm ... somehow strangled yourself, the outcome remains the same. The ceiling may have caved in, but the damage had already been done. By the time an elderly neighbour discovered you, you had already passed away.' Agatha rubbed her hands, satisfied. 'Right, that's it. Introductions over. Thank you for your patience. Now, we'll get down to the real business. Why you're all here for a start.'

'Here?' Lucas looked around at the bare brick walls. 'Where is *here*?'

'This is just an empty room above a wedding-dress shop,' explained Agatha. 'I have access to a number of places like this, dotted all over. If possible I like to talk without prying eyes and open ears.'

Lucas scowled. 'We are still in London, aren't we?'

Agatha shook her head. 'No, we're in Stainmouth.'

'Stainmouth? Where the fuck is Stainmouth?' cried Tommy.

'It's still in England if that's what you're worried about, Mr O'Strife,' said Agatha.

'I've fought in Stainmouth before,' said Mercy, nodding to herself. 'It was a long drive. Three or four hours. She was a big girl if I remember right. Hands like shovels. Beat her in two rounds, though. I think we went for a curry after—'

'Great story,' chipped-in Tommy. 'You ever thought about starting your own travel show?'

Mercy closed her eyes tight. Took a deep breath. She wasn't fooling anybody, though. They all knew she could lash out at any moment.

Agatha, wary that the mood in the room may turn sour at any moment, began to speak. 'Thank you, Miss Mee. Has anybody else ever been to Stainmouth?'

'Almost,' said Lucas. 'I nearly got transferred here once. Thank God I didn't. Stainmouth has the least funded police force in the whole of the country—'

'You what?' Tommy sat forward, his interest piqued. 'Why has nobody ever told me that before? I could've made a killing round these parts. You know, before I … erm … got killed myself.'

'That could quite possibly be true,' Agatha had to admit. 'Stainmouth police are struggling. Underfunded and overwhelmed. They need help—'

'There is no way I'm joining the police!' said Tommy firmly.

'That won't be necessary,' insisted Agatha. 'Like I said before, you work for me. You're my team. Off the grid. Completely untraceable. You didn't just fall into my lap by accident; I handpicked you. Correct me if I'm wrong, but all of you have no immediate family and very few friends. You won't be missed. You're easily forgettable. Everybody you've ever known now thinks you're dead. We, however, know differently. That's the fine line between life and death. Don't look so glum. This is the beginning of the rest of your lives. Do as I say and I'm sure it'll be better than your first stab at things.' Agatha stopped suddenly. With that, she walked towards the door.

'Where are you going?' asked Lucas bluntly. 'We haven't finished yet.'

'I think you'll find we have,' replied Agatha. 'I'm going home. And so are you. I've found you some lovely accommodation out in the countryside. Miles will take you there. He'll also fill you in on what I want you to do next. It's a simple case of locating a missing person. Nothing too troublesome for the four of you. Not if you work together and play to your strengths.'

'And what if we refuse?' asked Mercy.

'That's your choice, Miss Mee,' said Agatha. 'But answer me this. If you refuse to cooperate then what was the point of me bringing you back to life?'

Mercy opened her mouth and then shut it just as quickly. Try as she might, she had no response to that.

'Very well.' Agatha hesitated in the doorway. 'This is nice, isn't it?' she said, smiling back at them. 'The four of you, together at last. My Nearly Dearly Departed Club. Ready to get to work.'

CHAPTER THIRTEEN

Miles eased the Saab smoothly around the country bends.

The four new recruits had all gone worryingly quiet ever since Agatha had spoken to them back at the wedding-dress shop. Even now, moments after Miles had revealed the exact nature of what she had planned for them, no one was speaking.

Which was strange.

Strange enough for him to feel for his gun. To his relief it was still there, in his inside pocket, safe and secure. What if they all jumped him without warning? Crashed the car and tried to escape? It was unlikely, but not impossible. He had to be ready.

The policeman was in the passenger seat beside Miles, whilst the other three were in the back. They had squeezed the data analyst into the middle. Good thinking. The boxer and the criminal had hardly seen eye-to-eye before. The last thing Miles wanted to do was break up a cat fight whilst he was driving. The fact they were still wearing their gowns would only have made things worse. There'd be bits flopping about all over the place. Very distracting.

'Any questions?' asked Miles, looking in his rear view mirror.

Tommy poked his head into the front of the vehicle. 'Just the one. Can you run through it all again please? And this time I promise to listen.'

Miles drew a breath as he scanned the roadside for the sign to Croplington. He had to remember who they were. Where they had come from. They weren't professionals; they were just nobodies. Dragged from the streets before they drowned in the gutter. 'We'd like you to find a boy called Benji Hammerton,' he began. 'He's twenty—'

'Twenty?' repeated Tommy. 'You're a man at twenty. Hairy balls and everything. Not a boy.'

'It's not important,' sighed Miles, concentrating on the road. 'What *is* important is that he's somewhere in Stainmouth. He moved here with a girl called Gina Pritchard—'

'A woman,' insisted Mercy. 'If he's a man then she must be a woman.'

'Yes, okay, fine,' shrugged Miles. This shouldn't have been this difficult. 'Benji's parents haven't heard from him in months. They think he could have split from Gina. There might even be a child involved. A baby girl. The facts are hazy I'm afraid, but it's all we've got to go on. One thing seems certain, though. Benji's got in with a bad crowd and his parents are worried about where it might lead to. Let's be serious. No one wants their son to end up as a lowlife criminal now, do they?'

Mercy turned to Tommy and smiled.

'What?' he grunted. 'I'm not a criminal. I'm an

57

opportunist. And, before you start, it's not my fault that all the opportunities that swing my way just happen to be illegal. If anything I'm a victim of circumstance.'

'Is that the same *circumstance* that's resulted in Benji getting mixed up with an *opportunist* of his own?' said Miles. 'In this case a local gangster called Vernon Gold. Find either Gold or Gina and you might just find Benji. Then it'll be your job to persuade him to go home, or at least call his parents and reassure them that he's okay.'

'You make it sound so simple,' remarked Lucas, his brow furrowing.

'It might be,' said Mercy.

'It won't,' grumbled Lucas.

Miles was about to argue when something caught his eye in the headlights. He braked hard and the Saab shuddered to a halt. 'Sorry about that,' he said, once they were back on the move. 'There was something in the road. A rabbit probably. The wildlife's insane around here. They don't care. They just run in front of you like they're on some kind of suicide mission.' Miles checked himself. 'Sorry. That came out wrong. I wasn't being—'

'I didn't try and kill myself,' mumbled Rose.

'What's that, Mouse?' said Tommy, patting her on the head. 'Did you squeak something?'

Rose turned to one side, keen to avoid eye contact. This was unbearable. The tight, confined space. The lack of air. The constant squabbling. Digging her fingernails into the palm of her hand, she hoped with all her heart that she could somehow make it stop. Everything. Forever.

'Are we nearly there yet?' moaned Tommy, breaking her concentration. 'I can't imagine you'll find many five star hotels in the middle of nowhere.'

'We're not going to a hotel,' said Miles, changing gear as he slowed his speed. 'You'll be staying with a woman called Proud Mary.'

'Like the song?' guessed Mercy.

'Perhaps … or maybe it's because her name is Mary and she likes to keep her house clean,' replied Miles drily. 'Agatha showed me a photograph. She seems quite … intimidating. A force of nature you might say. If I was in your shoes I'd be on my best behaviour.'

'We're not children,' snapped Lucas. 'We'll act accordingly when we're in her home. Listen, all I want to do is get this over with as quickly as possible. Then I can get back to my old life.'

Miles resisted the urge to burst his bubble. Instead, he took a tight turn onto a bumpy dirt track. This was it. They had arrived. 'Welcome to Cockleshell Farm, set deep in the sleepy village of Croplington,' he announced, minus the travel guide. 'Your new home for the foreseeable future.'

'Our home?' Mercy peered out the window. 'But I thought … you said … this is a farm!'

'Yeah, no shit,' smirked Tommy.

'Ah, there's plenty of shit,' shot back Mercy. 'They call it manure round these parts.'

'We'll probably be having some of that for breakfast,' said Tommy, sticking his tongue out. 'Vegans have been eating it for years.'

Miles stifled a smile. O'Strife was an annoying little prick, make no mistake, but he also had a way about him that made him hard to truly despise. Maybe Agatha was right. The four of them *would* all gel over time. Maybe, given half a chance, this Nearly Dearly Departed Club of hers could actually work.

Or maybe not.

Miles was about to speak when a tiny *crack* appeared in the windscreen before his eyes. His first response was to slam on the brakes. It was enough to send the Saab skidding across the dirt track before it eventually ground to a halt.

'What was that?' asked Lucas, gripping hold of his seat belt. 'Not another rabbit?'

'If so, then *that's* one huge fuckin' rabbit!' blurted out Tommy.

Miles followed his gaze. Tried to focus. The Saab's headlights had illuminated the entrance to the farmhouse. Tommy was right; there was something there. Something big. Big enough to fill the doorway.

No, not something.

Someone.

Miles ducked down behind the steering wheel as the *someone* lifted a shotgun, aiming it at the Saab for a second time.

'That's Proud Mary,' he said, breathing hard. 'So much for a warm welcome …'

CHAPTER FOURTEEN

'You've got ten seconds to turn around and leave. Ten …'

Proud Mary was stood on the doorstep with the shotgun in both hands. She was dressed in a flowery head-scarf, green wax jacket and black wellies. Legs apart, shoulders back. A deep scowl etched across her face.

'What now?' asked Mercy, peeking out the window.

'Nine …'

'Somebody needs to go and speak to her,' said Miles. 'Any volunteers?'

'Eight …'

'I'll go.' Lucas was about to open the passenger side door when Miles grabbed his arm.

'Seven …'

'No, *I'll* go,' Miles insisted. 'I brought you here. It's up to me to sort this mess out.'

'Six …'

With that, he opened his door. When no gunshot came, he climbed out of the vehicle, careful not to expose too much of his body. 'There's no need to panic,' he yelled. 'We come in peace.'

'And you'll leave in pieces,' Proud Mary shouted back. 'I'm not afraid to shoot. Five …'

'I can see that,' sighed Miles, examining his windscreen. Slowly, so not to alarm the old lady, he shuffled away from the Saab. Not forwards in case it spooked her, but to one side. If she decided to fire now he would have nowhere to hide. He would have to dive for cover and hope for the best. 'I thought you were expecting us.'

'I was expecting *someone*, but that was almost thirty minutes ago,' Proud Mary revealed.

'That was me,' admitted Miles. 'I'm not familiar with these roads and got held up. I didn't know I was on a time limit, though.'

Proud Mary swung the shotgun across her body, pointing it straight at Miles's chest. 'Why should I believe you? Prove it.'

'I was sent by my boss,' said Miles hastily. 'Miss Pleasant—'

Proud Mary responded with a snort. 'Never heard of her.'

'Agatha.'

'Still never heard of her.'

'Agatha Pleasant!' cried Miles, suddenly on edge.

'Now, her I have heard of.' At the same time Proud Mary lowered the shotgun. 'You should've said that to begin with, you silly man. It would've saved all the confusion. I was told you'd be bringing four more, though. Where are they?'

Miles gestured towards the Saab. 'In there.'

'Get them out then,' Proud Mary demanded. 'Let's see what we're working with, shall we?'

Miles made his way back to the car and opened the doors. One by one, the others exited, forming a line beside him.

'This is Proud Mary,' announced Miles. 'Be nice to her and she'll be nice to you.'

'That's not what you said a minute ago,' grinned Tommy. 'You called her a—'

'Landlady,' finished Miles. 'Mary will cook for you, clean for you, look after you. She'll basically do what you want, when you want, as long as it's within reason.'

'Don't do no personals, mind,' Proud Mary piped up.

Miles pulled a face. 'Sorry?'

'Underpants … knickers … bras,' Proud Mary listed. 'Personals around your privates. Not for me, thank you kindly. You wash those yourselves.'

'Of course,' nodded Miles. 'But everything else is fine, right? You are getting paid, after all. Probably more than me.'

'Peanuts and monkeys spring to mind.' With that, Proud Mary headed back into the farmhouse. 'Don't just stand there looking gormless, you lot,' she called out. 'Let me show you to your rooms.'

CHAPTER FIFTEEN

Rose sat on the edge of her bed and took in her new surroundings.

Her room at Cockleshell Farm was small in size and desperately in need of a fresh lick of paint and a new carpet. It was clean, though. And tidy. Perfectly adequate if truth be told. No worse than her bedroom back in her apartment.

No. Her *old* bedroom. In her *old* apartment. In her *old* life.

She stood up. Tip-toed over to the wardrobe. There were clothes in there. Not a great deal, but enough to last a week or so. Smart not casual. Blouses and skirts. Jackets and trousers. All black, even the underwear. Rose changed out of the gown without thinking, selecting the first things she had laid her hands on. To her surprise, the sizes were spot on. Somebody had clearly done their homework.

Okay, so the clothes weren't exactly to her taste, but then how would a complete stranger know what her taste was when she didn't even know herself?

A pounding on the door was enough to make Rose start. 'Yes,' she said quietly.

'Miles wants us outside. Says it's important.'

That was the other woman. The boxer. She frightened Rose a little, but then they all did. They were so different from her. Coarser. Brasher. Bolder. Not for the first time she felt like the odd one out.

Fearful of being the last to arrive, Rose bundled out of the room and set off down the stairs. She had almost reached the bottom when she heard movement behind her. Turning sharply, she saw the man with the bird nest hairstyle.

'Wait for me, Mouse!' said Tommy, hopping down the steps two at a time.

Rose took a breath. Built up the courage. 'Please don't call me that. I don't like it …'

The man stopped at the foot of the stairs and leant into her. 'Sorry. You'll have to speak up a little. I can hear you squeaking something, but I can't quite make it out.'

And, with that, he was gone. Skipping straight out the front door. Laughing as he went.

Rose followed him outside. The others were already there, stood in a circle. Like her, they were dressed in black. Miles was in the middle of them.

'It looks like Christmas has come early,' he began. 'Hold out your hands and you'll all get a present.'

The four new recruits did as they were told as, one by one, Miles passed them a small, rectangular box.

'What's this?' grunted Tommy, fumbling to get it open. 'It looks like a phone. A *shit* phone.'

'And that's because it is,' replied Miles. 'It's a Nokia 105 to be precise. Admittedly, it's not the smartest of—'

'These are donkey's years old!' Tommy blurted out. 'I wouldn't be seen dead with it.'

'What an ironic turn of phrase considering your circumstances,' sighed Miles. 'Listen, you don't have to be seen anywhere with it. Just keep it in your pocket. These phones are only to be used in emergencies. There are five numbers stored on them and that's the five of us. Not Proud Mary and certainly not Agatha.'

A confused Mercy jabbed furiously at the buttons. 'Can you get on the internet?'

'Why would you want to get on the internet?' frowned Miles.

'Why do you think? To look at things—'

'Porn,' said Tommy, winking at her.

'No, it hasn't got the internet,' said Miles sternly. 'In fact, you can't get the internet anywhere around Cockleshell Farm. Proud Mary's got a TV if that helps. I'm sure she wouldn't mind you joining her in the sitting room on those cold winter evenings. Don't look like that; she won't bite. Anyway, let's get back to the matter at hand. I've not finished with your presents yet.' Reaching into his coat pocket, Miles removed a thick roll of bank notes. 'You'll each get a daily allowance—'

'Bit old for pocket money, aren't we?' remarked Lucas.

'You can always go without,' Miles replied. Starting with Tommy, he peeled off three notes and placed them into the palm of his hand.

'Thirty quid?' Tommy counted it again. Just to be sure. 'Is that all? I've got expensive tastes.'

'Not anymore you haven't.' Miles continued to distribute the money equally amongst the four. 'Thirty pounds a day for as long as this takes. Proud Mary will sort you out after today. Don't ask her for more. I mean, what else do you need? You've got clothes in your wardrobes. Toiletries in the bathroom. Food in the kitchen. And a full tank of petrol.'

Lucas perked up a little as he glanced over at the Saab.

'Think again,' smiled Miles. 'That's mine. And I don't like sharing. You have got a car, though. It's over there. Beside the cowshed.'

Miles pointed beyond the farmhouse towards a series of barns. There, hidden slightly from view, was a cherry red Fiat 500.

'That's a woman's car,' frowned Tommy.

'Sexist pig,' snarled Mercy.

Miles rolled his eyes as he handed the keys to Rose. 'I'll let you have these. You seem like the most responsible. Right, I think that's all,' he said, addressing them altogether. 'You've got my number for emergencies. I'll be in touch soon.' Miles walked over to the Saab and opened the door. He was about to climb inside when he felt a tug on his sleeve.

'Please,' whispered Rose, edging closer to him so the others couldn't hear her. 'This is a mistake. I shouldn't be here.'

Miles waited for her to let go. She didn't. 'You'll be fine,' he insisted. 'They need you as much as you need them. I've done my research. You've got skills.'

'I haven't,' whimpered Rose. 'I can't do anything. And ... I'm scared. So scared.'

'The rest of them will take care of you.' Miles wasn't sure he believed that, but what else could he say? 'I know it's a shock to the system, but this won't just go away. You *have* to do it. That's why you've been brought back from the dead.' Miles finally shook her off. 'I don't make the rules,' he said, resting a hand on Rose's shoulder. 'This goes way above my head. Good luck.'

A desperate Rose watched as Miles climbed into the Saab and drove away. She stayed like that for almost a minute, staring gloomily into the darkness, before eventually turning around. To her horror, the man who called her Mouse was stood right behind her.

'What's wrong?' mumbled Rose, shuffling away from him.

'Keys,' demanded Tommy.

Rose weighed them up in her hand. She was about to pass them over when Mercy moved between them. 'What do *you* want the keys for?' she asked suspiciously.

'Let me see.' Tommy pretended to think. 'You can't drive the car without the keys. And we won't find this Benji boy unless we get in the car and start searching.'

'I thought this Benji boy was a man,' said Mercy.

'Nah, *I'm* a man,' insisted Tommy, puffing out his chest. 'And I'm willing to prove it. You only have to ask. Now, keys please, Louise,' he said, holding out his hand. 'And I know that's not your name but it's the only way to make the rhyme work.'

Lucas yawned out loud as he stretched his arms above his head. 'We're not going anywhere tonight. It's dark and cold and we don't know where we are. Whatever you think we're going to do can wait until tomorrow.'

'But the night's still young,' pleaded Tommy.

Mercy glanced at her Nokia. 'It's nine.'

'Exactly,' nodded Tommy. 'A quick freshen up and we can be in Stainmouth town centre before the hour's out.'

The farmyard fell silent.

'Think about it, people,' Tommy persisted. 'None of us want to be here, but there is an escape plan. The sooner we find Benji, the sooner we can go home. So, who's with me? And who'd rather go back inside and cuddle up on the sofa next to the old battle axe?'

'Well, when you put it like that …' sighed Mercy.

Lucas took a breath. 'Yeah, okay, let's do this. I don't like cuddling at the best of times.'

'What about you?' asked Mercy. She was staring at Rose. 'What do you think?'

Rose stumbled over her reply. 'I don't … I can't … I mean … I'll do whatever the rest of you decide.'

'Three out of three.' Lunging forward, Tommy snatched the keys from Rose's grasp. 'Congratulations. You've all made the correct decision … whoa!'

He was twirling the keys around his finger when Mercy plucked them out of the air. 'You're still not driving,' she said firmly. 'I don't even know you. And I certainly don't trust you. There's got to be a better alternative,' she added, turning towards Lucas.

'Not on your life!' argued Tommy, following her gaze. 'He crashed his cop car, remember. What about you?'

'My head's still a little fuzzy from the fight,' Mercy had to admit. 'I'll probably be okay in a day or—'

'Brilliant. And then there was one …' Tommy switched his attention to Rose. 'Looks like you're the designated driver, Mouse. I hope you've passed your test.'

CHAPTER SIXTEEN

Lucas tried *and* failed to get comfortable on the back seat of the Fiat 500.

He was too big and the car was too small. That was a fact. He had only sat in the back so they could separate the other two. In hindsight, he'd have preferred it if they were still squabbling and he didn't have his knees lodged under his chin.

Proud Mary had informed them that the journey from Cockleshell Farm to Stainmouth town centre took about fifteen minutes at most. The landlady, however, had clearly never been in a car driven by the quiet one. At that very moment she was pushing twenty at most, and that was the fastest she had gone. Some people may have called her careful, but Lucas would've disagreed with them vehemently. To go this slowly made her a danger to other drivers. A liability.

He wasn't the only one who thought that either.

'Any chance we can go any faster, Mouse?' piped up Tommy. 'The speed we're farting along at isn't even top whack in an old folk's wheelchair race.'

'Don't call her Mouse,' snapped Mercy from the passenger seat.

'Why not?' Tommy shrugged. 'That's what she is. A little squeaker—'

'Well, you're a gobby prick,' spat Mercy, 'but I don't spend every second of every day reminding you of that, do I?'

Tommy was about to reply when Lucas beat him to it. 'Oh, come on. All this arguing … it's getting tedious. For the time being at least, you two have to find a way to get on with each other. So, let's start at the beginning. I don't think we've been properly introduced, have we? I'm Lucas.'

'Mercy,' said Mercy, refusing to turn around.

'Cool name,' said Tommy, patting her gently on the head.

Rose cleared her throat. 'Rose.'

'Yeah, not so cool,' Tommy frowned. 'Dull as dishwater—'

'Cut it out!' said Lucas firmly. 'That … shit banter or whatever you think it is … has to stop. From now on, we work together. Like it or not, we're a team.'

'Too right,' grinned Tommy. 'I've always wanted my own gang. What did Pleasant Agatha call us again? The … um … Deadly Dudes of Death or something …'

'The Nearly Dearly Departed Club,' said Mercy.

'Ah, that's it,' groaned Tommy. 'Bit naff really. We sound like a bunch of geriatrics nibbling shrivelled-up fish-paste sandwiches on a park bench. Let's put it this way. I won't be using it in any of my chat-up lines. Not that I need chat-up lines, of course. I just let my face do the talking.' He glanced over at Lucas. The big man was silently fuming. 'Sorry, I seem to have strayed off course. That's a sure sign of having too much to say and not enough time to say it. Right, I'm Tommy. Tommy O'Strife. I'm a good boy really. Ask my mum.'

Mercy finally looked behind her. 'You've got a mum?'

'Not exactly.' Tommy lowered his head. Pretended to wipe a tear from his eye. 'I *had* a mum. Yes, I know I said you could ask her, but I never said she'd reply, did I? She's quite ignorant in all honesty. But then you would be too if you were six foot under. Poor old girl. Nobody could believe it when she slipped in the shower and smashed straight through the bathroom window.'

'Seriously?' The breath caught in Rose's throat. 'That's … that's horrible.'

'It's also a lie,' said Lucas, rolling his eyes. 'It's what he does. He can't help himself. I thought you would've realised that by now.'

Tommy snorted. 'Chill out, man. It was just a joke. Thanks for your concern, though, everybody. Much appreciated.'

Lucas stared at the other man until he took the hint and stopped talking.

'Okay, correct me if I'm wrong, but as far as I can tell we've got two leads,' Lucas began. 'The girlfriend and the shady boss. Miles has given us addresses for them both. The girlfriend's in a block of flats at the top end of town, whilst the boss seems to spend much of his time in a nightclub close to the centre. Looking at this map of Stainmouth they're a couple of miles apart. Anybody got any preference as to which one we visit first?'

'Kind of,' said Tommy. 'I say we split up. No, hear me out. Whatever happens, we don't want to go in mob-handed, do we? It'll cause a scene. Arouse suspicion.' Tommy sat forward. Rested his chin on Mercy's shoulder. 'Why don't me and you go and drop in on this nightclub owner. We can have a few drinks whilst we're there. A bit of a boogie.'

'I'm not going anywhere with you,' scowled Mercy.

Tommy pulled a face. 'Ah, worried you can't keep your hands off me, eh?'

'Fists … not hands,' replied Mercy. 'No, I'll go with Lucas and visit the girlfriend. Rose can drop us off first and then the two of you can take the car.'

'Fine,' sighed Tommy, falling back into his seat. 'I'll go with … erm … Rose. I'm sure we've got lots in common.'

'That's the spirit,' said Lucas, smiling to himself as the Fiat maintained its steady twenty miles per hour. 'You're bound to have plenty to squeak about.'

CHAPTER SEVENTEEN

Rocketway Heights was a seventeen-storey tower block to the north of Stainmouth.

A drab concrete erection, it consisted of one hundred and thirty-six flats, one of which just happened to be the home of Gina Pritchard.

Hopefully. Fingers crossed.

Rose dropped Lucas and Mercy off at the main entrance. The door had been left ajar, an open invitation to all manner of waifs and strays. Once inside, they were greeted by a low ceiling, stained walls and a dirty concrete floor. And graffiti. It was everywhere they looked. Most of it downright rude. Offensive even. Especially if your name was Hannah and you lived on the second floor.

Lucas set off for the lift, stumbling to a halt when he spotted the *Out of Order* sign draped across its doors. He responded with a groan. Of course it was faulty. Why would he expect anything less?

'Remind me what number she lives at again,' he said, fearing the worst.

'Flat ninety-eight,' replied Mercy.

'Yeah, thought so. And what floor is that on?'

'The thirteenth.'

'It gets better.' Lucas veered towards the stairs. At first, they walked in silence. By the time they had reached the fifth floor, however, he felt the need to speak up. 'Quick question. Why is there always a different smell on every landing? Weed and sick. Weed and beer. Weed and dirty nappies—'

'Have a bit of compassion, why don't you?' said Mercy. 'It's easy to judge, but you don't know these people. Life's tough when you've got nothing.'

'I'm not talking about money,' insisted Lucas. 'I'm talking about personal pride. Morals. Respect. When did we ... society as a whole ... let those old values die out?'

'Bit self-righteous. Try living in the real world.'

'I'm not stirring for an argument.'

'No, not much!' Mercy held her tongue as they passed a boy on the stairwell. Twelve or thirteen at best. He was carrying a mountain bike. The back wheel had been removed, whilst a steel lock swung limply from the frame.

'Stolen probably,' muttered Lucas under his breath.

Mercy couldn't help but bite back. 'There you go again. Judging people. It could always be *his* bike. He might have lost the key to the lock. Or forgotten the combination. Not everyone's a criminal.'

'I said stolen *probably*,' stressed Lucas. 'I'm not one hundred-per-cent certain. Just ninety-nine ...'

Shit joke or not, Mercy let it go. They were on the seventh floor. Past halfway. The last thing she wanted was to keep on arguing the rest of the way. Besides, maybe Lucas had a point. Not about the bike; about the smell. Curiously enough, it did seem to change with every floor. And, yes, it was revolting. Not that she'd ever tell him that.

'What was your childhood like?' asked Lucas, out of the blue. 'Were you happy? Did you have much?'

Mercy hesitated. She had never felt comfortable talking about herself. Her life. Her past. What she'd been. What she was now.

Lucas sensed her unease. 'Sorry. I wasn't being nosey—'

'It was pretty grim if I'm being honest,' revealed Mercy, surprising herself in the process. 'I never knew my mum, and my dad died when I was twelve.'

'Oh.' Lucas fiddled awkwardly with his trousers. They were a little too tight around the waist and pinched when he climbed the stairs. 'You don't have to talk about it,' he mumbled. 'If it's … you know … still raw.'

'It's not,' said Mercy. That much was true. 'It was a long time ago now. More than ten years. My dad was both a useless father and a massive drinker. He used to live in our local pub. No, really. He had a bed in the back bar. I only saw him once … twice a week. If anything it was a relief when he finally died. Don't look at me like that; he wasn't a good man. The drink made him violent and his fists got him into trouble. I mourned him for about ten minutes and then came to a decision that changed my life forever. I decided to keep his death quiet. Got two of his old drinking mates to bury him under a bridge. They probably forgot about it the next day. The three of us were the only ones who even knew he had popped his clogs so my secret was never exposed.'

'Fuck me, that's bleak,' frowned Lucas. 'And I thought I'd had it rough going into care at fifteen. What happened to you after that?'

'Nothing,' said Mercy. 'I looked after myself. I could cook and clean by then so it wasn't too much of a hassle. I kept on claiming my dad's sickness benefits and always went to school so the authorities didn't suspect a thing. Parents' evenings were a bit tricky, though. There's only so many times you can pretend your dad has to work late.' Mercy paused. It felt funny to speak about this now, after all this time. Funny in a good way. A release even. 'I suppose things only really changed when I turned sixteen,' she continued. 'I left school and got a job. Just shop work. Then I discovered boxing. Better than that, I got good at it.'

Lucas began to smile. 'There you go. You've just backed up my argument. You rejected the hand you were dealt and turned things around. You found a way to get yourself out of it.'

'What? By bare-knuckle boxing?' laughed Mercy, barely noticing that they had reached the thirteenth floor. 'Dodgy fights in dingy basements? Taking a dive for a few extra quid? Yeah, very glamorous. I'm a role model for kids everywhere.'

'Don't put yourself down,' said Lucas. 'That was *a* way. *Your* way. That's better than most. As an aside, sniff the air and tell me that's not weed and lamb kebab.'

Mercy did as he asked. 'Chicken – not lamb,' she said, trying not to smile. 'There's a difference.'

They stopped soon after at a wooden door with peeling

paint and a lop-sided handle. Their destination of choice. Flat ninety-eight.

Lucas clenched his fist and pounded on the door.

'Steady,' said Mercy. 'You're not a policeman anymore.'

Lucas glanced nervously over his shoulder. 'Keep it down, will you? Given half a chance the locals would probably string me up by my balls if they ever found that out.'

Mercy pushed past him and knocked herself. Not so loud. Less threatening. The result, however, was the same. 'I guess there's nobody home.'

A door along the corridor opened a few inches and a head popped into view. It was an elderly woman. Suspicious eyes hidden behind thick-rimmed spectacles.

'Sorry to disturb you,' began Lucas, edging towards her. 'You don't happen to …' The door closed quickly before he could finish his sentence. 'Charming.'

'You can't blame her,' grinned Mercy. 'You'd do the same if you saw us two lurking about.'

'Why? Because we're black?'

'No, because we're bloody ugly,' said Mercy. 'You more than me. I've just got a few cuts and bruises from fighting. You look like someone's hit you in the face with a hammer. Repeatedly. Day and night.'

'I would blame it on the accident, but I looked like that before,' smiled Lucas. 'Some people call it rugged. Handsome even.'

Mercy shook her head at him. 'Talking to yourself in the mirror doesn't count.'

Next thing she knew, Lucas was shifting her to one side so he could crouch down by the door. He lifted the letterbox. Peeked inside the flat. Sighed.

'We've got a problem,' he said, standing up.

'What kind of problem?'

Lucas pulled a face. 'The dead kind.'

CHAPTER EIGHTEEN

Rose parked the Fiat across the road from the Everything's Electric nightclub.

Vernon Gold's list of businesses was as long as your arm, but they had to start somewhere. And this was as good a place as any.

'Better late than never.' Tommy admired himself in the rear view mirror. Ran a hand through his hair. 'Give me half-an-hour tops. This shouldn't take long.'

Rose turned to him. 'Pardon?'

'Do I really have to repeat myself? This shouldn't take long.'

'What shouldn't take long?' Rose cleared her throat. Chose a different approach. 'Where are you going?'

'In there.' Tommy gestured towards the nightclub. 'I thought that was obvious. We haven't just come here for a recce.'

Rose stared at him, confused.

'A reconnaissance,' explained Tommy. 'This isn't the early learning centre. I don't just want to look and listen. I want to get up close and personal.'

'What about me?'

'What about you? You're not coming if that's what you're thinking. This is my area of expertise. Nightclubs are my natural habitat. I fit in. And you ... well, you don't. Seriously, leave this to me. I'll be in and out before you know it.'

Rose was overly aware of her heartbeat. 'So, what am I supposed to do?'

'Settle down and enjoy the peace and quiet.' Tommy pushed open the door as he spoke. Hopped out onto the pavement. 'You might want to keep the motor running, mind. Just in case I get into a spot of bother and we have to make a quick getaway ...'

Without another word, he slammed the door shut and marched across the road. Rose had seen enough. He clearly didn't care, so why should she? Instead, she locked the doors, closed her eyes and allowed herself to breathe.

What had Tommy said? *Settle down and enjoy the peace and quiet.* Fine. Then that was what she would do.

Or, at the very least, try to.

If there was one thing Tommy couldn't stand it was being stuck in a queue.

One minute or one hour, it didn't matter. A queue was still a queue. And *this* was a queue. And that was why Tommy disregarded it completely as he wandered straight up to the doormen who were stood by the entrance.

There were two of them. One had more facial fuzz than was socially acceptable, whilst the other was hideously ugly in a warthoggy kind of way. Beardy and the Beast then. Yes, that would do nicely. It was always good to put a name to the face.

Tommy drew to a halt beside Beardy. Tapped him on the shoulder. 'Daz in tonight, fella?'

Beardy viewed the interference with a look of sheer contempt. 'Daz?'

'Yeah, Daz.' Tommy rested a hand on the doorman's arm. Firm enough to prove a point. 'Everybody knows Daz. He's a Stainmouth legend. Been working the doors for years.'

'Never heard of him,' said Beardy, pushing Tommy's hand away. 'You know anybody called Daz?' he asked, turning towards his colleague.

The Beast shook his head, choosing, instead, to concentrate on the stream of eager clubbers who were desperate to get inside.

Tommy pondered his next move. That line had never failed him before. There was always a Daz working the door of every nightclub he had ever been to. Not Stainmouth, though. Typical.

'There's Baz,' announced the Beast.

A lifeline.

'Yeah, Baz,' shouted Tommy, over the hubbub of the crowd. 'We're good buddies. Known each other for years. He told me he could get me in for free if I was ever in town.'

'Really?' nodded Beardy. 'Maybe I should go and fetch him. You know, so he can confirm it.'

Tommy began to squirm. 'Well … yeah … if you must—'

'Not possible,' grinned the Beast. 'Baz doesn't exist. I made him up. Now fuck off.'

'Or just queue up,' suggested Beardy, offering a less aggressive option. 'It's what everybody else does.'

Tommy looked back along the line. It was a young crowd. Late teens, early twenties. Student night most probably. There were some quite tasty girls in there if he was being honest. He patted the notes in his pocket, deep in thought. He could afford to get in … couple of drinks … sniff out the dealers, no pun intended … get some gear on tick … and … and …

Stop.

'I'll just fuck off,' said Tommy, smiling at the doormen. 'Give my love to Baz, won't you?'

He walked away without another word. It was either that or risk a good pasting from a couple of steroid chomping meatheads. The most frustrating thing of all was the fact he had wasted at least five minutes failing to get into the club. He had told Rose he would be back within half-an-hour. The last thing he wanted was for her to come looking for him like some over-protective mother hen. Clucking around the dancefloor. Cramping his style.

Tommy took a sharp right, continued on until he reached the next turning then took a right again. He was out of sight, away from the crowds. He assumed he was at the back of the nightclub, an assumption that was proven correct when he scrambled up a seven foot wall and peered over the top. There was a square-shaped yard with industrial waste bins in one corner and empty barrels stacked high in the other.

There was also someone stood smoking by the fire exit.

Tommy ducked out of sight. He waited a minute or two before he heard a *swoosh* and then a *clunk*. He guessed it was the sound of a door opening and then closing in quick succession. Climbing up the wall, he was relieved to see that the smoker had ventured back inside. The coast was clear.

Tommy moved swiftly. Swinging his legs over the top, he dropped down onto the other side and hurried across the yard. He had a plan. Of sorts. Not perfect, but possible. With any luck, the fire exit would lead to a corridor which, in turn, would lead to the manager's office. There'd be a filing cabinet in there somewhere with all the employees' details. Crack it open and rummage about a bit. All alphabetical, touch wood. H for Hammerton. Name. Age. Address. Bingo.

Easy-peasy, lemon fuckin' squeezy.

Tommy was almost within touching distance of the fire exit when the door burst open. He stepped back, half-expecting another smoker to emerge from inside.

What he didn't expect to see, however, was blood.

Lots of blood.

Ah, shit …

CHAPTER NINETEEN

Crouching down by the door, Mercy lifted the letterbox and peered inside the flat.

She could see a poorly lit, narrow hallway. A swirly patterned carpet and tobacco-stained walls. Stuff everywhere. Empty bottles. Takeaway cartons. Newspapers and magazines.

And a body.

A woman. Over-sized t-shirt and tight shorts. Bare-footed. Eyes closed and mouth open. She was in the bathroom at the end of the hallway. Sprawled out in a crumpled mess by the toilet.

Mercy had seen enough. 'Are you sure she's dead?' she asked, standing up.

'We'll soon find out.' Lucas took a step back. 'Move to one side.'

'You can't just knock the door down,' frowned Mercy, refusing to shift. 'You'll make a right racket. The neighbours will call the police.'

'And the police won't get here for another twenty minutes at least,' finished Lucas. 'I should know. If needs be we'll be long gone by then.' He hesitated. 'We can't just leave her in there, can we? Have a bit of compassion.'

'Oh, very funny.' A reluctant Mercy moved away from the door. 'Go on then. Do your worst. Just try not to put your back out in the process.'

'As if.' Leaning back, Lucas lifted his leg and kicked out at the door. He was aiming for the lock. The lock, however, held firm.

Mercy didn't bother to conceal her smile. 'Is that all you've got? I thought the police were good at this sort of thing.'

'They are … *I* am.' Lucas shook his foot. Either in pain or frustration. It was hard to tell. 'It's these shoes … I need something heavier … work boots would do the trick … a solid heel …'

'Maybe I should have a go,' Mercy suggested. 'Put a bit of muscle behind it.'

That was the cue for Lucas to take another step back. He kicked again, striking the door with as much force as he could muster. This time the wood splintered and the lock broke.

'My hero,' grinned Mercy, pushing the door to one side. Lucas hurried past her into the flat, stopping only when he reached the bathroom. Kneeling down, he lifted the woman's wrist. Felt for her pulse.

'Is she still alive?' asked Mercy. She hadn't moved from the doorway, her eyes peeled for any nosey neighbours who chose to investigate.

'Just about,' replied Lucas. 'She's practically foaming at the mouth, though. And she stinks of sick. Help me carry her through to the bedroom, will you?'

Mercy took one last look along the corridor and then entered the flat, careful to close the wonky door behind her. Joining Lucas in the bathroom, she grabbed the woman by her arms, raising her slowly into the air. They carried her together through to the bedroom, laying her gently on a dishevelled bed.

'I don't like this.' Lucas repeatedly shook his head as he turned the woman onto her side. 'She might have choked on her own vomit. We should probably take her clothes off—'

'Whoa!' Mercy spluttered. 'This isn't some kind of fetish thing, is it?'

'I'm not joking,' insisted Lucas. 'We don't want a dead body on our hands, do we?' Taking hold of the woman's t-shirt, he started to pull it roughly over her head. He had barely begun, however, when a bare foot flew out and caught him right between the legs.

'Try that again and I'll scratch your eyes out!'

Lucas backed away, clutching his testicles. At the same time, the woman leapt up onto all fours, snarling and growling like a wild animal.

'Relax,' said Mercy, trying to keep her at arm's length. 'We're not here to hurt you. It's Gina, isn't it?'

'Why you asking?' spat the woman. 'Who are you? Police?'

Lucas was still struggling to catch his breath as he stood upright. 'If only. At least I'd have a taser to zap you with.'

That was the trigger. Without warning, the woman launched herself off the bed. She hit Lucas hard and the two of them toppled over onto the bedroom carpet. Fighting back, Lucas placed the palm of his hand flat against the woman's face, another layer of protection in case she tried to bite him.

'Get this psycho off me!' he cried out.

Get this psycho off me *please*, thought Mercy. Bending down, she grabbed the woman around her waist and dragged her to her feet.

'Calm down,' said Mercy. 'You'll only do something you regret.'

Eyes ablaze, the woman spun around in anger and swung wildly. Mercy blocked the blows and then clenched her fist. No, not a punch. That would do far too much damage. I mean, it wasn't as if she wanted to hurt her.

Okay, maybe just a little …

Shifting to one side, Mercy waited for the right moment and then slapped the woman across the face. Not full power, but firm enough.

Firm enough to stop her in her tracks.

Every ounce of fury vanished in an instant as the woman collapsed onto the bed, defeated.

'You are Gina, right?' asked Mercy. The woman nodded. 'We just want to talk,' she continued. 'That's all. Nothing more. Can we get you a drink? Glass of water? Cup of tea?'

'Not thirsty.' Gina wiped the back of her hand over her eyes. 'Wouldn't mind something stronger, though. Something to take the edge off.'

Mercy pursed her lips. She didn't like the sound of that. 'What do you mean exactly?'

'Let me think.' Gina sat up straight. Held out her hand. 'Pills or powders would be nice,' she said, her fingers trembling in anticipation. 'I'll let you decide.'

CHAPTER TWENTY

Tommy staggered backwards as a globule of blood arced across the nightclub yard and landed on his left shoe.

He looked towards the fire exit. There were three of them coming through the door. All men. Two different doormen from Beardy and the Beast, and a young guy in a Hawaiian shirt. One of the doormen was incredibly thin with razor-sharp gnashers, whilst the other was almost his exact opposite. Double the size with a huge belly and great big saggy man boobs.

Teeth and Tits. Perfect.

Compared to the other two, Hawaiian shirt seemed to be at something of a disadvantage. Bent double, he was being dragged along on his knees, clearly against his wishes. His head was bowed, his shoulders slumped. The blood was all his. It was streaming from both corners of his mouth. Running from his nose.

The doormen stopped suddenly when they saw Tommy. 'What you doing?' snarled Teeth.

'Having a smoke.' Tommy tried not to draw attention to his empty hands. 'I've just finished.'

'Yeah, well, run along then,' panted Tits. 'There's nothing to see here.'

'Fine by me.' Tommy swerved around the pool of blood that had formed on the ground as he veered towards the fire exit.

'You new?' asked Teeth.

Tommy shook his head. 'New to you perhaps, but then don't they say a stranger is just a friend you haven't met yet?'

Teeth's stare intensified. 'What's that supposed to mean?'

'Yeah, I'm new,' said Tommy hastily. 'Not been here long at all. I've worked at some of the other bars, though—'

'Alright, mate, I didn't ask for your life story,' Teeth sneered. 'You can go now. Leave us to it.'

A relieved Tommy was back on the move. That was easy. *Too* easy.

'Wait.'

Tommy waited.

'Pass me that knife, will you?' Teeth demanded. 'I've got my hands full here.'

Tommy didn't have to look far to locate the weapon in question. It was resting on one of the empty barrels, exposed to all weathers. Stainless steel with a long, sharp blade, it reminded Tommy of a chef's knife. Capable of cutting through meat and vegetables with precious little effort. The same probably applied to human flesh if and when required.

Tommy picked up the knife before turning back towards the guy in the Hawaiian shirt. The doormen had already knocked him about a bit, but the spirit was still intact.

'What did he do?' asked Tommy.

'He stole from Mr Gold,' said Tits. 'Young Dylan here knew the consequences before he dipped his fingers in the till. An eye for an eye and all that shit.'

Tommy nodded. Held out the knife. Teeth was all set to take it when it began to fall.

'Whoops. Butter fingers,' said Tommy, hopping backwards as it landed by his feet. 'Purely accidental, of course. I can be so clumsy sometimes.'

He waited for Teeth to crouch down to pick up the knife before he barged into him from behind. Tommy wasn't the biggest, but he still had a huge weight advantage. Sure enough, Teeth went down in stumbling slow motion. First, he lost his balance. Then he toppled over. Then he loosened his grip on the Hawaiian shirt.

Sensing his opportunity, Dylan wriggled furiously until Tits had little choice but to let go as well. Free from his shackles, the youth raced across the yard until he was close enough to throw himself at the wall. In no time at all he had scrambled over. Vanished from view.

Tommy put a hand to his mouth in mock horror. 'You'd better give chase,' he said, pointing both doormen in the right direction. 'I'm sure Mr Gold won't be a happy bunny if you just let him get away scot free.'

With that, Teeth and Tits hurried towards the wall. Tommy watched as they helped each other over before kicking the knife to one side.

Go on, Dylan lad. Do us both a favour and keep running.

Back on track, Tommy opened the fire exit door and peeked inside. As expected, it led straight into a darkened corridor. He could hear music coming from the club itself. The same repetitive pounding beat, accompanied by high-pitched vocals and tinny electronics.

Set me free … lift me up … take me higher … baby, baby, baby …

Nineties dance. Two-and-a-half minutes of pure cheese. Inoffensive and instantly forgettable.

Tommy tried to blank it out as he chose right over left and set off along the corridor. There were closed doors every few metres or so. *Store Cupboard. Staff Room. Staff Toilet.* He came to a halt at the next in line. He had found what he was looking for. The door to the *Manager's Office.*

He pressed down on the handle. It was bound to be locked.

Think again.

The handle dropped and the door opened. He was in.

CHAPTER TWENTY-ONE

It didn't take Mercy long to decide.

Decide that the last thing Gina Pritchard needed was more drugs.

Instead, she headed through to the kitchen and made her a cup of tea. Or the closest thing she could manage to a cup of tea. Mercy found a used teabag in the sink and some lumpy milk that was on the turn in one sad corner of the fridge. At least the kettle worked, even if it was clogged up with lime-scale. As a final flourish, Mercy added two heaped teaspoons of sugar, partly to hide the taste, but mostly because Gina looked as if she needed perking up a little.

When Mercy returned to the bedroom she found the other two in roughly the same positions as when she had left them. Lucas was leant against the wall, arms folded, a scowl on his face, whilst Gina was sat cross-legged on the bed, her attention drawn to a particularly fierce-looking scab on her left ankle.

'You two the best of friends now?' smiled Mercy. Silence. 'Well, at least you're not fighting anymore. That's a start.' She placed the cup down on the table beside Gina. 'There you go. It'll make you feel better. Sorry about your face. I shouldn't have slapped you.'

Gina touched her cheek. 'Don't matter.'

'I asked her about Benji, but she's refusing to talk,' said Lucas. 'Says she wants a tenner before she'll tell us anything. I didn't know smack was so cheap these days.'

That was all it took to make Gina fly off the handle. 'I don't touch smack,' she growled, holding out her arms. 'See. Where are the track marks? There aren't any, pal. And that's because I've never done it. Yeah, I like getting off my head, but I'm not a fuckin' junkie.'

'Okay,' snorted Lucas. 'I believe you. Thousands wouldn't.'

Gina was raging now. 'You don't know a thing about me!'

'I've got eyes.' Lucas made a point of looking her up and down. 'I can see what you are. What you've become. It's a shame really. How old are you? Twenty? Twenty-one? You've got your whole life ahead of you—'

'Oh, it's that simple, is it?' hissed Gina.

'It should be,' said Lucas. 'I'm talking about the basics. You could be quite pretty if you made an effort. Took a shower. Washed your hair and put some make-up on. You might want to think about cleaning this dump up once in a while as well—'

Gina lunged forward. 'Why you—'

'Whoa!' Mercy put an arm across the other woman's chest, easing her back onto the bed. 'We only want to ask you a few questions and then we'll be on our way. We're not here to cause trouble.'

'Well, tough shit 'cos I ain't saying a word,' spat Gina. 'Not whilst he's in here.'

Mercy nodded. There was one way to solve that particular problem. 'Wait outside,' she said, steering Lucas towards the door.

'Seriously?' Lucas pulled a face. 'What have I done?'

'Everything,' said Mercy. 'And all of it wrong. Listen, just leave this to me. I won't be long.'

Lucas hesitated before heading back into the hallway.

'Sorry about him,' said Mercy, sitting down on the bed beside Gina. 'He can be a little … confrontational at times.'

'He's a prick,' said Gina bluntly. 'You're alright, though. You understand.'

Mercy forced a smile. She wasn't sure she did, not really, but there was no point arguing about it now. 'So, you'll tell me what I want to know, yeah?'

Gina sat forward. 'Course I will … for a price.'

Her eyes widened as Mercy removed a ten pound note from her pocket.

'Do you want me to pretend that I'm going to buy milk and bread with it?' Gina grinned, snatching the note from Mercy's fingers.

Mercy shook her head. 'It's yours to spend now, however you see fit. Right, I think you know by now that we're … *I'm* looking for Benji—'

'What's he done now?' asked Gina. Her tone had softened a little. 'He's not in any trouble, is he?'

'We're not sure. That's why we came to you first. You're the closest tie we've got to him.'

ANTHONY GRACE

Gina shrugged. 'I *was* the closest. Not anymore, though. I haven't seen him for ages.' She paused. 'We shouldn't have come here. To Stainmouth. It was a mistake. Things were going well before then. We were in love.'

'So, why *did* you come here?'

'Money,' said Gina. 'We couldn't afford to live in London. Everything costs a bomb. Oh, and we wanted to get away from his parents. Especially his mum. She kept nagging Benji, telling him I wasn't good enough. Moving to Stainmouth was the best way to throw it back in her face.'

Mercy nodded. Fair enough.

'We had only been here a few months when me and Benji split up,' Gina continued. 'We were arguing all the time. Middle of the night, first thing in the morning, it didn't matter. We had grown apart. Benji had started working for a snake called Vernon Gold. He was hardly ever around. That's why I began mixing with some of the neighbours. They opened my eyes to … recreational pursuits, shall we say. It helped to take my mind off things. You can't blame me. I've had a rotten life. People have always treated me like shit.'

Mercy stayed silent. She had no wish to go down that particular route. 'Tell me about Gold.'

'I've only met him a few times. Yeah, he appears friendly at first, charming even, but it's all an act. Once he's got his claws into you, you're doomed. He got Benji mixed up in all manner of bad stuff. I'm guessing Gold will know where he is, but there's no way he'll tell you. Not without a fight.'

Yes, that was always an option, thought Mercy. The one

that came naturally. 'Is there anybody else we can talk to about Benji? Friends? Acquaintances?'

'There was one lad he was really tight with,' said Gina. 'Eddie something-or-other. Always down the boxing club on Marlowe Street. He might've worked for Gold too for all I know.'

Mercy made a mental note of that. 'Is that it? There's nothing else you can tell me.'

'There is something.' Gina scratched her face so hard that Mercy could see the marks from her jagged fingernails. 'We had a kid, me and Benji. A girl. Amelia.'

Mercy raised an eyebrow. Miles had told them that there might be a child involved, but it had completely slipped her mind. 'Where is she?' asked Mercy, glancing back into the hallway.

'Not here if that's what you're thinking,' said Gina. 'Benji took her when we split. Said I wasn't fit to be a mother.'

'And you just accepted that? You didn't try and stop him?'

'Didn't like the kid anyway,' smirked Gina. 'Too much fuss and bother. Besides, I had other things going on. Like your mate said, I've got my whole life ahead of me. Don't need no baby dragging me down. Ruining my fun … hey, where you going?'

Mercy walked out of the bedroom without another word. It was time to leave. There was nothing to be gained from staying a moment longer. Besides, she had heard enough.

Enough hate and spite to last a lifetime.

CHAPTER TWENTY-TWO

Rose drummed her fingers repeatedly on the steering wheel.

Tommy had been gone for nineteen minutes. And twenty-three seconds. Twenty-four … twenty-five … twenty-six …

She didn't know why she was counting. To pass the time perhaps. Or maybe because she was actually concerned. Not about Tommy as such. About *this*. Her situation. Stuck in the Fiat 500. Outside a nightclub. All alone in a strange town.

This – whatever *this* was – was as far removed from the norm as Rose could possibly imagine. She didn't go out much. Not even when she was alive. Why would she start now that she was dead?

Dead.

It felt odd to think of herself that way. She wasn't dead. Fact. This wasn't a dream. It wasn't even a nightmare. She didn't need to pinch herself to wake up. No, if anything, this was simply the hand she had been dealt, however unfair.

An alternative life. Set in a different part of the country. Starring people she had never met before.

She didn't have to play a role herself, though.

What was to stop her from putting her foot down and driving away? The tank was full. She could go anywhere she desired. Vanish in the blink of an eye. Nobody would even know she had gone.

Except she couldn't, could she? Not really. Not whilst she was Rose Carrington-Finch. Her life may have changed, but some things remained the same.

Twenty-one minutes and forty-seven seconds … forty-eight … forty-nine … fifty …

Tommy closed the door gently behind him.

There was a key dangling from the keyhole. He turned it once and then tossed it across the room. Bad move. He would have to get out at some point. Enter first, exit later. Standard practice. With that in mind, he crouched down and picked it up. There was a moral to that particular series of events. *Think before you act.* Still, why change the habit of a lifetime? Act now and don't bother to think at all. Yeah, that was more like it. The perfect formula by which to live a life most unpredictable.

Tommy gave the Manager's Office a quick once over. It was a square room with black walls, a red carpet and gold furnishings. Tacky as fuck and twice as garish. Quite big, though. Too big for a poxy office. There was a desk at one end and a black leather sofa at the other. The desk was wooden, old and battered, also known as antique to those in the know. Tommy's eyes wandered towards a glass decanter set amongst the mounds of paperwork. It was filled with a glorious reddish-brown liquid. He licked his lips. That would be his reward if … *when* he found Benji Hammerton's address. Give him something to look forward to. A little treat to make the drive back with Rose slightly more tolerable.

It was only when he shifted his gaze away from the desk that he spotted it. Hidden away in a corner. A free-standing filing cabinet. Tommy almost patted himself on the back as he walked over to it. He had guessed correctly. Things were going to plan.

He pulled at the top drawer. Locked. Damn. There was still work to do before he could take a drink.

He returned to the desk, poked around a bit until he found what he was looking for. A small box of odds and ends. Stationery mostly. Pens and pencils. A hole punch. Stapler. And … paperclips. Bingo.

Tommy took two of the clips and headed back to the filing cabinet. He straightened one of them out, but left an end still bent. He then straightened out the other, this time making three little bumps at the point. Pliers would've come in handy for that, but beggars can't be choosers. Once he had finished he had two deformed-looking paperclips. Or, to be precise, a tension wrench and a lock pick.

He was ready to get to work.

Tommy inserted the tension wrench first and applied light pressure. He followed it with the pick, squeezing it inside the lock until he felt resistance. He began to move it back and forth. He had done this before. Many times. And it had never failed him.

Back and forth …

It was only a filing cabinet for pity's sake. Nothing too

challenging. If in doubt, blame it on your tools. Maybe the paper clip was too thin. Too weak. Too … paper-clippy.

Back and forth …

It had never failed him. Why had he thought that? It was bound to go wrong eventually. Everything did.

Tommy had already turned his attention to Plan B (give the filing cabinet a bloody big kick) when the pins inside the lock finally dropped. He held the clips steady whilst he opened the top drawer. Satisfaction turned to disappointment in a flash. The drawer wasn't exactly empty, but it wasn't full either. Not with what he expected. There were several notepads in there, half-a-bottle of Scotch and fifty pounds in notes. Tommy grabbed the cash without thinking. Better in his pocket than somebody elses. Especially when that *somebody else* was Vernon Gold. He switched to the notepads, casually flicking through them. They were full of numbers. Not accounts as such; just random digits dotted around on each page. No use to the untrained eye.

Tommy was all set to close the drawer when a series of sounds distracted him. They were coming from somewhere outside the office. Footsteps along the corridor. Distant chatter.

Without warning, the door handle began to jerk up and down. Somebody was trying to get in. Tommy relaxed a little when he remembered he had locked the door. That was a stroke of luck. If nothing else it would buy him some time.

The next thing he heard was the sound of a key rattling around in the keyhole.

So much for a stroke of luck.

His time, from that moment forth, was up.

CHAPTER TWENTY-THREE

'What sort of mother just abandons her own child?'

Lucas stared intently at Mercy as they made their way towards the stairs. If he was waiting for an answer though, he'd be waiting a long time. Mercy had nothing. No explanation or excuse. No good reason why somebody would ever behave that way.

'You didn't give her any money, did you?' pressed Lucas.

Mercy hesitated for a moment too long before shaking her head.

Lucas, thankfully, didn't pick up on it. 'Good. She'd only buy drugs with it if you had. There's no helping some people.'

Mercy refused to bite. Okay, so maybe he had a point. Sort of. He didn't have to keep banging on about it though, did he?

'Listen.' Lucas stopped at the top of the stairwell. 'I've seen it so many times before it's unreal. You try and do everything you can and they just throw it back in your face. We can't change those on a path to destruction; they have to change themselves.'

'I know that,' muttered Mercy. 'It's just … oh, forget it.'

Lucas opened his mouth and then closed it just as quickly. By the look on Mercy's face he was starting to irritate her. Fair enough. He was starting to irritate himself if he was being honest. All this ranting and raving. Preaching about random strangers he barely knew. He blamed it on the job. The *old* job. It was hard not to be cynical when all you ever came across were the lowest of the low.

Still, that was all in the past. Maybe he could make some changes. Lighten up a little. Smile from time to time. Starting … now.

'Race you to the bottom,' he said, nodding towards the stairs. 'Last one down is a rotten egg.'

'A rotten egg?' Mercy began to laugh. 'How old are you?'

Turning away, Lucas was about to start his descent when the lift – the same lift that was supposedly out of order – reached the thirteenth floor. He watched as the doors slid slowly to one side.

Three men emerged onto the landing.

Lucas took them in. No, not men. Almost, but not quite. Youths. Late teens, early-twenties. Tall, well built. Not massive, but big enough. Two white, one black. Tracksuits. Not Adidas or Nike. More expensive than that. Gold jewellery and spotless white trainers. Hoods and face masks. Not for surgical purposes either. Just so they couldn't be identified by the police.

Two of the youths stopped suddenly, shocked by the mere sight of mysterious strangers. The third, meanwhile, wandered straight up to Mercy, drawing to a halt when they were eye to eye. 'You good, girl?'

Mercy held her ground. Nodded.

Satisfied, the youth turned to Lucas. 'And you?'

Lucas shrugged. 'And me *what?*'

'Are … you … good?' drawled the youth slowly.

'Sorry, I can't quite make out what you're trying to say,' replied Lucas, deadly serious. 'Your voice … it's all muffled. That mask doesn't help, of course. Maybe you'd like to remove it. Your face can't be that ugly.'

Mercy glared at him out the corner of one eye. This wasn't the time for smart arse comments; this was the time for getting out of there with as few a complications as possible. Yes, boys like these might not be as tough as they think, but they could still pull something without warning. Something sharp. Something life-threatening.

To Mercy's surprise, the youth lowered his mask before going one step further and pulling down his hood. His face was pale, but scarred with pockmarks, no doubt the result of bad acne when he was younger. He had hair shaven to the skin at the back and sides with a Caesar fringe at the front, and a slit in one eyebrow.

'Just for you,' he said, smirking at Lucas. 'I'm Cutz.'

'With a *z*, I'm betting,' said Lucas. 'I'll be disappointed if it's not.'

Cutz strode forward. Pushed out his chest. 'You got a problem with me, bruv?'

'Bruv?' Lucas sighed. 'Somebody else calling me that recently. He's a lot like you. Jumped up. Too big for his boots.'

'What's your problem?' Cutz growled. 'This is my manor. The Rocketway belongs to me—'

'Then you might be able to help us,' chipped in Mercy, quick to intervene before things escalated. 'We're looking for someone. Benji Hammerton. Do you know him?'

Cutz made a point of pretending to think. 'Benji Hammerton? That ain't ringing no bells, but if we ever meet I'll be sure to pass on your regards.'

'Fine.' Mercy made to leave, but didn't get far before Cutz halted her progress with an arm across her chest. 'What do you think you're doing?' she asked, her voice calm yet firm.

'We have rules,' Cutz began. 'Strangers can't just roll into the Rocketway uninvited, not without a contribution to the cause. Get your phones out.'

Lucas shook his head. 'Trust me, you really don't want us to do that.'

'Get … your … phones … out!' Cutz demanded. 'I ain't asking again.'

'Have it your way.' Lucas took the Nokia from his pocket. There was a moment's silence before the three youths started to laugh.

'Are you joking?' cried Cutz.

'Not intentionally,' said Lucas.

'It's all we've got,' shrugged Mercy. 'You can take it or leave it.'

'I think we all know the answer to that,' grinned Cutz. The grin vanished in an instant, only to be replaced by an ugly sneer. 'No one leaves the Rocketway without contributing to the cause. If you've nothing to offer then maybe I'll have to take something myself. I never did tell you why they call me Cutz, did I?'

With that, he reached into his tracksuit and removed the *something* that Mercy had feared most. The something sharp. The something life-threatening.

The other two followed suit immediately.

Three youths.

Three knives.

One colossal problem.

CHAPTER TWENTY-FOUR

Agatha Pleasant ended the call.

She was sat in her makeshift office in the empty room above the wedding-dress shop, deep in the heart of Stainmouth town centre. She was pleased with what Miles had told her. By all accounts, the four new recruits had settled in relatively well at Proud Mary's. Few arguments. No more violent outbursts. No cause for concern. If anything, they seemed to have accepted their fate. Agatha corrected herself. It wasn't a fate. It was a future.

What surprised her most, however, was the fact they were already on the move. The Fiat 500 had made its way out of Croplington before stopping in Stainmouth. Yes, they could've been trying to escape, but Agatha doubted that very much. More likely, they were getting straight down to business. They were searching for Benji Hammerton.

Her Nearly Dearly Departed Club was no longer the stuff of dreams. It was a reality.

A wave of optimism swept over her that was so powerful it made Agatha lift her phone and scroll through her list of contacts. She stopped at *S*, hesitated, before placing the phone back down on the desk. She tried to find ways to build up the courage. Took a breath or two whilst waiting for the right moment.

The same right moment that never seemed to come.

There was a call she had to make, not through choice, but through necessity. Obligation even.

Just do it, you silly woman.

Agatha jabbed at the button. Pressed the phone against her ear. Listened whilst it started to ring. And ring. And …

She was about to give up when the call was finally answered.

'Hello.'

'Hi, Sabby.' Agatha paused. 'It's me. Your mum.'

'Yes, I know who you are. What's up? It's quite late.'

'It's not *that* late,' chuckled Agatha. Why was she laughing? 'It's only half-nine.'

'Exactly,' Sabby grumbled. 'It's been a lousy day. We're over-run at work and I couldn't get away until dark. Then, when I get home, I find that Digby has been shitting all over the place.'

Agatha frowned. 'Digby?'

'Our dog,' explained Sabby. 'He's a French bulldog. We got him a few months ago. He can't seem to control his back passage …'

'I didn't know you had a dog.'

'You mean I didn't tell you,' snapped Sabby.

'No, I mean I didn't ask. I don't ask about much, do I? I've been busy—'

'We're *all* busy. Not just you.' Sabby fell silent. 'Is there something that you *actually* want?'

'No … no … not really,' mumbled Agatha. 'Just … you know … a chat.'

'A chat?' Sabby snorted. 'You don't do *chats*. I suppose you're going to tell me that you've changed. That this is the new you.'

Agatha recognised the condescending tone in her daughter's voice. 'No, nothing like that. It was a spur of the moment thing.'

Liar.

Agatha waited for her daughter to speak. She didn't.

'How's Dean?' asked Agatha, filling the silence herself.

'Good.'

'Is he still working nights?'

'He's not worked nights for three years.'

'Really?' Agatha rubbed her eyes. 'Next thing you know you'll be telling me he doesn't like football anymore.'

'He's never liked football. Just rugby.'

'Oh, yes, rugby. My mistake. And the twins. Are they both okay?'

'They're fine. Hold on … I think I can hear them now.' Sabby's voice seemed to fade as if she had turned away from her phone. 'I'd better go and—'

'Maybe you could fetch them,' suggested Agatha. 'I'm sure they'd love to speak to Grandma.'

'Not tonight. They're in bed. Like I said, it's late.'

Agatha nodded. And that was that. There was nothing more to say. 'Of course. I should probably leave you to it. Give my love to everybody, won't you? Tell them I called.'

'Will do. Bye.'

'Wait.' Agatha squirmed in her chair. 'Love you.'

'Yeah. Bye.'

Agatha ended the call. Yes, that went well. Better than usual. She took a deep breath and tried to clear her mind.

Obligation over, now she had work to do.

But then she *always* had work to do.

CHAPTER TWENTY-FIVE

Fifty-eight … fifty nine … sixty …

The thirty minutes were up.

Rose nibbled at her fingernails as she tried to recall Tommy's exact words.

Give me half-an-hour tops. This shouldn't take long.

She had done everything he'd asked. And he still wasn't out yet. What else had he said? That he might get into a *spot of bother*. Rose had no idea what constituted *bother*, or even how you'd measure a *spot*. An argument? A fight?

Or worse?

She had to do something. Didn't she? Well, not necessarily. From the moment she had first cast eyes on him, Rose knew that Tommy O'Strife was everything she despised in a man. In a human being, to be precise. He was cocky and overbearing. So full of himself he could pop at any moment. The only times he seemed to acknowledge her existence was when he wanted to ridicule her. Mouse. That was worse than Roxanne. No, he was just like all the others. Every last person she had left behind in Norwich. All of them just disregarded her with a casual glance. Boring. Plain. Vanilla.

Move on. Nothing to see here.

Rose's attention shifted towards a boy staggering along the pavement. Eighteen at most. Designer t-shirt and black jeans. Completely inadequate clothing on such a cold evening. Maybe it was the alcohol that was warming him up. He was clearly drunk. Either that or he had simply forgotten how to walk.

Drawing level with the Fiat, the boy dropped his head, leant forward and threw up all over the car's bonnet. It was nothing more than liquid. He waited until he had finished before wiping his mouth on his bare arm. At the same time he locked eyes with Rose. There was a moment's delay whilst his befuddled brain struggled to process the situation. Once he had done so, he held his ground. Laid down the challenge.

Go on. Say something. I dare you.

Rose studied the gear stick with a painful intensity, all the while continuing to count. She left it twenty seconds before raising her head. The boy may have gone, but he had left the sick behind as a lasting memento. The sight of it was enough to make Rose feel both disgusted and angry in equal measures. Disgusted with the drunk. Angry with herself.

When you're scared of living, but afraid to die.

Rose had heard that in a song. She couldn't remember which, but then it was only the words that mattered. They were her all over. Summed her up perfectly.

Do something. For once in your pitiful life, just do something.

Tommy had been in there thirty-four minutes now. And

seventeen seconds. Maybe he was enjoying himself so much that he had forgotten all about her. Or maybe he was lying in a pool of his own blood. There was no middle ground with Rose.

Did she really hate him? Or did she just hate herself?

Do something.

Do something.

Do something.

Opening the door, Rose climbed out of the car and set off towards the nightclub.

This was it.

This was something.

Tommy needed a hiding place. Somewhere he couldn't be spotted in the Manager's Office. His options were seriously limited, but not entirely non-existent. Behind the sofa. Under the desk. Inside the filing cabinet. No, don't be stupid.

He checked himself. This wasn't him. Panic-stricken and petrified. Running away like a frightened child. What was the point in that? Whoever was outside, they were bound to find him eventually. Surely it was better to beat them at their own game. Ask anyone. The element of surprise was half the battle.

The key stopped jangling in the keyhole. Skipping over the carpet, Tommy sat down behind the desk and poured himself a large brandy from the decanter. Leaning back in the chair, he put his feet up as he took a sip.

The door opened a moment later.

'Good evening.' A smiling Tommy raised his glass, toasting the new arrivals. 'Can I get you a drink?'

CHAPTER TWENTY-SIX

Agatha stood up from her desk and stretched.

It was gone eleven. A long, laborious day was drawing to a close and she was exhausted. She was booked in at The Nightingale Hotel, well within walking distance of the wedding-dress shop. The only five star hotel in Stainmouth, it was the perfect location for her to set up base. She didn't usually stay *on site*, but on this occasion she was prepared to make an exception. She wanted to be close by, just in case. No, not wanted to. *Needed to*. At least she had Miles to call upon if things went belly up. He was across town in a slightly less swanky establishment. If required, he would be there in a flash. He was good like that.

Agatha closed her laptop, picked up her belongings and made her way towards the exit. She was all set to leave when a dull vibration in her handbag brought her to a halt. It was her phone. One of many. Reaching inside, Agatha rummaged around until she found the culprit. She studied the screen as it continued to vibrate. *No caller ID*. That made sense. Not many people had that particular number. Only those above her in the pecking order. The kind of caller that you shouldn't really ignore.

Agatha answered before it was too late. 'Hello.'

'Well, bugger me. I'd almost given up on you.' A man. Gruff in tone. Blunt in approach. 'Sorry for the late interruption, but there's nothing I hate more than noddin' off on a problem. Wouldn't want to have any nasty dreams now, would I?'

'I guess not.' Agatha paused. 'Who is this exactly?'

The caller brayed like an agitated donkey. 'This is exactly Clifford Goose, madam. Chief Constable of Stainmouth police force.'

Agatha rested her phone against her shoulder. She had been expecting a call like this at some point. Stainmouth's top dogs were bound to come sniffing eventually. Shame it was so early in proceedings, though. They had only been in town a day for heaven's sake.

'You still there, Miss Pleasant?' Goose bellowed. 'Bloody signal. Don't know why I chuffin' bother sometimes …'

'Yes, sorry, I'm here. I lost you for a moment, but it's fine now. And, please, call me Agatha.'

'Suit yourself … Agatha. This isn't a social call, mind. Purely business.'

'Doesn't mean we can't be friendly.'

'Pleased to hear it.' Goose made a strange gargling sound, before following it up with a burp or two. 'Now, just so you know, I'm the kind of fellow who chooses to pop a blister with a flamethrower. I'm like a bull in a Chinese shop—'

'A *china* shop,' said Agatha, jumping in. 'A bull in a china shop.'

'Is that so?' Goose seemed to mull it over. 'Makes sense,

117

I suppose. What's a Chinese shop then?'

'No idea. A supermarket perhaps … a restaurant … takeaway—'

'Well, I'm like a bull in all of those and then some,' hollered Goose.

Agatha should really have let that go. And yet … 'You mean you're incredibly clumsy. You make mistakes. Cause damage along the way.'

'Not bloomin' likely!' barked Goose. 'Listen, don't get bogged down in the details. All you need to know is that I don't beat around the bloody barbecue. That's why I called when I did. I've got a question. A question that can't wait 'til the morning. What are you doing?'

'What am I doing?' Agatha played dumb. 'I'm talking to you—'

'What are you doing *here*?' pressed Goose. 'In Stainmouth? On my patch?'

Agatha ignored the question. Asked one of her own. 'How did you get this number?'

'I didn't; *it* came to me,' said Goose cryptically. 'I got a call about an hour ago. From a woman. Very la-di-da, she was. Called herself Lady Jane. It's not often I get to talk to the aristocracy. Plenty of nobs. Just not nobility.'

Agatha sighed. 'Her name's not Jane and she's certainly not a lady. Not the last time I checked, anyway. Did she also inform you that she was very high up in the British Government?'

'Something like that,' muttered Goose, the irritation evident in his voice. 'I drifted off if I'm being honest. My ears did prick up, however, when she told me that one of her underlings was coming to Stainmouth with an elite squad for a top secret operation.'

Agatha tried not to laugh. *Elite squad. Top secret operation.* That was something of an overstatement. The *underling* bit annoyed her, though. Lady Jane was only slightly higher up in the chain than she was. Less of a boss. More a senior colleague.

'It's not a top secret operation; just a favour for an old friend,' Agatha explained. 'A missing son gone off the rails. It shouldn't be too much of a stretch for my … elite squad.' The cogs began to turn. 'What do you know about a man called Vernon Gold?'

Goose groaned out loud. 'Vernon Gold? That shitehawk? He's not the son, is he?'

'No. He's just a person of interest.'

'Thank the sweet lord for that. Gold's a scum bucket. A sewer rat who's fought his way up from the gutter. He's been on our radar for a while now, but we've never been able to pin anything on him. Nothing concrete anyway. Nothing to get him banged up. What's your interest?'

'The son was working for him last we heard,' said Agatha. 'Some of it legal, some not so. That was a few months ago now, though. For all we know he might have found other employment since.'

'Or he might be one of Gold's top boys,' remarked Goose. 'A pusher in his Gold Squad. In it up to his ball sack. What's his name? I'll see if I know him.'

'His name?' Agatha hesitated. She didn't want to involve the police. Not unless she really needed to. 'Harry Benjamin,' she lied.

'Never heard of him. But if he's tight with Gold then he's bound to be an unscrupulous bastard.' Goose drew a wheezy breath. 'This isn't going to end badly, is it? For me, I mean. I've no time for folk shitting on my doorstep and then asking me to clean it up with my bare hands.'

Nice image, thought Agatha. Very classy. 'Clifford, you really don't have to worry,' she said calmly. 'Like you'd imagine, my team are highly trained specialists. Skilled professionals. I might be wrong, but I doubt you'll hear a peep out of them all the time we're here …'

CHAPTER TWENTY-SEVEN

Strike first, ask questions later.

Or just don't ask questions at all.

Cutz was staring straight at Lucas. That was where his attention was focused. Nowhere else. Certainly not at Mercy.

That was his second mistake. His first was touching her chest.

Lunging forward, Cutz was about to lash out with the knife when Mercy made her move. There was no back swing. Just a jab. Power and precision in a single punch.

She hit him hard on the jaw.

Too hard.

Cutz dropped the knife before he dropped himself. It was enough to make the other two youths re-evaluate the situation. Despite their masks, the shock was evident in their eyes. This didn't happen. Not to them. Not in the Rocketway. Their home turf. And certainly not by a girl.

Time seemed to momentarily stall before Lucas broke the silence. 'This is the police! You're all under arrest!'

That was the cue for the two remaining youths to scatter. One scarpered down the stairs whilst the other ran along the length of the corridor before disappearing from view.

Mercy threw her arms up in despair. 'Why would you say that? It's not even true.'

'Old habits die hard,' shrugged Lucas. 'I can't help myself.'

Doors began to open up and down the corridor. Twitching curtains and flickering lights. They had caused a commotion.

'Nothing to see here,' called out Lucas. 'You can all go back inside now.'

Mercy pointed at a pitiful Cutz. Laid flat on his back, he was out cold. 'What do we do with him?'

'Leave him where he is.' At the same time, Lucas took to the top step. 'He'll wake up soon enough, hopefully with a massive bruise and a throbbing headache. He got a taste of his own medicine, that's all. As for his two mates, they'll be back before long with reinforcements. And, trust me, we don't want to be here when that happens.'

Mercy took one last look at Cutz before she set off down the stairs. Lucas was right; the youth had almost certainly deserved it. He had a knife and he wasn't afraid to pull it. Still, there was a tiny part of her that felt sickened by the speed with which she had struck out. It was almost as if she was waiting for something like that to happen. The thrill of the fight. Desperate for the adrenaline rush to take hold.

That was her job, after all. It came naturally. It was what she was paid to do.

Was. Not anymore.

'That was one hell of a punch,' said Lucas, as the two of them hurried between the floors. 'You hit him so hard I thought I saw his teeth poking out his nostrils.'

Mercy began to frown. 'I know.'

'You could've broken his jaw. Put him in hospital.'

The frown deepened. 'I know.'

'Bit much maybe. Yes, he's a lowlife, but no one wants to be sipping soup for the rest of their days, do they?'

The frown had reached breaking point. 'I know.'

'Listen, I'm grateful … you know I am … he was going to stab me, remember … thing is, you might want to think about … calming down a little. Controlling that temper of yours—'

Mercy came to a sudden halt. Grabbed Lucas by the arm. 'Yes, I know!' she snapped. 'I know all of that. I'm not stupid. But that moment … with the boy … Cutz … it's been and gone now. I can't turn back time. So stop going on about it, will you?'

Lucas waited until her grip had weakened. 'I'm just pleased we're on the same team,' he said, continuing down the stairs. 'Call me boring, but I prefer my brains fixed inside my head, not scrambled or fried.'

Mercy held her tongue as they reached the bottom. They slowed down without deliberation. No need to rush now. Take it nice and easy. They were almost out the exit when Lucas recognised the familiar stomp of pounding feet on concrete. He had heard it so many times it had etched itself in his brain. At football matches. Riots. Gang fights. The precursor to violence of some kind, the sound chilled him to the bone. Scared the life out of him if he was being honest.

He had been right. The call had gone out. Reinforcements had arrived.

Without missing a beat, he steered Mercy under the stairwell, opposite the lift. She was about to protest when he put a finger to his lips, hushing her. Surprisingly, Mercy did as he asked.

A swarm of youths charged into the Rocketway soon after. Twenty at least. Boys mostly, mixed with the occasional girl. Hoods and masks as standard. Armed to the hilt with knives and baseball bats.

To Lucas's relief, nearly all of them took to the stairs.

Nearly ... but not all.

Four of them stopped at the lift. Lucas had a clear view of them from under the stairwell. They were stood with their backs to him. But if they were to turn ...

Word would've spread quickly. Two strangers, a black man and a black woman, had attacked Cutz. That was all the description they would need. If they saw them now they would know it was Lucas and Mercy immediately.

The lift was still yet to arrive when heads began to turn. The four youths must've sensed a presence behind them, lurking in the shadows. Lucas knew what he had to do. Seizing Mercy by the shoulders, he pulled her towards him, kissing her full on the lips. She tried to resist, but Lucas beat her to it by tightening his grip. The youths, who had spotted them by now, broke out into a chorus of cheers and jeers. Mercy's response was to push against him harder. Lucas couldn't hold onto her for long, not when there were so many ways she could fight back. A punch to the stomach. A knee to the balls. A heel scraped down the ankle. A combination of all three.

THE NEARLY DEARLY DEPARTED CLUB

Please, don't ...

The kiss continued whilst Lucas listened carefully. He was waiting for the lift to *ping* as it made it to the ground floor ... the doors to open ... the youths to dive inside ... the abuse to fade away. Only then could he let go of Mercy's shoulders.

At last.

Mercy spun away, fists raised, ready for the payback. If she was going to hit him it would be now. Lucas risked a glance at the lift, nevertheless. The doors had closed. The youths had gone. They were in the clear.

Well, one of them was.

'Whoa!' Lucas scurried to one side, careful not to bang his head on the stairs. 'That's not what ... I didn't ... let me explain ...'

The expression on Mercy's face changed as she slowly lowered her fists. 'You thought they'd see us so you did everything you could to distract them.'

Lucas nodded.

'And the best you could come up with was kissing me?'

Lucas nodded again.

'That better be the truth—'

'It is,' insisted Lucas, still nodding. 'I promise. I'd never just force myself on a woman. Especially not you.' He checked himself. 'I mean, you're very nice and everything ... it's just—'

'Stop digging that hole,' said Mercy. 'You could've warned me, though. You're lucky I didn't head-butt you.'

A head butt. Of course. Lucas added that to his long list

of potential injuries as he stepped out of the shadows and made his way outside. There was nobody there. Not that strange when you considered what time it was and how many youths had just run past them.

'Call Rose,' said Mercy, as the two of them hurried away from the apartment block. 'She can pick us up.'

Lucas pulled out his phone. Scrolled through the contacts until he found her name. 'It's ringing.'

Mercy had no idea where they were going, but they had to put some distance between themselves and Rocketway Heights. Glancing behind her, she wondered what was happening now on the thirteenth floor. Had Cutz woken up yet? She certainly hoped so. The last thing she wanted was to seriously hospitalise someone she barely knew.

'Rose isn't answering,' muttered Lucas. 'That's not something we need to worry about, is it?'

Mercy looked at him. 'She's with Tommy. Of course it's something we need to worry about.'

CHAPTER TWENTY-EIGHT

There were two men stood in the entrance to the Manager's Office.

One was of average height and build with a jet-black ponytail, dark eyes and an incredibly tanned face. The tan seemed natural though, as if he'd recently returned from holiday, not just a spray or sun bed. He was flashily dressed in an open-collared black shirt, white trousers and tan loafers. And jewellery. Lots of jewellery. Enough to make him sink if he was pushed into deep water.

The other man had a bald head, pointed chin and a handlebar moustache, none of which compared to his one striking feature that caught the eye immediately. He was huge. Both in height and width. Muscle on top of muscle on top of muscle. Straight off the cover of a body-building magazine. It came as no surprise that the clothes he was wearing only served to accentuate his sheer enormity. The tight black t-shirt he had squeezed into would no doubt rip if he sneezed too loudly, whilst his trousers were so snug they appeared to have been painted on.

Ponytail was first to speak. 'Who the hell are you?'

'Thomas William O'Strife,' replied Tommy. 'Tommy to my family and friends. Not that I've got many of those, mind. If any …'

'How did you get in here?' Ponytail glanced over his shoulder. 'This door's supposed to be locked.'

'Maybe I can walk through walls,' grinned Tommy. A thought struck him soon after. 'No, seriously, maybe I can. That's what ghosts do, right? And I'm a ghost. I do not exist.'

Ponytail seemingly ignored that as he wandered casually into the office, stopping only to wave his hand at the man mountain, who closed the door behind them.

'There. It's just the three of us now,' smiled Ponytail, displaying a dazzling set of white teeth in the process. 'You seem to have made yourself comfortable, Thomas. Too comfortable, some might say. Tell me. Have we met before?'

Tommy shook his head. 'Unfortunately not. I'm what you'd call an alien on foreign soil. Besides, I'm far too sophisticated for Stainmouth.'

'And yet you seem to think it's perfectly acceptable behaviour to enter my office uninvited,' Ponytail remarked. 'Plonk yourself down in my chair. Drink my Cognac.'

Tommy wagged a finger. 'Don't be like that. Didn't your mother tell you it's nice to share?'

'My mother didn't tell me anything,' said Ponytail, settling on the leather sofa. 'She died in childbirth. Such a horrible way to go. I think she'd be rather proud if she saw me now, though. What I've achieved. The man I've become. My name is Vernon Gold. And that's Doberman,' he added, gesturing towards the third person in the room.

Tommy let his eyes fall on the man mountain. 'Like the dog?'

'Just like the dog,' nodded Gold. 'Doberman's loyal and obedient. He'll do anything I say—'

'Does he shit in your garden and lick his own balls?' asked Tommy, deadly serious. 'Because if he does, I'd love him to show me how. The balls bit, I mean. Not the shitting. That seems fairly straightforward.'

Doberman tensed up.

'You have a lot to say for yourself, Thomas William O'Strife,' Gold began, 'but now it's my turn. Let me make things simple for you. Either you tell me what you're doing in my office, or I let Doberman off his leash. Do I make myself clear?'

Tommy was barely listening as he sipped at his drink. 'This is bloody marvellous by the way. Very smooth. Only the best for our Mr Gold and his pet pooch.'

Without warning, Doberman stomped towards the desk. By the look on his face he wanted nothing more than to rip Tommy's head off his shoulders and kick it around the office.

'Whoa there, big boy!' Tommy raised a hand in defence. 'You need to learn to take a joke. Make him roll over, Mr Gold, and I'll tell you everything you want to know.'

Doberman looked towards his boss, who nodded for him to do as Tommy had asked. He didn't roll over, of course. Or sit. That was too risky. Especially in those trousers. Instead, he held his ground, just waiting for the word.

The word to attack.

'Right, if … *most* of us are sitting comfortably then I'll begin,' said Tommy, leaning back in his chair. 'Let's start at the beginning, shall we? No, not the day I was born. My memory's not that sharp. I'm talking about the day I died …'

Rose joined the queue to the nightclub.

She found everything about it unbearable. The close proximity of so many people. The smell of cheap aftershave, sweet perfume and stale alcohol. The threat of violence that hung unnervingly in the air, just waiting to rear its ugly head. Rose tried to ignore it all as she shuffled forward. There was just one problem to overcome now.

Well, *two* problems.

The doormen stood by the entrance were the same pair that had stopped Tommy from going in.

Beardy and the Beast.

Right on cue, Beardy stepped in front of Rose. Studied her with intent. 'Been a long day, has it, love? Come straight from work?'

Rose shook her head, confused. 'No.'

'You're not a tax inspector, are you?' laughed the Beast, keen to join in. 'Mr Gold tends to keep most of his cash stuffed down the back of his sofa if you are.'

'Nah, she's health and safety,' said Beardy. 'I'd stay away from those toilets if I was you. They're bloody toxic.'

'I-I-I just want to go in,' stammered Rose.

Beardy ushered her forward. 'We're only pulling your leg. You have a nice evening. A few drinks and you might even think about undoing your top button …'

Both doormen were laughing as Rose squeezed between them. She didn't care. Feeling inside her pocket, she produced a ten pound note and handed it to the girl behind the counter. She received a stamp in return. The word *ELECTRIC* in bright red ink on her left hand. The noise increased as she pressed on, swept along by the crowd. Dance music was blaring out from the main room. She didn't like dance music. Not to worry. She wasn't there to enjoy herself.

She was there to find Tommy.

So, where was he?

'Is that supposed to be funny?'

Tommy shook his head. 'Not in the slightest. It's all true. Every last bit of it.'

'You've come back from the dead,' frowned Gold. 'And now you're looking for—'

'Benji Hammerton,' repeated Tommy. 'If I can find him then I can go back home. They're already missing me in London. I can sense it. My toenails are tingling. That's one of my special powers. Proper super-hero shit.' He shifted his attention to the human beast that was Doberman. The big goon was just stood there, primed and ready to go. 'I'm starting to think I may have outstayed my welcome,' said Tommy. 'Let's get straight to the point. This Benji ... does he work for you or not?'

'I neither know nor care,' shrugged Gold. 'But there is one thing of which I am sure. You've over-stepped the mark, Thomas William O'Strife. You've treated me like a fool in my own club and now there has to be some form of ...

retribution.' Gold turned to Doberman. 'Take him outside. Nothing too savage. Just teach him a lesson.'

Doberman didn't need telling twice. Striding forward, he was already reaching over the desk when Tommy leapt to his feet. 'Wait! You never answered my question.'

Gold whistled and the man mountain came to a halt. 'What question?'

'A drink?' Without warning, Tommy picked up the decanter and launched it across the office. 'Would you like a drink?'

CHAPTER TWENTY-NINE

The decanter hit its target, striking Doberman firmly on the side of the temple.

He staggered and swayed, managing, somehow, to stay upright as the golden liquid spilt out over the carpet. He was all at sea. Not completely out of it, but not completely with it either. Vernon Gold, meanwhile, looked more shocked than anyone. Shrinking into the sofa, he was no longer a threat.

Tommy saw his chance.

Scrambling around the desk, he made a beeline for the door. One yank on the handle later and he had left the office behind. He was all set to head back the way he had first come when he saw two of the doormen from earlier, Teeth and Tits, enter through the fire exit. Tommy changed direction. There was another door at the end of the corridor. He had a feeling it might open up into the nightclub.

Fingers crossed.

Tommy raced towards it. Slammed down on the handle.

Bright flashing lights greeted him instantly, alongside a barrage of pounding beats. And people. Lots and lots of people. Too many to count.

He had done it.

Tommy was about to blend in with the crowd when he felt an arm around his neck. Next thing he knew he was being dragged backwards. The door closed and, with it, his hopes faded. The lights, the music, the people, had all disappeared.

He was wrong. He hadn't done it.

He hadn't done it at all.

Rose made her way anxiously around the perimeter of the club.

Not only was it packed to the rafters, but the carpet felt sticky beneath her shoes, making it harder than it should've been to get around. She couldn't hear anything beyond the music, and was starting to wish she couldn't smell either. The entire place reeked of an ungodly combination of fetid body odour and sickly sweet, brightly coloured drinks. Watermelon or passion fruit? Take your pick. Rose barely drank anyway but, if she did, they were the last things she would have chosen.

She was about to start a second lap of the club when a door marked *Staff Only* burst open in front of her. A figure appeared in the opening.

Tommy.

Rose hurried towards him. She had almost filled the gap between them when someone else beat her to it. A giant of a man, he grabbed Tommy around the neck and pulled him back into the shadows. The door shut tight. Blink and you might just miss it.

Rose hadn't blinked, though. She had caught every frame. Seen the anger carved into the giant's features. Jaw clenched, nostrils flared, eyes wide. Huge veins popping out of his forehead. All of it in stark contrast to the look of horror on Tommy's face when it dawned on him that something bad was about to happen.

Happen to him.

Rose stared at the door. She couldn't just leave him in there. She had to do something.

Again.

Out of sight, Doberman's first move was to curl his fist and smash it into Tommy's stomach.

Tommy doubled up as the pain swept over him. That was some punch. He could barely see and he certainly couldn't breathe.

'Silly boy,' said Gold, wandering slowly along the corridor towards them. 'You've just made a bad situation even worse. Doberman, take him into the yard and deal with him appropriately.'

Doberman's mouth fell open as he spoke for the first time. 'Appropriately?'

'Rough him up,' explained Gold. 'Enough so he remembers, but not so much that he ends up in hospital. On second thoughts, a few nights in Stainmouth General might do him some good …'

Turning on his heels, Vernon Gold began to snigger as he headed back towards his office.

'Shit in the garden, do I?' hissed Doberman, his lips close

to Tommy's ear. 'You won't even be able to shit at all when I've finished with you!'

Tommy wasn't listening. Unbelievably, there was something else bothering him. Something more pressing than the threat of violence to come, however brutal.

The power of Doberman's punch had had disastrous consequences. Not only had the bandages around his chest come apart, but the wound from the gun shot had opened. He didn't need to look to know that he was leaking blood. Lots of blood.

Feeling faint, Tommy let himself be dragged along the corridor. They were heading away from the lights and music. Away from the clubbers. Towards the fire exit.

Towards retribution.

Rose weaved in and out of the young, happy, smiling people.

There were so many of them, shoving and straining as they stumbled their way to the bar or dance floor. Whooping with joy. Screeching at one another. Rose couldn't think of anything worse. She hated the noise. The commotion. The close contact and indiscreet touching.

She stopped at the door. Rested her fingers on the *Staff Only* sign.

What now?

No, seriously, Rose. What now? What do you think you can do to help?

She saw it by chance. It was to the left of the bar in a tiny alcove, practically hidden from view. A legal requirement in nightclubs up and down the land.

Nobody noticed as Rose moved swiftly towards it, but then nobody ever did. She clenched her fist before deciding against it. The last thing she wanted was to break a bone. Instead, she looked for something heavier. Stronger. More suitable for the job in hand.

There was an empty bottle on the bar. Rose reached out.

Please be glass, not plastic …

Glass.

Shielding the bottle behind her back, Rose made sure no one was watching before she shuffled into the alcove. It was perfect for amorous couples in need of privacy. Or more illegal activities perhaps.

Rose fell firmly into the latter category.

Turning the bottle upside down, she discreetly lined up her shot. On three.

One … two … two-and-a-half …

Smash.

A seething Vernon Gold charged out of his office.

'Some stupid prick has set off the fire alarm,' he raged. 'Doberman, get out there and see what all the fuss is about.'

Doberman nodded at Tommy. 'And him?'

Gold threw up his hands, exasperated. 'He's nothing. Toss him out into the club and let the doormen take care of him. You've got more important things to worry about than that maggot.'

Tommy felt his stomach turn cartwheels as his body performed something of an unexpected U-turn. He was still being dragged, but now he was heading in the opposite direction. Along the corridor. Through a door. Into the open.

He slumped to the ground when Doberman let go of him. He was in the nightclub. The lights were on full power, but the music seemed to have stopped. All he could hear was a persistent ringing in his ears. A constant reminder that his brains had been scrambled beyond repair.

He was on his way out. Fading fast. And this time there'd be no coming back. No second chances. No resurrections or reprisals.

Tommy closed his eyes. Succumbed to the inevitable.

Game. Set. Match.

Goodnight.

CHAPTER THIRTY

Tommy had almost drifted off to somewhere else entirely when he felt a hand on his face.

Somebody was trying to rouse him from his mortal slumber. Didn't they know it was rude to wake the dead?

'Tommy, it's me. You're … you're bleeding. We have to go.'

Me. Tommy struggled to think. 'Who …?'

'Rose,' replied a trembling voice.

'Rose.' Tommy mustered a smile. 'My mouse in shining armour.'

Rose ignored that as she hauled him ungracefully to his feet. The nightclub was emptying and they had to get out of there. With one hand around his waist and the other under his arm, she led him slowly towards the exit. Tommy was barely able to walk, struggling to place one foot in front of the other, but that was nothing out of the ordinary at that time of night. Just another lightweight who couldn't handle his drink. Look a little closer, however, and the signs were easy to spot. His face had turned a deathly shade of white and there were patches of blood all over his shirt. Rose pulled his jacket across to hide the stains, all the while encouraging

Tommy to keep his head down as they passed the doormen on their way out.

As if things weren't bad enough already, Rose's phone began to ring. She removed it carefully from her pocket, wary of dropping Tommy as she did so. It was Lucas. Rose wanted to answer it, but knew she couldn't.

Exiting the nightclub, she avoided the crowds who had gathered in the road and made her way towards the Fiat 500. She opened the door, pushing Tommy headfirst onto the backseat. A little clumsy perhaps, but there was no time to waste. Skipping around the car, she got in the driver's side and glanced over her shoulder. Tommy was curled up in a ball, worryingly silent.

'Seatbelt,' said Rose. That wasn't going to happen so she reached behind her and did it herself. To her relief, Tommy groaned as it pressed against his chest. She was pleased that it hurt. At least it meant he was still alive.

Rose started the car and crept away from the kerb. The clubbers were still there, unsure whether or not to hang around any longer or find somewhere else to spend the rest of the evening. Rose had almost crawled past when she spotted the giant. He was stood in the entrance to the club, arms folded whilst he surveyed the scene. The sight of him was enough to make her shiver.

The shiver turned to a jump when her phone rang again. Placing it in her lap, Rose prodded the receive button before returning both hands to the steering wheel.

'Where have you been?' barked Lucas. 'I've been trying to call you.'

'I know.' Rose's voice was shaking as she took a sharp left, unsure if that was the right way to go.

'You know? Good. I'm pleased about that,' Lucas muttered. 'We really need you to pick us up.'

'Yes … of course … I'm coming,' mumbled Rose. 'It's just … I don't know the way …'

'Ask Tommy.'

Rose glanced at the lifeless lump on the backseat. 'That might not be possible.'

'What's happened?'

'I'm … I'm not entirely sure,' spluttered Rose. 'Tommy went into the nightclub, but never came out. I followed him in … eventually. There was a man … a giant of a man … and so much blood …'

'Shit.' Lucas paused. 'Is Tommy okay?'

'I think so,' said Rose unconvincingly. 'He's here with me now. He's very quiet.'

'Quiet?' Lucas snatched a breath. That didn't sound good. 'You really need to pick us up. And fast.'

Rose nodded to herself. She could do this. 'Where are you?'

'Stainmouth's got a church,' said Lucas. 'I can see a tower in the distance. We could be there in a few minutes if we get a shift on. Do you think you can find it, Rose?'

'I don't … yes!' Rose had spotted a road sign as she took another left and turned onto a winding hill. She was heading in the right direction. 'I'm not that far away.'

'Good. We'll see you there.' Lucas ended the call. Turned to Mercy. Frowned.

'What was all that about?' she asked.

'Quick question,' said Lucas. 'You've not grown too attached to Tommy, have you?'

'What do you reckon?' shrugged Mercy.

'Ah, that's a relief,' said Lucas, breaking into a jog. 'At least you won't be too upset when I break the bad news …'

Rose parked the Fiat 500 by a low wall that ran around the perimeter of the church.

Tommy was as pale as milk and uncomfortably still. She pressed the back of her hand against his forehead. He felt both cold and clammy.

'They'll be here in a minute,' she said softly. 'We'll get you to hospital.'

'No … hospital,' hissed Tommy through gritted teeth.

Rose was about to reply when the passenger-side door swung open.

'What have we missed?' panted Lucas, as he climbed inside.

Rose took a moment to compose herself. 'He doesn't want to go to hospital.'

'And he's right,' insisted Mercy. She jumped in beside Tommy. Looked him up and down. 'Remember what Agatha said. We don't exist. We need to stay out of trouble. Going to hospital will only result in a whole bunch of questions that nobody wants to answer. I say we head back to Proud Mary's and patch him up ourselves.'

Rose opened her mouth to argue, before quickly deciding against it.

'Follow the signs for Croplington,' said Lucas. 'We'll be back at the farm in no time. You can fill in the gaps whilst you drive. And, if you're lucky, Mercy will even tell you how she laid out some wannabe bad boy with a single punch.'

Rose collected her thoughts as she started the engine, angling the car back down the hill. Then, in meticulous fashion, she recited the events of their time at the Everything's Electric nightclub. Before she knew it, she had finished her account and they were driving up the bumpy dirt track on their way to Cockleshell Farm.

A furious Proud Mary stepped out of the farmhouse the moment Rose brought the Fiat to a halt. The landlady had changed into a yellow dressing gown, matching it with a pair of black wellies like the ones she'd worn before. She had removed the head scarf too, choosing, instead, to tie her greying hair back into a messy bun. 'I've a good mind not to let you in,' she raged. 'A curfew is not to be ignored. It's way past eleven … what's the matter with your man?'

'His wound's opened up,' explained Mercy, as she and Lucas half-carried, half-dragged Tommy towards the door.

Proud Mary didn't miss a beat. 'Take him through to the kitchen and lay him on the table,' she said firmly, moving to one side so the three of them could pass. 'There's an airing cupboard at the top of the stairs,' she said, resting a hand on Rose's shoulder. 'Fetch me as many towels and blankets as you can manage.'

With that, Proud Mary marched back into the farmhouse. Rose did as she was told without hesitation. She could hear screaming as she hurried up the stairs. When she finally made it back to the kitchen, weighed down with as much as she could carry, Tommy was laid out on the table with his shirt off. There was blood everywhere. Mercy was leant over him, working hard to force a tea towel between his teeth, dampening his screams to nothing more than a muffled cry.

'Put the towels on the floor,' said Proud Mary, snapping Rose out of her trance.

'What do you want us to do?' asked Mercy, pressing down on Tommy's shoulders as she struggled to keep him still.

'Get out,' replied Proud Mary bluntly.

'Get out?' Lucas screwed up his face. 'You think you can cope on your own?'

'Oh, I've coped with worse than this before,' said Proud Mary, pulling on a pair of plastic gloves. 'Now, let me work in peace. And that's an order!'

DAY TWO

CHAPTER THIRTY-ONE

It was gone ten when Rose finally dragged herself out of bed.

She never slept in that late. Then she remembered the horrors of the previous evening and almost wished she had slept in later.

She wanted to cry, but the tears wouldn't come. She just felt numb. Dead all over.

Rose dressed quickly in the same clothes as yesterday and opened the door to her room. The farmhouse seemed quiet. Creeping down the stairs, she found both the sitting room and kitchen were empty. She looked out of the window, surprised to see that the Fiat 500 had gone.

Where was everyone?

She was about to head back upstairs when the door flew open and in stomped Proud Mary from outside.

'Good morning, young lady.' She stopped suddenly. 'And what are you intending to do with that?'

Rose glanced down at her hands. Or, to be precise, at the bread knife she was carrying. 'I panicked … I didn't know who it was—'

'So, you thought you'd just stab me?' said Proud Mary bluntly.

'No … no … never.' Rose placed the knife back down on the table. 'I couldn't … I wouldn't do that …'

'I'll give you the benefit of the doubt,' said Proud Mary, cracking something that almost resembled a smile. 'You had quite a time of it last night. No wonder you're feeling jittery.'

'My …' Rose struggled to find the right word. 'My … colleague,' she settled upon. 'Tommy. Is he—?'

'Dead?' Proud Mary hesitated for a second too long before she shook her head. 'Not the last time I looked. He's outside in one of the barns, talking to the pigs. I'm not sure what they've done to deserve it, though.'

Rose took a breath. What was that feeling? The one that crawled up from the pit of her stomach. Was it relief? Perhaps. Just a smidgen. She stopped analysing it and peered around the kitchen instead. 'Where are all the towels and blankets?'

Proud Mary gestured out the window. 'I started a fire. There'd be no getting all that blood out. If I'm being honest, I needed some new ones, and I'm sure Miss Pleasant will be keen to reimburse me.'

Rose nodded. 'Where's the car? And my other … colleagues?'

'They left ages ago,' Proud Mary revealed. 'They didn't tell me where and I didn't ask. Don't look like that, dear. Not everyone stayed in bed until ten. Life goes on, with or without you. Now, can I get you some breakfast? Thomas wolfed down a full English, but I'm guessing you're more of a muesli kind of girl.'

'Some toast would be nice,' said Rose. 'Thank you.'

'On its way.' Proud Mary turned her back as she busied herself around the kitchen. 'You should probably go and speak to your friend. If nothing else, it'll give those pigs a break.'

Rose walked towards the door without another word.

'You can borrow some wellies,' Proud Mary added. 'I've got enough to go around.'

Rose studied the shoe rack on the wall. There were at least twenty pairs there. Some black, some green, some blue. All were caked in mud. She chose a green pair without over-thinking it and slipped into them. They were too big, but it didn't matter. She wouldn't be out there for long. Truth is, she didn't have much to say.

Tommy was in the third of three barns behind the farmhouse.

It was his voice that gave him away. Loud and incessant. On and on and on. Did he ever pause for breath?

'And that was how I got shot. Yeah, I know. Unacceptable behaviour by anyone's standards. I handed that money to Kamil in good faith and he responded by blowing a hole in me. Right here. In my chest. Any lower and he would've hit me in the heart. Then it would've been game over, my stinky chums. No more Tommy O'Strife. You'd miss me, right?' Tommy must've sensed someone approaching because he turned the moment Rose entered the barn. 'Ah, it's you,' he said, grinning from ear to ear. 'Sleeping beauty has finally awoken.'

Rose stopped when she drew level with him. He was leant over the pen with half a dozen pigs gathered around him.

Curiously, they seemed to be hanging on his every word. 'Are you okay?' she asked.

'Thanks to you, I am,' said Tommy. 'That's what the others reckon anyway. They say you pulled me out of that nightclub before I got a good kicking. I still need some convincing, though. I'd like to hear it from the horse's mouth. Not that I'm calling you a horse. You've neither the long face nor the teeth. Besides, I prefer pigs. Look at 'em. They're so cute. They don't give a damn either. They just go about their piggy business without a care in the world.' Tommy stopped. 'What were we talking about again?'

'You,' said Rose.

'No, *you*,' said Tommy, correcting her. 'I owe you one, don't I?'

'Something like that,' shrugged Rose.

Tommy held out his hand for her to shake. She didn't. She just stared at it.

'Would you prefer a hug?' Tommy shuffled closer. 'A kiss and a cuddle?'

Rose couldn't help but smile as she finally took his hand. 'You're insufferable.'

'I don't even know what that means,' Tommy had to admit. 'But it can't be any worse than most things I've been called. Maybe you could write it on my gravestone.' He stopped to think. 'We have got gravestones, haven't we? I mean, we should have, being dead and all that. I'd like to visit mine. Graffiti it. Here lies Tommy O'Strife, the best shag I ever had—'

'Where are the others?' asked Rose, keen to shift the

conversation in a different direction.

Tommy pointed into the distance. 'They've gone to some boxing club on the other side of Stainmouth. There's a mate of Benji's there. He might know where he is. Oh, there's something else. Well, *someone* else. Benji's definitely got a kid. A daughter. Kinda' makes things awkward, don't you think?'

'Very,' said Rose. She looked around the farmyard, unsure what to say next. 'So … what do we do now?'

'We cheer up these little porkers.' Tommy leant over the pen so he could stroke the pigs one by one. 'I don't know about you, Rose, but I prefer my bacon to come from a happy home.'

CHAPTER THIRTY-TWO

'Who goes to a boxing club at this time in the morning?'

Lucas rested on the sign for *Marlowe Street* and waited for Mercy to reply. She didn't, but that was largely because she didn't need to. Not when a scrawny youth with floppy hair and a baggy tracksuit walked straight up to the double doors and disappeared inside.

'He doesn't count,' Lucas added hastily. 'He probably wandered in by accident. Couldn't see beyond his fringe.'

Mercy was barely listening as she peered up at the sign above the entrance. *Come Fight With Me.* Yeah, clever that. A play on words for somewhere that usually shied away from humour. It certainly made a change from Big Barry's Boxing Club or something equally banal. If Gina was right, this was where they would find Eddie surname unknown. Benji's best mate. Perhaps. Time rolled by and friendships drifted. Still, it was worth a shot. Better than sitting in Cockleshell Farm waiting for Tommy to regain his strength and Rose to just wake up.

'Are we going in, or are we going to stand here all morning until we've built up the courage?' asked Lucas, breaking her train of thought.

Mercy responded with a roll of her eyes. 'Don't worry about me. I've spent half my life in places like this. It'll be like a second home.'

With that, she pushed opened the doors, walked inside … and immediately realised that this was nothing like a second home at all. Not unless her second home reeked of stale sweat, last night's beer and criminally toxic farts.

Lucas followed her in, his eyes shifting from left to right as he quickly took in his surroundings. The club was well lit with a low ceiling. One large room with several much smaller rooms coming off it. Two boxing rings in the centre and numerous punch bags and free weights scattered around the edges. Lucas did a head count. Eleven people at a glance. All of them male. All of them pumped full of raging testosterone and small town frustration.

All of them staring at the two new arrivals.

Lucas stopped in the doorway. Drew a breath. 'We're looking for Eddie,' he called out.

Silence.

'We heard he comes here. Comes here a lot.'

The silence lingered.

Lucas sighed. 'You can talk, you know. I mean, I *hope* you can. Maybe knocking seven shades of shit out of each other on a daily basis has rendered you all mute.'

'You tryin' to be funny?' That came from the scrawny youth they had watched enter. He stepped forward at the same time. Chest out, chin back, arms flailing by his side. 'You think you're a big man or somethin'?'

'Not particularly,' shrugged Lucas. 'I mean, I'm bigger than you. And way more intelligent. I've learnt how to buy clothes that fit me for a start …'

Mercy turned sharply. 'Stop it!' she hissed at Lucas. 'Don't make me send you outside again!'

Somebody sniggered. That was a good sign. Now she just had to press home her point.

'Seriously,' she said, holding up her hands, 'we're not here to cause trouble. Feel free to ignore my friend, though. He's just nervous being around so many men. It's a macho thing. He's also got a really tiny willy, but we don't like to talk about it.'

A cheer went up around the boxing club. Laughter and lots of it. Mercy tried not to smile herself. That was how to do it. You didn't wander into somewhere like *Come Fight With Me* and start throwing your weight around. You had to win them over. Charm them. She glanced at Lucas, who looked fit to explode. He was about to speak when she raised a finger.

Don't ruin things now. Leave this to me.

'We just want to find Eddie,' Mercy continued. 'That's all we've got to go on. No surname or address. It is pretty important, though.'

'Important, you say.' Mercy watched as a small, egg-shaped man appeared from one of the side rooms. He was dressed in a bright-red tracksuit and a checked flat cap. Big eyes and a wide mouth. 'The name's Nimble,' he said, bowing theatrically. 'Stainmouth's finest featherweight back when I was beautiful. These days I'm a trainer to the stars.' Nimble gestured towards the assembled boxers. 'And these losers,' he added, straight-faced. 'Come Fight With Me is open to everyone. I don't discriminate. But I don't gossip either.'

'So, this is your club?' Mercy looked around, impressed. 'You've got a decent set-up here.'

Nimble smiled. 'Thank you kindly. About twenty-five years I've owned it now. I've seen all sorts in here.'

'You should be proud,' said Mercy.

'I am,' nodded Nimble. 'Very. Even if it does stink like a cesspit at the moment. That's not my lads by the way. It's the sewers. The council keep promising to get it sorted.' Nimble stuck his tongue into the side of his mouth. His thinking pose. 'Listen, we do know Eddie,' he said eventually. 'And we could tell you where to find him. But what would be the fun in that? No, I've got a better idea. We have a code of conduct here. And one golden rule. We don't chat shit. We let our fists do the talking. So, if you want to know something, you'll have to beat it out of us.'

Lucas sighed. 'What's that supposed to mean?'

'A boxing match,' announced Nimble, rubbing his hands together. 'Win and we'll tell you everything you need to know. Lose … and we won't. It's that simple.'

'Sounds it,' groaned Lucas.

'That's not all.' Nimble pointed over at the biggest man in the club. Fair hair. Square jaw. Huge shoulders. 'That's who you'll be fighting, me old mucker. The Exterminator.'

'Great.' Lucas began to mutter under his breath as he took off his jacket and unbuttoned his shirt. 'Right, let's get this over with.'

'After you,' said Nimble, pointing towards the closest boxing ring.

'No, after *me*.' Without warning, Mercy pushed past Lucas and climbed between the ropes. 'He's not fighting – I am!'

CHAPTER THIRTY-THREE

'You look concerned?'

Agatha had been studying Miles for a while now and his expression hadn't changed once.

'This is my normal face,' he frowned. 'I thought you would've got used to it by now.'

'I have,' insisted Agatha. 'And it's not. It's not normal at all. Did something happen last night?'

Miles gazed out across the rolling lawns of the Sanctuary. He had stumbled upon it by accident when out for an early morning run, instantly deciding it was the ideal place to meet Agatha later that day. Back then, of course, it had been quiet and perfectly serene. Now, as Stainmouth had woken, it was a little less chilled. Miles blamed the dog walkers. Not the dogs themselves. Just the idiots who couldn't control them.

He knew without looking that Agatha was still staring at him. He was going to have to tell her the truth. It was unavoidable.

'I got a call from Proud Mary,' he began, shifting about on the wooden bench. 'Late last night. Or early this morning, depends how you look at it—'

'Go on,' pressed Agatha, her body tensing as she sat up straight.

'Our … team went out after I'd left them,' continued Miles. 'I followed them with the tracker on the Fiat 500. They seemed to head into the town centre.'

Agatha ran a hand across her forehead. 'You told me all that last night. Surely that's a good thing.'

'You'd think so, wouldn't you?' said Miles. 'And then you'd change your mind pretty damn sharpish when you find out what actually happened. According to Proud Mary, O'Strife ended up on her kitchen table, leaking blood. His wound had burst open.'

Agatha took a breath. 'How is that even possible? Had he been fighting?'

'Not fighting – just losing,' said Miles. 'He went to Everything's Electric. It's a nightclub. Probably as bad as it sounds. He was looking for Vernon Gold. He never came out, though, so the quiet one—'

'Rose.'

Miles nodded. '*Rose* had to go in and get him. She smashed the fire alarm and emptied the club.'

Agatha resisted the urge to smile. 'She's a clever girl. And O'Strife? Is he okay?'

'He'll live.' By the look on Agatha's face that wasn't enough. 'Yes, he's fine,' said Miles. 'Proud Mary patched him up again and packed him off to bed with a couple of paracetamol and a hot water bottle.'

'Good.' Agatha waited for a middle-aged couple with a

black Labrador to pass before she spoke again. 'They've not tried to escape yet, have they?'

'No. Not as far as I'm aware. Do you think they will?'

'Possibly. It's hard to tell. It'd make things easier if they didn't.'

Miles rolled his eyes. 'Since when have things ever been easy. I thought that's how you liked it. Bloody awkward and impossible to predict.'

Agatha snorted. He had a point. It wasn't deliberate, of course, but events did often seem to turn out that way. 'What do you make of Stainmouth?' she asked.

'Adequate,' replied Miles, barely able to muster the enthusiasm. 'I mean, we've only been here a day or so. Seems nice enough, though. Very hilly. Lots of … erm … grass.'

Agatha didn't buy it in the slightest. 'You want to go home, don't you? Back to London?'

Miles hesitated. Only a fraction of a second, but it was enough for Agatha to pick up on.

'Not until the job's done,' he said stiffly. 'That's what I get paid for, isn't it? And that's why you'll agree to that pay rise I've been hankering after.'

'Good answer.' Agatha stood up to leave. 'Right, there's somewhere I need to be. I think it's time I acquainted myself with Stainmouth's dark side. It's always best to introduce yourself to the enemy. Put a face to the criminal record …' Agatha paused. 'You still look concerned,' she said, frowning at Miles.

'Maybe it's nothing,' he shrugged. 'It's just … you and I, we're professionals, right? We surround ourselves with professionals. We always have, ever since I've known you. Now, I get the whole dead-not-dead thing. Ghosts who walk in the shadows … impossible to trace … all that nonsense. But what I don't get is why these four? We could've had anyone. Soldiers from the special forces. Spies with twenty years' experience—'

'Robots,' chipped-in Agatha. 'Drones. No human touch. No social skills. Unable to mix and mingle. Blend in. Hide in plain sight—'

'I meant highly trained and disciplined,' said Miles. 'Instead, we end up with these muddled misfits.'

Agatha could feel her hackles starting to rise. 'Are you doubting me, Miles?'

'No.' Miles shook his head. And then shook it again to prove his point. 'Not you … the system. I mean, come on, Agatha. One day in and they're already ruffling feathers. It's hardly very discreet, is it? They're a blunt tool when what we really need is a razorblade. It's like happy hour at the bar. Karaoke time. Come and have a go. All welcome. They're nothing but a rag-tag bunch of nobodies who just happen to have one thing in common. They all *almost* died on the same day.'

'And you think that was an accident, do you?' snapped Agatha.

Miles let that soak in for a moment. 'What are you trying to say?'

'Nothing.' Agatha took a moment. *Breathe.* 'You're such a snob, Miles,' she said, shaking her head at him. 'Have a little faith please. If not in the system, then in me. They may not be perfect, but they're a work in progress. And, yes, O'Strife may be a little unconventional in his methods, but the others balance him out. A ying to his yang. Honestly, they're not as disruptive as you seem to believe. The way you go on you'd think they were out causing trouble every second of every day. It's ten o'clock in the morning, Miles. Do you really think they're out there fighting even as we speak?'

CHAPTER THIRTY-FOUR

Mercy dodged smartly to one side as the fist flew past her face.

That was close. Closer than she intended. If the Exterminator connected with a punch like that it would be lights out. The fear of that happening was enough to make Mercy refocus. Stay on her toes and concentrate. Be alert to all possible dangers at all times.

Everyone in the Come Fight With Me boxing club had objected when she had insisted on fighting instead of Lucas. She was a woman, after all. Delicate and dainty. Far too frail for something so rough.

Okay, if you say so …

'I don't want to hurt you,' the Exterminator had whispered when they touched gloves.

'You won't,' replied Mercy.

That had resulted in a few giggles from the other boxers. Smirks and sniggers and a room full of smiles. Two rounds in, though, and who was laughing now? Mercy had danced around the ring and the Exterminator had failed to make contact with her once. Granted, Mercy hadn't hit him either. But she would do. That was a fact.

Mercy stepped back as another huge fist came hammering towards her. The Exterminator was a big man, make no mistake. At least 6'3 in height. Bulging chest. Thick, throbbing veins popping out of his forearms. Look a little closer, though, and not all of it was muscle. Mercy had spotted the wobble under his vest as he climbed into the ring. The gut that refused to vanish however many times you hit the punch bag.

Yes, there was no denying that the Exterminator was a big man. But that didn't necessarily mean he was a fit man.

A respite came for the two boxers when Nimble rang the bell. The third round was over.

Mercy walked back to her corner where Lucas was waiting with a towel and a bottle of water.

'You're doing great,' he said, his voice little more than a murmur as he wiped the back of her neck. 'Maybe ... and I'm no expert here, so don't take this the wrong way ... maybe you could always try and ... you know ... hit him.'

'Don't,' hissed Mercy.

Lucas held up his hands. 'Don't what?'

'Don't try and give me advice. Not ever. I've got things under control. I know what I'm doing.'

'I realise that. It's just—'

'Just nothing.' Mercy ended the conversation by marching back into the centre of the ring. It took the Exterminator a little longer before he joined her. He was tiring; that was clear for all to see. It was in the way he walked. Head down and shoulders hunched. Short, shuffling steps and gasping breaths. It doesn't matter how powerful you are, thought Mercy, bouncing from toe to toe. When your lungs have gone there's no coming back.

The Exterminator had but one chance now. End it with a single punch. And fast.

The bell rang and the big man lumbered forward. Mercy had time to step back and watch the action play out in front of her as he swung wildly. It was the kind of punch you only ever saw in films. The kind that knocked you all the way across the room and straight through the window.

The kind that never connected in real life.

The Exterminator didn't stop there. He swung again and again and again. He had lost all technique now, his training having long since deserted him. He was desperate.

Desperate for a miracle that wasn't going to happen.

Mercy skipped across the ring, waiting for the right moment. Draw him in. Let him come closer. And then end it once and for all.

She stopped moving.

The Exterminator threw his last remaining strength behind a haymaker that, if it made contact, would've knocked Mercy's head right off her shoulders.

It didn't, though.

It was so slow, so telegraphed, that Mercy had time to shift to one side. This was it. Mercy hovered over the big man as he bent double and tried to catch his breath. He was blowing out his arse. The second he stood up straight Mercy would hit him. One jab and it would all be over. It was as easy as that.

The Exterminator, somewhat predictably, would be exterminated.

Mercy moved in close as he lifted his head. An uppercut was her best option now. Right under the chin. Not too hard. She didn't want to cause him any permanent damage.

The hairs on the back of her neck had begun to prickle. The red mist was descending, but she didn't mind. If anything, she actively encouraged it. It was what she lived for.

No.

Not anymore.

Mercy's feet took over and she hopped backwards until she felt the ropes behind her. 'Had enough?'

'What do you think?' panted the Exterminator, dropping to his knees. 'I'm done in. I can't even lay a glove on you.'

With that, Mercy climbed out of the ring. She had barely raised a sweat. Better than that, though, she had somehow controlled her anger. She winked at Lucas, but he was barely looking, his attention already switched to Nimble.

'Mercy won,' he said, striding towards the trainer. He slowed his step when the other boxers gathered round. Ten on one were never the best odds. 'She won fair and square,' repeated Lucas. 'That was the deal. Now tell us where we can find Eddie.'

'Chill out, fella,' grinned Nimble. 'All in due course. I don't think you quite understand the situation—'

'Oh, I understand alright,' said Lucas. 'No more pissing about. Where's Eddie?'

'I'm here.' Lifting himself up off the canvas, the

Exterminator leant on the ropes whilst he tried to catch his breath. 'I'm Eddie. Eddie the Exterminator. How can I be of assistance?'

CHAPTER THIRTY-FIVE

Agatha climbed out of the Audi A8 and closed the door behind her.

Her driver, Olaf, was as competent a man as she had ever met. Competent and mute. In all the time she had known him – a little over two years now – he had barely spoken to her. Just the odd word or two. If anything, he preferred a half smile or gentle nod. On this occasion, though, he had grunted. He never grunted. Agatha started to wonder what it could mean as she made her way across the car park of The Meadows Private Hospital. Maybe he was unhappy with his lot in life.

Or maybe he just wanted to grunt. Everybody likes a good grunt from time to time. Even someone as competent as Olaf.

The Meadows was a one-storey, L-shaped building situated to the west of Stainmouth. Surrounded by fields, it offered a peaceful alternative to the hustle and bustle of the town's general hospital. That's only if you had the money, of course. One night's stay would set you back a week's salary. And heaven help you if you actually wanted something removing or stuffing back in. That would be more than a fortnight abroad in a five-star hotel.

Agatha knew all this because she had read the brochure on her way there. Eighteen private rooms, all with en-suite bathrooms and flat screen televisions. A swimming pool, jacuzzi and steam room on site. Very nice. Like a health spa for the sick and unwell.

The moment Agatha entered the premises her persona changed completely. She ditched the confidence, the calm and collected demeanour, and transformed into someone else entirely. Someone old. Someone decrepit.

It was all an act. An act that people easily fell for.

'Can I help you?'

Agatha slowly lifted her head as she drifted aimlessly around the hospital foyer. A woman had stepped out from behind the reception desk to greet her. Middle-aged. Smartly dressed. Forward yet friendly.

Agatha looked at the name badge without staring.

'Yes … no … I'm not really sure, Penny,' she mumbled, nervously rubbing her hands together. 'Do you mind if I call you Penny? One's never too sure these days …'

Penny smiled. 'Of course not. It is my name, after all.'

'And a lovely name at that,' said Agatha, smiling back at her. 'I had a dog called Penny. The sweetest, most kind-natured Golden Retriever you're ever likely to meet. Dead now, unfortunately.'

'I'm sorry to hear that.'

'Don't be. It was over fifteen years ago. Besides, I'm not here because of my dog.' Agatha rested a hand on the receptionist's arm, deliberately placing her weight on it. 'It's my husband. Derek Trueman. He was checked in yesterday. Acute angina.'

'Derek Trueman?' Penny bit her lip as if she was thinking. 'I'm fairly certain we haven't got a Mr Trueman staying with us at the moment.'

'Really? How embarrassing.' Agatha fumbled about in her handbag with a trembling hand. 'I hope I haven't made a mistake … it does tend to happen … I'm always getting things mixed up … oh, my eyes … I'm starting to feel a little faint—'

'Please. Take a seat,' said Penny, guiding Agatha towards a row of chairs beside the reception desk.

'Yes, that's a good idea. You really are a lovely—'

Agatha stumbled forward, her knees buckling beneath her. That was the final touch. The icing on the cake.

Unsurprisingly, Penny moved swiftly to grab her around the waist. The panic on her face was evident. The last thing she wanted was someone keeling over. Not on her watch.

'There,' she said, easing Agatha down onto a chair. 'Would you like some water? I could always fetch a doctor—'

'No, no, I don't want to be a burden,' insisted Agatha. 'You're so nice, Penny. So caring. I can't imagine what you must think of a batty old dear like me.'

'Don't be daft,' said Penny, trying not to blush. 'I'll tell you what I'll do. I'll get the manager and we can track down your husband together. I'm sure it's nothing to get worked up about. Just a simple misunderstanding.'

Agatha perked up a little. 'Oh, that'd be wonderful.

You're an absolute treasure. It's not true what they say about young people these days.'

'I'm not that young,' laughed Penny, as she headed towards a door behind the reception desk. 'Now, don't you go anywhere. I'll be back before you know it ...'

Agatha waited for Penny to disappear from view before she stood up. There was no one else around. No one to see what she was up to.

Leaning over the desk, she found a thick leather-bound book by the telephone. It was open. Agatha cast an eye over its contents. She struck lucky first page. The left-hand column was made up of room numbers with the names of the occupants beside it.

Room 8 – Jackie Carmichael.

Agatha moved away from the desk. She could hear noises coming from somewhere behind the door. The last thing she wanted was to still be there when Penny returned. If she vanished now the receptionist would just assume that the old lady had absent-mindedly wandered off. She was hardly a threat so she wouldn't go searching for her. She would just leave it at that.

Tiptoeing across the foyer, Agatha passed smoothly through the first door on her left. It wasn't a spur of the moment decision nor a calculated guess. She had studied a floor plan of the hospital beforehand. If she had read it right, the next corridor she found herself in would be made up of the first nine rooms.

She *had* read it right.

There was a *1* on the door beside her. And then *2 ... 3 ... 4 ...*

Agatha stopped suddenly. There were two men at the end of the corridor. Both were well turned out, suited and booted, perfectly respectable. Something didn't quite sit right, though. The men were too large for visitors and far too smart for hospital security. No, they were hired muscle. There to guard their employer.

Agatha rested a hand on the nearest door to her, unsure of her next move. The men were pacing up and down now, talking, laughing. Fearful of being spotted, Agatha was about to turn back the way she had come when one of the men flashed a packet of cigarettes. That was the cue for them both to head in the opposite direction. There was a Fire Exit there. A smoker's escape route.

Agatha waited until they were out of sight before hurrying along the corridor. She stopped at *Room 8* and knocked twice. Just in case.

There was no answer so she pressed down on the handle.

The door opened and she walked in.

Agatha surveyed the room. It was clean and brightly lit with dried flowers and an abundance of soft furnishings. There was a bed in the centre of the floor space. It was occupied by a man. *Jackie Carmichael.* Probably. Agatha couldn't be certain. She had seen a picture or two on the internet, but none of them conclusively matched the man who was laid before her now.

Flat on his back, eyes closed and mouth open, Carmichael was rigged up to all manner of machines that were designed to keep him alive. He looked terrible. Pallid and unnaturally still. Practically dead. Agatha edged closer. He was younger than her, mid-fifties at a guess, but a life of wining and dining Stainmouth's glitterati at charity dinners and gala functions had clearly aged him. Whiskey, champagne and all the cigars you can suck on. The respectable face of crime.

Not anymore.

Agatha mentally put a cross against his name. Jackie Carmichael, the head of a powerful criminal family, was no longer the man he once was. No person of interest. If anything, he was barely even a person.

Agatha had seen enough. She was all set to leave when the door opened behind her. Without turning, she hunched her back, bent forward and reverted to character. She took a breath, ready to reel off a list of excuses.

Oh, silly old me ... I was looking for the lavatory ... I've an awfully weak bladder ...

Agatha twisted her neck. There was a woman stood in the doorway, but it wasn't Penny, the receptionist.

Dressed in black, this woman was less than half Agatha's age with long dark hair and particularly striking features. Her eyes narrowed when she saw there was someone else in the room. A stranger. A threat.

'Who the hell are you?' the woman spat, slamming the door shut behind her. 'And what are you doing to my father?'

CHAPTER THIRTY-SIX

Eddie the Exterminator led Lucas and Mercy into one of the side rooms in the boxing club.

Lockers lined every wall whilst a long bench filled much of the floor space. Eddie grabbed a towel from a hook and wiped the sweat from his face.

'Take a seat,' he said, gesturing towards the bench. 'Better than standing.'

Mercy and Lucas did as he suggested. At the same time Eddie opened up one of the lockers and removed a plastic beaker filled with a frothy green liquid.

'You're good,' he said, nodding at Mercy. 'Please tell me you've boxed before.'

'Just a bit,' Mercy admitted.

'That's a relief.' Eddie took a sip of his drink as he sat down beside them on the bench. 'I don't know what's in this, but it's vile,' he said, shaking the beaker in a bid to improve the taste. 'Full of the good stuff, though. Nutrients and minerals and all that. Nimble reckons it'll make me a better boxer. I'm starting to wonder why I even bother—'

'Don't let me put you off,' said Mercy hastily. 'You're

good, too. Honestly. It's just—'

'You're better.' Eddie took another sip. Turned to Lucas. 'Right, I'm pretty sure we've never met before and yet I seem to have done something to upset you …'

Lucas shook his head. 'What makes you think that?'

'I don't know,' shrugged Eddie. 'I guess it's the way you just wandered into Come Fight With Me and started laying down the law. Not many people do that. Only gangsters. Oh, and the police.'

'We're neither of those,' said Mercy, glancing at Lucas.

'Well, that takes some balls then,' said Eddie. 'No offence.'

'None taken,' smiled Mercy. 'And, listen, you've done nothing to upset us. If I'm being honest, it's not even you we're interested in. We're looking for a friend of yours.'

'Benji Hammerton,' said Lucas.

'Benji?' Eddie seemed to momentarily freeze. Almost as if someone had pressed his pause button. '*Ex*-friend,' he said eventually.

'Really? You two not pals anymore?' asked Lucas.

Eddie pulled a face. 'Not as such. I mean, we never actually fell out. We just drifted apart. I got more involved in boxing, and put my time and energy into training and everything else that goes with it. And Benji … well, he got caught up in … you know … other stuff—'

'What kind of other stuff?' pressed Lucas.

'The dodgy kind.' Eddie stopped and sighed. He had started now. He would have to finish. 'Drugs mostly. He works … if you can call it work … for a man called Vernon Gold. Do you know him?'

'Not personally,' said Mercy, 'but some friends of ours had a run-in with him last night. It didn't end well.'

'He's a right horrible bastard,' growled Eddie, tensing up as he spoke. 'I only met him a few times, but I realised it immediately. Benji clearly didn't see things the same way. I suppose he liked the glamour of it all. The bad boy image. You know what it's like—'

'Do I?' said Lucas stiffly.

Mercy shot him down with a glare. 'I can imagine,' she said. 'I've had friends who've gone down that route. A life of crime. It seems so simple at the time.'

Eddie held out his arms. 'Benji used to come here. To the boxing club. Nimble loved him. Said he was a natural. He was smaller than me, not so heavy. It made him lighter on his feet. We were inseparable for a while. Then he stopped coming. I was absolutely gutted. Still, I guess that's life. Nothing ever lasts forever, does it?' Eddie paused. 'Listen, don't mention any of this to Nimble, will you? He won't like it. It'll stir up bad memories—'

'Don't mention any of *what* to Nimble?'

Heads turned at the sound of the chirpy voice. Sure enough, Nimble had poked his head into the side room.

'Nothing,' mumbled Eddie. 'Well, something. Somebody. Benji.'

'Benji? Benji Hammerton?' Nimble spat on the floor. And then instantly regretted it and tried to rub it off with his plimsoll. 'Why are you talking about that scumbag?'

'We weren't,' insisted Eddie. 'Not really. These two are looking for him—'

'You the police?' Nimble asked. 'They're the only folk interested in Benji. He's the lowest of the low. A cockroach—'

'He's not that bad,' muttered Eddie. 'He just went off the rails. Wrong time, wrong place—'

'Bullshit,' scoffed Nimble. 'It was his choice; nobody forced him. I gave him a purpose. A reason to get up in the morning. Some order to his life. All he did was throw it straight back in my face. And why?'

'Money at a guess,' answered Lucas. 'Dealing drugs is a whole lot simpler than digging holes for a living. Don't look at me like that, Mercy; it's true. We're all thinking it. I'm the only one who dares to say it, though.'

Nimble took a breath. Tried to settle himself. 'Right, you nearly finished in here, champ?' he said, grinning at Eddie as he raised his fists and shadow boxed on the spot. 'The best don't rest. The top don't drop. The elite don't cheat. Do you catch my drift?'

'Give me two minutes,' said Eddie, holding up the required number of fingers. He waited for Nimble to duck out of the room before he spoke again. 'Anyway, back to Benji. What do you want with him? Is he in trouble?'

'Not yet,' said Mercy. 'But it won't be long. His parents are worried sick about him. They think he's in deep with this Gold character. We went to see the ex, Gina, but she couldn't help us.'

Lucas snorted. 'She could barely help herself.'

'Yeah, I heard she had sunk pretty low,' nodded Eddie. 'I only met her a few times. She was alright back then, before she got a taste for it. Speed and Ecstasy at first. Could be anything these days.'

'She had a kid,' revealed Mercy. 'A girl. Benji's a father.'

'I knew she was pregnant, but that's all,' Eddie admitted. 'I suppose that shows how far we've grown apart. Makes me feel pretty shitty, though. Some friend I am.'

Lucas cleared his throat, keen to steer things back on track. 'Do you know where we can find Benji?'

Eddie took a moment to think. 'I don't know where he's living these days, but I know a few places he might be.'

The side room fell silent as the boxer took another sip from the plastic beaker.

'Any chance you can tell us?' pressed Lucas.

'I can do more than that.' Eddie climbed up off the bench. Walked towards the exit. 'I'm just going to square things with Nimble. He won't like it, but I've had an idea.'

'What is it?' asked Mercy.

'Why tell you where to find Benji when I can go one better?' replied Eddie. 'I just hope you've got a big enough car because the three of us are going for a drive.'

CHAPTER THIRTY-SEVEN

Agatha stood up straight.

There was no point pretending. She had been rumbled.

'You must be the daughter,' she guessed. 'Zara, isn't it?'

'That's none of your business!' Moving swiftly across the private room, the woman pushed past Agatha so she could get closer to the bed. 'What have you done to him?' she scowled, pressing her hand against Jackie Carmichael's cheek.

'Nothing,' insisted Agatha. 'I'm not the enemy.'

'How did you get in?' The woman was barely listening as she rearranged the bed sheets. 'Where are the guards?'

'What guards?' shrugged Agatha, feigning innocence. 'There was nobody here when I—'

The woman cut her off. 'I don't believe you. You're lying. How do you know my father?'

'So, you *are* Zara Carmichael then?' said Agatha.

'Of course I am.' The woman – Zara – tensed up. 'I won't ask you again. How do you know my father?'

'I don't,' Agatha admitted. 'But that's not to say I wouldn't like to. If I'm being honest, I had heard about his condition, but I had no idea he was in such a bad way …'

Without warning, Zara Carmichael reached into her coat and removed a small handgun. Agatha recognised it as a SIG P365. She had used one herself. Many times, in fact. A perfect fit for smaller fingers, it was easy to conceal with extended capacity for ammunition.

Lethal in the wrong hands.

Zara lifted the gun and aimed it at Agatha's forehead. 'Give me one good reason why I shouldn't shoot you dead.'

'I can give you plenty,' said Agatha, keeping her cool. 'You'll be arrested for a start, resulting in a life sentence at His Majesty's pleasure. That's a pretty hefty price to pay, don't you think? Yes, I've never met your father, but I know who he is. Jackie Carmichael. Businessman. Entrepreneur. Crime lord. I'm not here to judge, though. I'm here to talk. I think we might be good for one another.'

Zara held the gun steady. 'What are you? Police?'

'Not even close,' smiled Agatha. 'I operate largely in the shadows. Off the grid. Under the radar. Would you like me to carry on with the cliches?'

Zara shook her head. 'MI5? MI6?'

'You're getting warmer,' nodded Agatha. 'At this very moment I'm running a small team who don't officially exist. They're ghosts. Practically untraceable. I'm only telling you this because I want you to trust me.'

Zara lowered the gun. Slipped it back inside her coat. 'You never told me your name.'

Agatha was about to reply when the door crashed open and in stumbled one of the two heavies who had been guarding the corridor.

'Where have you been?' asked Zara sternly.

The man struggled to get his words out. 'Me? Nowhere. I mean … I did just nip off. I was desperate … you know … for the toilet.'

'You were desperate for the toilet? And what about your partner? Was he desperate, too?' Zara jabbed a finger at the heavy. 'You're here to protect my father. That's what you get paid to do. And paid well. Don't ever forget that. Now, get out there and do your job!'

'Yes, of course, Miss Carmichael.' The heavy hesitated in the doorway. 'What about her?' he asked, nodding towards Agatha.

'What about her?' replied Zara sharply. 'She's a friend of the family. Imagine if she wasn't, though. Imagine if she had an ulterior motive. Any more questions?'

The heavy quickly shook his head before closing the door behind him.

'Take a seat,' said Zara, gesturing towards two chairs beside the bed. 'You can have hard and plastic, or plastic and hard. It's a tough decision.'

'I'll have hard and plastic.' Agatha sat down and then waited for Zara to do the same before continuing. 'You're new to this, aren't you?'

'Is it really that obvious? I thought I dealt with that meathead quite well.'

'You did. Honestly. No, I was talking about the family business. The business of crime. How old are you? Twenty-five? Twenty-six? You're barely out of university.'

'I'm not a kid,' said Zara, clearly put out. 'I've been

involved for years. Listening and learning. Waiting for the right opportunity.'

'Which is …?'

'If … *when* my father dies then it'll be my job to take over,' explained Zara. 'I'll be head of the Carmichael family. It's what's expected of me. I won't let anybody down.' Zara drew breath. 'So, what can somebody like me possibly do for somebody like you? Surely we're at opposite ends of the table. We should be enemies.'

'Not necessarily,' argued Agatha. 'Good and bad are rarely as clear cut as we'd like to think. The line between both tends to merge seamlessly. All I know for sure is there's a storm blowing through Stainmouth even as we speak. A dark storm. Violent and unpredictable. At times like this I'd prefer to get to know my opposition, rather than fight them with my hands tied.'

Zara had listened carefully. 'That's understandable.'

'Your father may not have led the purest of lives, but at least he had a moral code. Loyalty and honour above all. He didn't deal drugs. He swerved women and children. Times have changed, though. That's the dark storm I'm talking about.'

Zara raised an eyebrow. 'And what are you? The sunshine?'

'No, I'm more like an umbrella,' said Agatha. 'I can't get rid of the rain clouds for good, but at least I can offer some kind of protection from their downpour. Are you aware of a man called Vernon Gold?'

Zara took a moment. 'Vaguely. Like you said, I'm new to this business. Is he the dark storm?'

'Let's just say he's looming on the horizon,' said Agatha.

Zara turned towards the bed. Reached out and grabbed her father's hand. 'So, what do you want from me?'

'Nothing,' Agatha admitted. 'Not yet. I just wanted to introduce myself. When the time comes, however, I think it would be beneficial for the two of us if there were less clouds in the sky. Stainmouth's gloomy enough already, don't you think?' Agatha stood up without warning. 'I've outstayed my welcome,' she said, moving towards the exit. 'Once again, sorry about your father. Until the next time—'

'Wait!' called out Zara. 'You still haven't told me your name. How am I supposed to contact you?'

'You're not.' Agatha opened the door and stepped outside. 'I'll contact you. I promise.'

CHAPTER THIRTY-EIGHT

The Fiat 500 wasn't big enough.

Not for someone as tall and as cumbersome as Eddie. Try as he might, he couldn't help but sit hunched over with his chin resting on his knees. He told everyone within earshot that it was more uncomfortable than it looked. And yet, funnily enough, it looked really uncomfortable.

'Are you sure you're okay?' frowned Mercy from the passenger seat. 'It's a shame we haven't got a sun roof. You could've poked your head out the top.'

'I'll be fine.' Eddie rested a hand on Lucas's shoulder. 'Just try not to go over any bumps. And don't brake too hard.'

Pulling away from the kerb, Lucas touched the brakes a little too sharply as they reached a junction.

'Yeah, like that,' laughed Eddie. 'I nearly went through the windscreen. Take a left.'

'Where are we heading?' asked Lucas.

'Gold likes to call his … employees the Gold Squad,' revealed Eddie. 'I know a few of their hangouts. Been there once or twice with Benji. They've got a house on St. Gerald's

Mews … Mermaid Street … Eastern Avenue … Rocketway Heights—'

Lucas pulled a face. 'Oh, we spent a lovely evening in Rocketway Heights. That was where we found Gina.'

'Gold's got a couple of flats in the Rocketway that they use as a front for dealing drugs,' said Eddie. 'Always pays to be right on the doorstep when you've got so many hungry punters in one place. Mermaid Street's closest, though, so we'll start there. Remember to keep your door locked, mind. You never know who might try and steal your car whilst you're still sat inside of it …'

Mermaid Street was nowhere near as bad as Eddie had made out.

Okay, so it was hardly the most salubrious of areas, but Lucas had certainly known worse. Boarded-up windows and broken fences were hardly a match for petrol bombs and sporadic gunfire. For a Friday morning it actually seemed quiet. Just a few youths loitering by the roadside, waiting for something to happen. The occasional stray dog searching for a home.

Join the club, thought Lucas. Tell me when you find one.

On Eddie's instructions, he parked the Fiat a stone's throw away from number fourteen. It was a mid-terrace, two up, two down. In need of a good makeover, much like the rest of the street. Lucas knew it was empty at first sight. The curtains were open for a start. That was a tell-tale sign. In his experience, dealers didn't tend to do their business in full view of the neighbours.

'Shall we move on?' Lucas suggested.

'Move on,' agreed Eddie.

St. Gerald's Mews was next up.

A huge council estate near the centre of Stainmouth, Eddie seemed unsure which house he was looking for. As a last resort he told Lucas to pull up by the bus shelter.

'I'm not sure Margaret waiting for the number sixty-six would be willing to spend a huge chunk of her pension on coke,' sneered Lucas, shaking his head in frustration.

'You don't know what the pensioners get up to round here,' Eddie smiled. 'Drug-fuelled orgies were all the rage at one time. Anything's got to be better than bingo.' Eddie waited for a reply that wasn't forthcoming. 'I'll shut up, shall I?'

'It's probably for the best,' said Mercy. 'Let's go.'

It was only when they reached Eastern Avenue that their luck finally changed.

Despite his obvious restrictions, Eddie threw himself forward and smashed his fist on the dashboard. 'Stop!'

Lucas reacted instinctively. Slammed on the brakes. 'You're not going to be sick, are you? Have you had too much of that sloppy green slime?'

'What? No ... I hope not.' Eddie pointed out the window, the focus of his attention the last in a row of new builds. 'That was Benji,' he cried. 'I'm sure of it. He just entered the house with another lad. Ah, I can't remember his name ... not his real name ... his nickname. It made him sound like a shit barber.'

Lucas got there first. 'Cutz?'

'Yeah, Cutz,' said Eddie, surprised. 'How did you know?'

'We've met before.'

Eddie turned his nose up in disgust. 'He's nothing much. Just a wannabe gangster. I don't think he'd last a minute in a ring with you,' he added, nodding at Mercy.

'It's funny you should say that ...' began Lucas.

'Leave it,' said Mercy, cutting him off. 'Right, what do we do now? We can't just knock on the door and introduce ourselves. Not with Cutz in there ... where are you going?'

'Me?' Eddie was already halfway out the door. 'I'm done. I told you I'd help you find Benji and I have. Now I've got to get back to Nimble. He'll blow his top if I leave it any longer. The best don't rest, remember.'

'Do you want a lift?' offered Mercy. 'It's the least we can do.'

'Nah, you're alright. I'll run,' grinned Eddie. 'Build up my stamina for our re-match. Besides, now you've found Benji you'd better not lose him.'

With that, Eddie closed the door behind him before jogging back the way they had come. He turned once and waved. Mercy returned the gesture. He was a nice guy. Joining Come Fight With Me boxing club might not be such a bad option if she had to stay in Stainmouth any longer than expected. She wouldn't mind lending a hand if asked. Teaching them a few tricks of the trade.

When she turned back to Lucas, he was flicking through his contact list. 'Who are you calling?'

'Dumb and dumber,' he replied, pressing the phone to his ear. 'Also known as the other two.'

CHAPTER THIRTY-NINE

They tossed a coin they had found in the glove compartment of the Fiat.

Heads.

'Bad luck,' said Lucas, resisting the urge to smile as he climbed out of the car.

Mercy took the defeat on the chin as she started the engine. She had lost the toss so now it was her job to pick up Tommy and Rose – also known as the other two – from Cockleshell Farm. She felt well enough to drive, the fuzziness in her head slowly fading with every day that passed.

Lucas was the lookout. If anyone left the house he had to follow them. If they left by car, well, then he was really in the shit.

Not my problem, decided Mercy, as she drove away. She just hoped he was a fast runner.

Twenty minutes later, she returned.

'Look at that dickhead,' said Tommy, as the Fiat crept along Eastern Avenue. 'He's hiding behind a tree trunk. Who hides behind trees except for perverts and weirdos?'

'Birdwatchers,' replied Mercy.

'Yeah, like I said, perverts,' nodded Tommy. 'You'd better turn away, ladies. Any moment now he's going to leap out into the open with his old fellow swinging between his legs.'

Mercy tried not to laugh as Lucas did just that, albeit with nothing of any note swinging between his legs.

'You took your time,' he moaned, once the others had joined him on the pavement.

'Keep your voice down.' Mercy guided them towards a nearby side street, both out of sight and out of earshot of the house. 'Benji Hammerton's still in there, yeah?'

'As far as I know,' shrugged Lucas. 'I mean, no one's left, but we don't actually know what Benji looks like, do we?'

That particular remark was greeted with an awkward silence.

'Why did nobody give us a photograph?' said Mercy eventually. 'I should probably call Miles and ask him to—'

Tommy shook his head. 'I'm not waiting for that posh fart to pull his finger out. We're here now so we might as well get the ball rolling.'

'What do you suggest?' asked Lucas, fearing the worst.

'I'll take one for the team and buy some gear off them,' said Tommy matter-of-factly. He followed that up with a wink. Bad move.

Lucas's jaw tightened. 'Pardon?'

'My mistake,' said Tommy. 'I'll *pretend* to buy some gear off them. Think about it. They won't deal on the doorstep, will they? They'll have to invite me in. Then I can see what's what. Get the lie of the land. Rate the threat level. More importantly, I can find out which one's Benji—'

'No way!' Lucas turned to Mercy. 'Back me up.'

She didn't. 'I mean, it's not the worst plan I've ever heard. And it's not as if we can take his place, is it? Cutz is bound to recognise us.'

'Well, he's not going in there on his own,' grumbled Lucas, shifting his gaze to Rose.

'Forget it!' blurted out Tommy. 'No offence, but there's not one dealer alive that would believe that Rose is either a cokehead or a pill freak. They'd think it was a trap … and they'd be right. That's the sort of stunt the police would try and pull. No, like it or not, I'm going in alone. It'll be safer that way.'

'You do remember what happened last time you flew solo, don't you?' frowned Lucas. 'Rose had to come and bail you out before you bled to death all over the dancefloor.'

Tommy gently stroked his wound. 'That was a one off. Nobody's perfect. Not even me.' He stopped stroking. Held out his hand. 'Go on then,' he said, rubbing his thumb and forefinger together. 'Give me what you've got.'

His request fell on deaf ears, largely because nobody knew what he was talking about.

'Pay up,' Tommy explained. 'I'll have a tenner off each of you please. Add a tenner from me and that's forty quid in total. Should be enough for a couple of grammes of coke if I ask politely.'

'Wait!' The lines that ran across Lucas's forehead were more pronounced than ever. 'You do know that you're not *actually* going in there to buy drugs, don't you?'

'The coke's just a sub plot; it's not the main event,' insisted Tommy. 'I have to play the role though, don't I? Otherwise I'll get rumbled immediately.'

'He's right … again,' sighed Mercy. Against her better judgment, she handed Tommy a ten pound note. The other two did the same, albeit with varying degrees of reluctance.

'This should be fun,' said Tommy, stuffing the notes into his back pocket before he set off across the road towards the house.

Lucas held his tongue for all of two seconds. 'I can't believe what we've just done. He'll probably come out completely off his nut. We'll have to scrape him up off the pavement.'

'He's not that stupid.' Mercy turned to Rose. 'He's not, is he?'

'I wouldn't like to say,' Rose mumbled.

The three of them watched as Tommy stopped at the front door. He knocked, waited a second or two, and then knocked again.

The door opened a fraction.

Shuffling from toe to toe, Tommy began to speak. Occasionally, he glanced over his shoulder. Even from a distance, he looked nervous. On edge. Maybe that was all part of his act, thought Mercy. Ever the performer. Sure enough, Tommy laughed out loud and the door opened a little wider. That was the cue for him to slip inside the house.

'Now what?' said Mercy, as the door closed behind him.

Lucas strolled back towards the Fiat. 'Now we cross our fingers … and then cross them some more because there's a very good chance things could go horribly, horribly wrong!'

CHAPTER FORTY

Tommy snatched a breath as the door closed behind him.

The man who had let him in was dressed in a white tracksuit and black trainers. He was barrel-shaped. Clean shaven beneath his hood. Puffy face and rosy-red cheeks. Tommy plucked an age from thin air. Early twenties. Something like that. Old enough to take care of himself, but too young to know what he was letting himself in for.

'In there,' grunted Barrel Belly, gesturing towards the first room off the hallway.

Tommy held his ground. 'Bit risky, isn't it?'

'What is?'

'Wearing white.' Tommy pointed at the man's tracksuit. 'Shows up all manner of stains. Practically unavoidable in this day and age. White underpants is the one that really gets me, though. You're practically walking a tightrope all day. One bad fart and it's game over—'

'In there,' repeated Barrel Belly. 'And less of the chat.'

Tommy did as he was told. The room he walked into was large in size, but badly in need of attention. The bare walls were begging out for a lick of paint, whilst the carpet had frayed so badly at the edges there was now more floorboard on show than fabric. Two well-worn leather sofas had been pushed up against the walls, with a round coffee table plonked somewhere in between. The table was covered in all manner of debris. Scrunched-up cans and empty bottles fought for space with congealed takeaway cartons and precariously stacked pizza boxes. Tommy looked a little closer. He could see a white powdery residue smeared across the table's surface and several half-smoked joints in a glass ashtray. Cocaine and weed. That was a relief. At least he'd come to the right place.

'Make yourself comfortable,' said Barrel Belly, as he left the room. 'I'll be back in a minute.'

Tommy settled back in the sofa. There was a TV directly in front of him. It was switched on to some dreary antiques show where the winners took home about fourteen quid in loose change and a shitty fleece that you wouldn't even do the gardening in. Tommy found the remote and turned it off. Looked towards the window. The room he was in was at the front of the house. He had a sudden urge to pull open the curtains and give the others a thumbs-up.

The urge passed when Barrel Belly re-entered the room. This time he had company. Another man. Same age, but a vastly different weight to his much chunkier friend. Dressed in black, his hair was shaven to the skin at the back and sides with a Caesar fringe on top. There were pock marks on his cheeks, no doubt the result of bad acne.

Oh, and a huge purple bruise on the side of his jaw.

Tommy's mind raced back to another time. A

conversation between the others. Mercy had flipped out and punched someone the previous evening. She was a loose cannon, that one. Now, what was his name again?

Think. It's important.

Ah, yes ...

Tommy jumped up off the sofa. 'You must be Cutz,' he said, holding out his hand to be shaken.

'Yeah, that's right.' Cutz ignored the hand. Looked Tommy up and down. 'Do I know you?'

'Me?' Tommy shook his head. 'No, not me. I'm a nobody. You're reputation, however, precedes you. You're one of the top boys round these parts. Practically a legend ...' Tommy forced himself to take a breath. There was sweet talking and then there was sweet talking with your tongue lodged halfway up someone's arse. Maybe he had gone too far ...

Or maybe not.

'Did you hear that, Jumbo?' Cutz, chest puffed out, began to swagger around the room. 'My man here speaks the truth. My reputation precedes me. I'm the top boy. Practically a legend.'

Barrel Belly – or Jumbo to those in the know – snorted like a stuck pig. 'He's taking the piss.'

'I'm not,' insisted Tommy. 'I'm nervous, that's all. I had to build up the courage to come here. I asked around and your name kept cropping up. They told me Cutz would see me right.'

'And they weren't wrong,' grinned Cutz. 'What about Jumbo here? Have you heard of him?'

Tommy pretended to think. Leave the crowd waiting. Comedy timing. 'No.'

'Bullshit,' muttered Jumbo, pushing past Cutz as he left the room and headed upstairs.

'Ha! That's music to my ears.' A beaming Cutz clenched his fist and punched Tommy gently on his shoulder. It was a friendly gesture, but it was still enough to make Tommy wince as the impact reverberated across his chest. 'Hey, let me get my boy in here,' said Cutz, turning towards the door. 'He's gotta' hear this. Benji … Benji …'

Tommy heard the familiar stomp of shoes on stairs before another man appeared in the room.

At first glance, Benji Hammerton was a mirror image of the other two. Tracksuit and trainers. Sneers and snarls. A second glance, however, suggested something else entirely. It was the eyes that gave him away. They were softer. Brighter. Whether he liked it or not, he had lived a different life to Cutz and Jumbo. A nice life. A family home and three meals a day. Clean clothes and hot running water.

Tommy could've laughed out loud. Some people don't even know they're born …

'My man here says I'm the top boy on the streets of Stainmouth,' began Cutz, bouncing up and down. 'A legend. Not Jumbo, though. Jumbo's a complete unknown.'

Benji smiled, showing too many teeth in the process. 'I've not seen you around,' he said, taking a good look at Tommy. 'You new to Stainmouth?'

Tommy nodded. 'I was living in London. Fancied a change of scenery, though. Somewhere a little more … sedate.'

'Stainmouth has its moments,' said Benji.

'Damn right it does!' Cutz stepped forward, filling the gap between the two other men, making himself the centre of attention. 'Listen, I don't like doing business on my own doorstep, but for you I'll make an exception.' He handed Tommy a card with a number on it. 'In future, you don't come to this house – I'll come to you. Give me a call and I'll deliver. It's all part of the service. And don't go fuckin' me off for any other dealers neither. They cut their gear with anything they can lay their thieving little hands on. Flour … talcum powder … rat poison … they ain't bothered. Not like us. Our coke's as pure as the driven snow. Whiter than white.'

Tommy doubted that very much, but held his tongue regardless. Truth be told, he was barely listening. No, he was formulating a plan. Unless he was mistaken there was only three of them in the house. Cutz, Jumbo and Benji. To speak to the latter he would first have to do something with the other two. Could he take them both on his own? With his bare hands? Probably not. What about a weapon then? You could do plenty of damage with an empty pizza box and a glass ashtray …

Whoa. Don't get ahead of yourself. Stick to the job at hand.
Buy the coke. Leave the house. Report back to the others.

Cutz crouched down by a wooden sideboard under the TV and pulled open the drawer. 'So, how much you after?'

Tommy leant forward. Glanced inside without making too big a deal about it. He could see a handgun, several bricks of cocaine and a dozen or so bags of weed in there.

And something else. Something to make his heart flutter.

Money. Lots of it. Huge wads of the stuff just sat there unattended. Thousands at a guess. Ten. Fifteen. Maybe more. Hard to tell from a distance. Enough to change his life, though.

Enough to bring him back from the dead.

Tommy took a deep breath in a bid to slow his heart rate. These boys had gotten cocky. Cocky *and* careless. He had seen it so many times before it was unreal. They had got so comfortable they had forgotten the one golden rule.

Don't take your eye off the ball.

Tommy had done that and got shot as a result. Now it was somebody else's turn for a nasty surprise.

'What's so funny?'

Tommy wiped the smile from his face when he realised Cutz was staring straight at him. 'Funny? No, nothing. Just excited, that's all. Tonight's going to be a good night. I can feel it in my bones.'

'Sure is, brother,' nodded Cutz. 'Now, how much you—'

'Cutz … Benji … you gotta' see this.'

That was Jumbo. Still upstairs, the tone of his voice suggested urgency.

Cutz hissed through his teeth. 'I'm busy.'

'This is important,' said Jumbo. 'We got a problem.'

'A problem?' Cutz closed the drawer. Stood up. 'What problem?'

'There's a man creeping about in the garden,' revealed Jumbo. 'And, trust me, he ain't here to clean the windows.'

CHAPTER FORTY-ONE

'Do you know what we've done?'

Mercy rested her forehead on the steering wheel. Sighed. 'No, but I'm sure you're going to tell us anyway.'

Lucas didn't appear to pick up on the sarcasm in her voice. 'We've sent a drug dealer into a drug den to buy drugs. What the hell were we thinking?'

'It'll be fine.'

'Will it? Because I'm not so sure. How long has he been in there now?'

'I don't know. Ten minutes—'

'Eleven minutes and thirty-three seconds,' said Rose from the back seat.

Lucas glanced at her out the corner of one eye. 'I'll take your word for it. Still, if nothing else it proves my point. Tommy's been in there ages. And it's not as if he's out of his comfort zone, is it? He practically does this as a day job.'

'*Did* this as a day job,' Mercy argued. 'Not anymore.'

Lucas ignored that. 'Do you remember what happened yesterday? If it wasn't for Rose he'd be laid out in a morgue by now.'

'Bit drastic,' said Mercy. 'I think Vernon Gold and his goons would've stopped at a good kicking. Listen, if you're so worried about Tommy's well-being, why don't you go and join him?'

'Good idea.' With that, Lucas flung open the car door and stepped out onto the pavement.

'I was joking,' said Mercy, leaning over.

'I'm not.' Closing the door, Lucas looked both ways before jogging across the road.

Mercy lowered the window, ready to call out, before deciding against it. The last thing she wanted was to draw attention to them. Besides, Lucas was an ex-policeman. He wasn't naive. He knew what he was doing.

Lucas knew what he was doing.

He had no intention of heading towards the front of the house. That was far too risky. Instead, he hurried down a narrow alley way that ran along the left hand side of the building. The wall that separated him from the property was six foot tall. Raising himself up onto his tiptoes, he peered over and took in the view. It was a small, rectangular courtyard with no grass to speak of, just roughly laid concrete slabs. Several overflowing rubbish bins and a battered old barbecue that had been left uncovered in all weathers took up much of the space. More importantly perhaps, the curtains, much like at the front of the house, were pulled to. He couldn't see in, but then nobody could see out.

Head down, Lucas walked all the way around the side of

the house until he reached the back wall. He smiled when he noticed the gate. He was still smiling when it opened without complication. That saved him climbing over the wall, meaning there was less chance of him being spotted. Or, worse than that, getting stuck at the top. A leg on each side. Genitalia trapped somewhere in-between.

Lucas closed the gate as quietly as possible and then waited. Ten seconds passed. If anybody had seen or heard him they would've come out by now to investigate. If they did, he could be out of the courtyard and halfway down the street in no time.

He gave it ten more seconds. He had waited long enough.

Senses on red alert, Lucas kept low as he made his way slowly towards the back door. He carefully avoided a tower of cigarette butts that had been crudely piled on top of one another, as well as several empty cans of some horrendously florescent energy drink. No dog shit was always a relief, and not just for fear of treading in it. No one wants some enormous beast sneaking up on them from behind. Taking their leg off whilst they're looking in the opposite direction.

Lucas froze. Just for a moment he thought he saw the curtains move in a top floor window.

He looked again. There was nothing there. Relax.

Lucas carried on until he reached the door. It was a white plastic frame with a frosted-glass window at the top. Ducking down, he pressed an ear to its surface. He could hear laughter coming from inside, coupled with the occasional shout. Nothing threatening, though. If anything, they sounded like they were getting on fine.

Maybe he should head back to Mercy and Rose.

Maybe Tommy had things under control, after all.

Lucas was still listening when he realised there was nothing to listen to. The laughter had been replaced by a lingering silence. Silence was never a good thing. Not unless everybody was asleep.

Or dead.

Lucas rested his fingers on the door handle, applied some pressure. Gently does it. Not too hard.

The handle moved and the door began to open. It was unlocked.

He tried to control his breathing as he poked his head inside the house. He could see an oven. A fridge. Kettle and toaster. And something else. Something that didn't belong in a kitchen.

Something like a gun.

CHAPTER FORTY-TWO

A large youth in a white tracksuit took several strides forward.

'Nice of you to join us,' he said, pressing the gun against Lucas's forehead. 'Unfortunately, all trespassers will be executed.'

Lucas cursed himself. That was amateurish. Just walking in like that. A man of his experience should've known better.

'Don't keep him to yourself, Jumbo,' shouted a voice from another room. 'Bring him in.'

The man called Jumbo was quick to comply. 'You heard. Shift.'

Lucas stood up straight. If he moved swiftly enough maybe he could disarm him. *Maybe.* That was the key word in that particular sentence. A combination of his opponent's sheer size and an itchy trigger finger meant it was a risk he wasn't prepared to take.

'Through there.' Jumbo gestured with the gun towards the door. Lucas started to walk until he found himself in a dark hallway. There was a door to his right. He passed through it and saw two tatty sofas and a litter-strewn coffee table.

And three more men.

One was Tommy. Lucas refused to meet his eye. He could tell he was smiling, though. Grinning even. Like this was all one big joke.

The second man he had never seen before. The third, however, was all too familiar. The Caesar fringe and pock-marked cheeks. Not to mention the huge purple bruise across the left-hand side of his jaw.

'Ah, shit, I know this guy,' scowled Cutz. 'He was up at the Rocketway last night.'

'Was it him who attacked you?' asked Jumbo.

Cutz shrugged awkwardly. 'Well … yeah … kind of—'

'No, I didn't,' Lucas argued. 'That was—'

Cutz lashed out with the back of his hand, striking Lucas firmly across his face, drawing blood as he shut him up mid-sentence.

'Alright, take it easy,' said Benji, resting a hand on Cutz's shoulder. 'He could be anyone.'

'He's police,' spat Cutz. 'He said so last night. Muzzy heard him.'

The house fell silent. Lucas glanced at Tommy. He was gently shaking his head whilst rolling his eyes. Not the easiest skill set to perform in all fairness.

'Get on your knees!' Jumbo kicked out at the back of Lucas's legs, sending him stumbling forward until he dropped to the carpet. 'Put your hands behind your head!'

'We need to think this through,' said Benji, trying to calm the situation. 'We've brought the police into the house. Pointed a gun at him. Now he's seen our faces. He might

even know our names.' Benji swallowed. 'We can't just …
kill him.'

'Can't we?' Cutz looked around the room. 'Ain't no one
here to stop us.'

'This is insane,' Benji cried. 'We're not just going to
murder someone—'

'At last,' said Lucas, spitting out blood as he spoke. 'A bit
of common sense.'

'Shut it, pig!' Cutz pulled back his arm, ready to strike
again.

'Wait!' said Tommy. He pointed at Lucas. 'He's not
police. He just likes to say that. To scare people.'

'You know him?' Cutz edged closer to Tommy. 'Who
the fuck is he?'

'His name is Lucas.' Tommy paused for effect. 'And he's
my boyfriend.'

'Your boyfriend?' Cutz backed away a little. 'What?
You're like … a couple?'

'Exactly like a couple,' nodded Tommy.

'I am not your boyfriend!' protested Lucas.

'Don't be like that, darling,' said Tommy, placing a hand
on his heart. 'We've been seeing each other for months now.
We're in love. That's why you're here, isn't it?'

'Bullshit,' Lucas blurted out. 'I'm not … I wouldn't … I
could do better than you for a start.'

'Well, *that's* clearly not true,' said Tommy. 'If anything,
you're punching above your weight. I'm a nine out of ten in
anybody's book. You're hovering somewhere between a four
and a five.'

'What do you mean *that's why he's here?*' pressed Cutz.

'He worries about me,' explained Tommy. 'Don't you, sweetheart? That's why he followed me all the way from London. I'm guessing that's why he was up at the Rocketway last night as well. Looking for me. Love can do that to a person. Make them do strange things.'

'I am not in love with you!' yelled Lucas. 'Oh, just shoot me now. Put me out of my misery.'

'Yeah, that can be arranged.' Crouching down beside the TV unit, Cutz pulled open the drawer and rummaged around inside. 'Where's my gun?' he said, jumping to his feet.

'What? This gun?' asked Tommy, waving the weapon in the air. He had grabbed it when Cutz and Benji had been summoned by Jumbo. Just in case something happened. Something like this.

Without warning, metal struck bone as Tommy brought the butt of the gun crashing down on top of Cutz's head.

'Night night, sleepyhead,' said Tommy, as the youth's legs gave way beneath him and his body crumpled to the carpet. 'Don't look so nervous,' he said, peering around the room. 'He'll wake up soon enough. Probably. I don't think I hit him that hard.'

'You did hit him *quite* hard,' argued Lucas. 'He deserved it, though. Now, what are you going to do about these other two?'

Tommy pointed the gun at Benji. 'That one's Benji Hammerton.'

'Is it really?' Lucas glanced up at him. 'Nice to meet you. Did my friend ... not friend ... and certainly not my boyfriend … partner then … not in a sexual way … tell you why we're here?'

'I thought he wanted to buy coke,' spluttered Benji.

'Life would be so much simpler if that was true,' Tommy sighed. 'Unfortunately, I've only got eyes … and nostrils … for you.'

'Me?' Benji frowned. 'What have I done?'

'Nothing,' replied Tommy. 'That's the problem. You've forgotten about your past. That can easily be solved, though. A quick phone call here. A flying visit there. A card for all appropriate occasions. Just come with us and—'

'Aren't you forgetting something?' piped up Jumbo, pressing his gun against Lucas's temple. 'Or someone?'

'You?' Tommy ran a hand through his hair. 'Yeah, I had kinda' forgotten about you. If I'm being honest, I was hoping you might have scuttled off to the fridge by now. Got yourself a snack.'

'I'm not going anywhere,' insisted Jumbo. 'I've got a gun. You've got a gun—'

'Ah, gun friends.' Tommy laughed out loud. 'That's the only thing we have got in common, though. Then there's the one major difference …'

'And what's that?' sneered Jumbo.

'You're afraid to pull the trigger.'

Jumbo bit too quickly. 'That ain't true.'

'Yes, it is.'

'No, it ain't! I've shot lots of people.'

Tommy shrugged. 'Go on then. Do it. Shoot him. I dare you.'

'What the hell are you doing?' wailed Lucas. 'You don't want him to actually shoot me, do you?'

'Shut it!' Jumbo's hand was trembling now. 'I'll … I'll do it.'

'Yeah, that's what we're all waiting for.' Tommy opened his mouth. Pretended to yawn. 'We haven't got all day, though.'

'Just put it down, Jumbo,' pleaded Benji. He was crouched down in the corner of the room, his head in his hands. 'I don't want to die. Not here. Not like this.'

'I ain't scared,' muttered Jumbo to no one in particular. 'I ain't scared of nothing.'

'Pleased to hear it,' said Tommy. 'Try not to confuse stupidity with bravery, though. It's an easy mistake to make. Listen, I'll tell you what I'll do. I'll give you three seconds. Three seconds to put a bullet in my friend's … no, boyfriend's … no, *ex*-boyfriend's brain. After that, it's my turn …'

'Don't tell him that!' barked Lucas.

'It's fine,' insisted Tommy, waving his own gun around like a cheerleader's baton. 'Three …'

'You don't tell me what to do!' Sweat was dripping down Jumbo's face. Blurring his vision. 'If I want to shoot, I'll shoot.'

'Course you will,' smiled Tommy. 'Two …'

'That's it!' Jumbo stamped his feet in a bid to energize himself. 'Him first. Then you. I'm going to—'

'One.' Tommy lifted the gun. Straightened his arm. Took aim. 'Too slow,' he said calmly. 'I told you it was risky wearing that white tracksuit …'

CHAPTER FORTY-THREE

Mercy practically jumped out of her skin at the sound of the gunshot.

Without missing a beat, she flung open the door and scrambled out of the Fiat. It was only when she was halfway across the road, however, that it fully dawned on her what was happening.

A gun had been fired inside the house.

There was movement up and down Eastern Avenue. Faces in the window. Bodies on the doorstep. People were coming to investigate. No doubt someone would've called it in by now. A gunshot in broad daylight wasn't an everyday occurrence on any street in any neighbourhood. Mercy knew she would have to act quick. Find Lucas and Tommy and get out of there.

That is, of course, unless she was too late. Unless only one of them was still standing.

Mercy came to a halt when she reached the house. Took a deep breath and slowly opened the door. The hallway was clear. She could hear voices, though. And sobbing. Somebody was hurt.

Mercy was about to edge forward when she sensed a presence behind her. Spinning around, she was all set to throw a punch when she realised who it was.

'Bloody hell, Rose,' she whispered. 'I almost took your head off.'

A terrified Rose mouthed some kind of mumbling apology.

'Fine,' frowned Mercy. 'You're here now. Just stay behind me.'

She crept forward, stopping at the first room on her left. Pushing the door to one side, she tried to take it all in at once. Lucas was the first person she saw. Sweat was trickling down his face as he climbed unsteadily to his feet. There were three men close to where he was. One of the men – Cutz – was face down on the carpet, out for the count. Another was hunched over in one corner, struggling to keep it together. The third man, meanwhile, was slumped against the wall, his fingers struggling to prevent a steady flow of blood from escaping from a wound in his leg. A *fresh* wound. The result of the gunshot no doubt.

'He'll never get those bloodstains out,' remarked Tommy.

Mercy found him stood by the window. 'What happened?' She noticed the gun in Tommy's hands and altered her line of questioning. 'What are you doing with that? Put it down.'

'Not likely,' said Tommy. 'This is evidence. If anything, we'll have to take it with us. Throw it in the river or something.'

Mercy breathed a sigh of relief as Tommy stuck the gun down the back of his trousers. At least it was hidden now. Out of sight, out of mind. 'Are you okay?' she asked, switching her attention to Lucas.

'Somehow.' Swaying slightly from side to side, it took all of Lucas's powers of concentration to stay upright. 'That's Benji Hammerton by the way. The one who's not unconscious or bleeding.'

Benji was on his knees now, tending to Jumbo the best he could with whatever he could find.

'This is a nightmare,' he whimpered. 'We need to clear this place out before the police arrive.'

Mercy held out her hand. 'Forget all that and come with us. We need to talk to you anyway. It's about your mum and dad.'

'My mum and dad?' Benji stopped what he was doing. 'Are they alright?'

'They're fine,' said Mercy. 'It's you that's the problem. You've not been in touch and they're worried.'

Benji looked over at Tommy. '*He* said something like that. I've just been busy. I've a lot going on.'

'So I see,' said Mercy. 'And all of it is going to land you in prison. Just come with us now and you can leave it all behind.'

Benji hesitated, unsure of himself. 'I want to. Honestly, I do. But I can't. Not yet, anyway. It'd be more than my life's worth. Gold would hunt me down if I tried to do a runner.'

'Time's ticking, Mercy,' called out Lucas. He had already

left the room, made his way along the hallway. 'We can't let anyone find us here. Especially not the police. We're ghosts, remember. We don't exist.'

Mercy threw the car keys to Rose, who was still waiting in the doorway. 'Go outside and start the engine. Don't run. And try not to panic either. You don't want to arouse suspicion.'

Rose set off without another word. Mercy had decided to follow when Benji clambered to his feet. Grabbed her by the arm.

'I will talk to them,' he said. 'My parents. Just not now.' He ran the back of his hand roughly across his face, wiping the tears from his eyes. 'Ah, man, this is fucked up. I thought it would be fun … you know, this life … but it's not. I'm sick of it now. I just want to go home.'

'We can sort that out,' said Mercy, resting a hand on his shoulder. 'You can be back in London before you know it.'

Benji nodded. 'Meet me tomorrow morning. Ten o'clock. There's a patch of wasteland behind the railway station. No one will see us there. We can talk in private.' Benji paused. 'Do you know where it is?'

'I'll find it,' said Mercy. 'See you then.'

Benji turned his attention back to Jumbo without another word.

'I can hear sirens,' shouted Lucas from the front door. That was his final warning. If Mercy didn't join him now then he would have to leave her to fend for herself.

Thankfully, it didn't come to that. 'Where's Tommy?' she asked, hurrying towards the exit.

'Don't know, don't care,' replied Lucas. 'The guy's a lunatic. He almost got me killed back there.'

'We can't just forget about him.' Mercy was about to head up the stairs when Tommy burst out of the room she had only just vacated. 'Where you been?' she asked tersely.

'Just checking on the injured party,' said Tommy. 'Wouldn't want him to bleed to death now, would I? And he won't. It's just a flesh wound.'

The three of them left the house without another word. They walked together, not too fast, not too slow. People had gathered in the street now. Nosey neighbours, huddled together in packs, desperate for something to talk about. Mercy could feel them looking, but that was all. Yes, they had heard a gunshot, but that didn't necessarily mean they knew where it had come from.

'Drive,' said Mercy, trying to keep her cool as she climbed into the Fiat's passenger seat.

Rose waited for Tommy and Lucas to jump in the back before she gently pressed down on the pedal. Her hands were shaking and it was difficult to control the steering wheel as she turned the first corner. The sight of a police car heading towards them only made things worse.

'Don't panic,' said Mercy, resting a hand on Rose's leg. 'You can do this.'

Staring straight ahead, Rose held her breath as the police car, first, drew level and then raced past on its way to Eastern Avenue. Another followed a moment later. Neither car stopped nor even slowed down. Fingers crossed, they were in the clear.

'Well done,' smiled Mercy. The smile vanished as she sat back and waited for the inevitable fireworks. She wasn't entirely sure what had happened back there, but things could hardly have gone much worse. Nobody was supposed to have got shot for a start. She studied Lucas in the rear view mirror. He was raging, primed to explode. It wouldn't take much to set him off ...

Tommy seemed to sense this, too. 'Feel free to thank me any time you see fit.'

Mercy turned sharply. 'Don't.'

'Don't what?' Tommy shrugged. 'Don't get inside the house ... don't find Benji Hammerton ... don't save his life,' he added, pointing at Lucas.

'Save my life?' Lucas was practically frothing at the mouth as he spun around in his seat. 'You told that kid to shoot me!'

'Now, that's not strictly true, is it?' argued Tommy.

'Yes. You told him to put a bullet in my brain.'

The Fiat swerved as a horrified Rose momentarily lost control of the car.

'Well, okay, maybe I did,' admitted Tommy. 'But I prefer to think of it as reverse psychology.'

Lucas shook his head. 'That's bollocks.'

'No, that's human nature. Think about it. Nobody likes to be bossed around, especially not someone like Jumbo. I just messed with his head by telling him to shoot you. And it worked. Tell me I'm wrong. Go on.'

Mercy felt obliged to speak up. 'Bit risky.'

'Not at all,' insisted Tommy. 'As I said before, risky was

wearing that white tracksuit. Listen, none of you have to thank me now, but you might want to think about showing me some gratitude later on tonight when we go out.'

'Tonight?' Lucas turned away. 'I'm not going anywhere with you tonight.'

'Don't be like that,' laughed Tommy. 'Tonight we celebrate. You heard Benji. He wants to go back to London.' A devilish grin spread across Tommy's face as he lowered his window and stuck his head outside. 'Fuck you, Agatha Pleasant,' he shouted at no one in particular. 'And fuck you, the Nearly Dearly Departed Club. We're done. By this time tomorrow it'll all be over.'

CHAPTER FORTY-FOUR

Nobody wanted to go out that night.

Tommy knew that. He also knew that he didn't care. Not one jot. The fact was, he had time on his hands and money in his pocket. Enough for a couple of pints and the odd chaser or three. That'd do nicely. Better than playing Twister with Proud Mary in her front room. On second thoughts, the old lady did look quite flexible for her age …

Rose took her foot off the pedal as she drove the Fiat into the car park of The Fig and Ferret. It was the only pub in Slepton-on-the-Mire, the next village on from Croplington. That probably explained why it seemed so busy, Rose decided. Worse luck.

'We'll keep it low key,' said Tommy, leaping out the back once they had come to a halt. 'Nothing too messy. Just a few drinks and pleasant conversation. What could be better than that?'

'Pretty much everything.' Lucas hesitated a moment before climbing out of the car. 'I'm starting to think I preferred it when I was dead.'

'Don't bring the mood down,' said Tommy. 'This is a

celebration. Tomorrow we meet Benji, twist his arm until he calls his parents and then it's job done. So long, farewell, auf wiedersehen, goodbye. Besides ...' Tommy pointed at a black chalkboard by the entrance to the pub. '*That's* why we're really here.'

Diamond Neil, Tonight 8pm had been scrawled all over the chalkboard in fancy lettering.

'It's a Neil Diamond tribute act,' Tommy added.

'Yeah, no shit,' muttered Lucas under his breath. 'Sometimes I wonder how we'll ever survive without you.'

Tommy slapped the other man on the back. Not hard enough to hurt, but hard enough for him to notice.

'You need to cheer up a bit. You're such a prick. I mean prickly.' Tommy turned to the others. 'Now, who doesn't love a spot of Neil Diamond from time to time?'

'I've never heard of him,' admitted Mercy. 'What is he? A magician?'

'Seriously?' Tommy rolled his eyes. 'You youngsters don't know what you're missing.'

'You're no older than me,' said Mercy. 'You've just aged badly.'

'Not older, but wiser,' grinned Tommy. 'Neil Diamond's a legend. You must know Sweet Caroline. And ... um ... some of his other songs.'

'I can see you're a massive fan,' Lucas groaned. 'Oh, come on. Let's get in there before I change my mind ...'

He returned the slap by giving Tommy a playful shove in the back, sending him stumbling through the door. Of the four, Rose entered last. She had never been particularly fond of pubs. Too many people. Too much noise.

The Fig and Ferret was no different.

The entrance led into a tight corridor which opened up into one large room. Rose took it all in as quickly as possible. There was wood everywhere she looked, from the beams on the ceiling to the boards on the floor. A curved bar ran along the entire right-hand side of the room. There were three members of staff stood behind it, two women and a man, all of whom were struggling to keep up with the ever increasing demand for drinks.

Rose tried to blank out the sounds that echoed around her. The raucous laughter. The shouting and swearing. Suddenly she longed to be back at Cockleshell Farm. In her room. Alone with nothing but her own thoughts to disturb her, however dark they may be.

'Looks like we're just in time.' Tommy gestured towards a make-shift stage that had been set up in one corner. It was home to a microphone on a stand and a small Marshall amp. Next to them was a tall, balding man in a white shirt and black trousers, both of which were at least a size too big for him. He was switching his attention from the microphone to the amp, adjusting the sound, checking the levels.

'Testing ... testing ... one, two, three-and-a-half ...'

Tommy licked his lips. 'Right, what we all having? Drinks on me.'

'Drinks on you?' frowned Mercy. 'You never gave us that money back from earlier, remember.'

Tommy raised his hands. 'Chill out, princess punch. You can have that when we get back to Proud Mary's. That's if we can still walk by then, of course.'

Lucas eyed the exit. 'I knew this was a bad idea.'

'Loosen up big fella,' said Tommy. 'That was just a joke. I've already told you what we're doing. A few drinks. Nothing more. Now, you look like a Guinness man to me—'

'Why? Because I'm black?' shot back Lucas.

Tommy's mouth fell open. 'Whoa! That's not what I—'

'Just a joke,' Lucas smirked. 'You did tell me to loosen up. Yeah, a Guinness will be fine.'

'Vodka and tonic,' said Mercy.

'Diet?' asked Tommy.

Mercy scowled. 'Are you saying I need to lose weight?'

'Shit, no,' replied Tommy hastily. 'Not at all. You've got a lovely … oh, I get it. That's a joke as well, right?'

The high-five that Lucas gave Mercy seemed to suggest it was.

'Very good,' said Tommy, rolling his eyes. 'It's banter central round here with you guys. What about you, Rose? What you drinking? And don't say a treble tequila because then I'll know you're taking the piss.'

'I'm good thank you,' said Rose automatically.

'Pleased to hear it,' nodded Tommy. 'But what are you drinking?'

'No … I don't … nothing,' mumbled a flustered Rose.

'Nothing?' Tommy screwed up his face. 'You can't have nothing. We're in a pub. They'll chuck you out for loitering.'

'Just leave her be,' said Mercy. 'She's the designated driver.'

'I'm the designated driver,' Rose repeated.

'Have a soft drink then,' sighed Tommy. 'Something fizzy. Lemonade? Coke?'

'I'll have water.' Rose hesitated. 'Tap water.'

Tommy stuck both his thumbs up. 'Ah, my kind of date. Cheap and cheerful. Well, cheap at least …'

Lucas watched as Tommy pushed his way to the front of the bar. There was something about his behaviour that didn't quite add up. He wasn't just excited; he was practically euphoric. Couple that with the wild eyes and fast mouth and Lucas was starting to wonder …

No, that wasn't possible.

Was it?

'We should probably think about getting a table,' said Mercy, nudging Lucas in the ribs, breaking his train of thought. 'There's one over there. By the stage.'

Rose tensed up. 'Not by the stage …'

'It'll be fine,' insisted Mercy. Taking Rose by the arm, she weaved a route through the throng of early evening drinkers until they reached the table. Rose grabbed the first stool she came to and sat down. Crossed her arms and stared straight ahead. Maybe things wouldn't be as bad as she feared. All she had to do was act as if she was interested. Smile occasionally. Nod in all the right places. She could do that. Yes, she could definitely do that.

What Rose didn't know, however, was that in less than half-an-hour's time all hell would've broken loose.

CHAPTER FORTY-FIVE

Tommy placed the drinks down on the table and took his seat.

'Cheers,' he said, raising his pint glass. 'It's been nice knowing you. Please do keep in touch in the future. Best friends forever.'

Lucas rubbed his eyes. 'You're full of it tonight.'

'Tonight, tomorrow and a week next Thursday,' said Tommy. 'I'm buzzing.'

Bad choice of words, thought Lucas, as he lifted his own pint to his lips.

'Are you okay?' asked Mercy, leaning into Rose. 'You seem on edge.'

'Not at all.' Rose took a ragged breath. 'I mean ... maybe ... just a little. I'm not that fond of small places with lots of people. I find it ... I don't know ... threatening. I can't relax.'

Mercy nodded. 'I can understand that. We won't stay here long. An hour or so with any luck. Just grin and bear it and it'll be over before you know it.'

Rose tried to do just that, even if her smile was more of a

grimace than a grin. When she turned back towards the stage, the balding man was no longer follicly challenged. Instead, he had applied a thick, brown wig which, against all odds, made him look both younger and older at the same time. He took the microphone off its stand and gestured towards the bar. The jukebox stopped suddenly and he began to speak.

'Good evening, ladies and gentlemen. My name is Diamond Neil, and this is …. yes, you've guessed it … a tribute to the greatest artist of our lifetime. So, sit back, take a drink and enjoy because you're in for a real treat. This one's called Forever In Blue Jeans …'

The music started and Diamond Neil soon joined in. He was an adequate singer, thought Rose, not that she had much of a point of reference.

The first few songs passed without incident. The crowd clapped at the end and then cheered when the next one began. Rose followed their lead. She was barely listening, but the songs sounded familiar. Maybe she had heard them somewhere before. On the radio at work. Certainly not at home. She didn't listen to any music at home.

A hand on her shoulder brought her out of her thoughts and back to reality.

'Not that bad, is it?' said Mercy, struggling to make herself heard over the music. 'Could've been worse.'

Rose nodded and then shook her head, unsure which of the two was the appropriate way to reply. Mercy was right, though. It wasn't that bad; it was almost bearable. Time was ticking by and nothing terrible was going to happen. It would be over soon.

And then, three songs in, Diamond Neil did something quite unexpected.

'Too kind, too kind,' he said, lapping up the applause until it finally faded away. 'Okay, around this time in the show I like to indulge myself in a little audience participation. Yes, that's right. One of you lucky people will be joining me here on stage.'

Two things happened simultaneously. The crowd cheered. And Rose's pulse began to quicken.

'I'm about to sing a favourite of mine,' Diamond Neil continued. 'Some of you might know it. It's called Cracklin' Rosie. Now, I don't suppose we've got anyone called Rosie in the pub tonight, have we?'

Rose drew a breath. *Rosie*. Not *Rose*. She was safe.

Or so she thought …

'You!' Tommy swivelled around on his stool, jabbing a wild finger in Rose's direction. 'Go on. Tell him.'

Rose visibly shrank. She could feel her face beginning to change colour as the heat overwhelmed her.

'Hey, don't be shy,' persisted Diamond Neil. 'There must be a Rosie somewhere. Or a Rose—'

'Rose!' Standing up, Tommy stuck his hand in the air. 'Yeah, Rose.'

Diamond Neil raised an eyebrow. 'I mean, you're not what I was expecting, but who am I to judge? Come on up, my friend, and we can—'

'Not me, dickhead – her!' Tommy was laughing as he gestured towards Rose. Everybody was laughing. The entire pub.

'Ah, my mistake.' Diamond Neil turned to Rose and smiled. 'Why don't you step on up, little lady, and join me for the next number?'

Rose stayed rooted to her stool. She couldn't move even if she wanted to. Why was this happening? This was everything she had been dreading and more. The stuff of nightmares.

'Don't just sit there,' urged Tommy, waving his arms about. 'Do … it. Do … it. Do … it …'

The crowd of drinkers started to join in. The chant was echoing around the pub. Over and over and over again.

'She doesn't want to,' shouted Mercy over the noise.

'Of course she does.' Diamond Neil hopped off the stage. Leant over the table. 'Come on, Rosie. It's only a bit of fun.'

'It's not Rosie,' mumbled Rose.

'I couldn't give a shit.' Diamond Neil was still smiling, but there was a hint of irritation in the way he spoke. 'Don't ruin it for everyone.'

He held out his hand for Rose to take.

Do … it. Do … it. Do … it …

'You can't force her,' said Mercy, pushing his hand away.

'Keep your nose out, bitch,' hissed Diamond Neil under his breath.

'Bitch?' Mercy tensed up. 'Bitch?'

Diamond Neil ignored her as he grabbed Rose by the wrist and tried to haul her up off her stool. 'Here she is, ladies and gentlemen,' he announced. 'Please give a big round of applause to—'

The pub singer stopped mid-sentence. There was something wet dripping down his face. Something like vodka and coke.

'That's your first and only warning,' growled Mercy, staring him out. 'If you don't let go of my friend this instant you'll be wearing the glass as well!'

CHAPTER FORTY-SIX

Rage.

That was all Mercy could feel. A burning, all-encompassing rage that she was trying – no, struggling – to control.

Diamond Neil didn't know how lucky he was. If she had truly let rip he would be laid out on the pub carpet with either a busted nose, a broken jaw or a black eye by now. Maybe all three, depending on how many punches she could get in.

With vodka and coke dripping from his chin, soaking into his shirt, the pub singer released his grip on Rose and switched his attention to Mercy. 'What the—?'

'Just you try it,' hissed Mercy, leaping to her feet. 'Go on. I dare you. Touch me once and I'll knock you clean off that stage!'

'You could've electrocuted me,' Diamond Neil spat.

'Good,' growled Mercy. 'I wish I had. Better luck next time.'

Mercy held her ground. Whatever happened, she refused to back down to a middle-aged karaoke clown with a shit wig and a damp face.

'Fun's over folks,' shouted Diamond Neil, addressing the entire pub. 'My microphone's completely wrecked. And it's all thanks to these two!'

As if it had been flicked at the switch, the atmosphere changed suddenly from jovial to toxic. Mercy didn't care. She was used to a hostile crowd. Bring it on. Rose, meanwhile, dug her nails into the stool beneath her. This was all her fault. She was to blame for everything.

'The natives are growing restless,' whispered Lucas. 'We should probably think about getting out of here.'

Mercy, to his despair, refused to budge.

Lucas was all set to repeat himself when he felt a shove in the back. Turning sharply, he found himself face to face with a Father Christmas lookalike in a checked shirt and baggy jeans. 'I love Neil Diamond,' he said gruffly. 'It's my birthday.'

Lucas shrugged. 'Are those two things related?'

'You've ruined my birthday.'

'What? Me personally?'

'Yes, you. You and your friends.' Lifting both hands, Father Christmas wrapped them around Lucas's neck and squeezed tight. 'You've ruined the best day of the year. My special day.'

Lucas tried to protest, but the words wouldn't come. He was starting to feel light-headed when Father Christmas emitted an almighty cry and let go. The reason for it became clear when Tommy shifted into view. He was wielding a bar stool like an over eager lion tamer, spinning it around his head, jabbing it towards anybody who dared to come too close. It was the stool that had knocked the stuffing out of Father Christmas, Tommy striking him firmly in the ribs, sending him sprawling back into the crowd.

Lucas stood up straight. He had barely caught his breath when he saw a table fly across the room.

Wait.

Somebody had thrown a table across the room!

This was insane. The Fig and Ferret was just a village pub. Fights like this weren't supposed to happen. And yet it had. The threat level had escalated quickly. It was time to disappear.

First things first, though, round up the others.

Lucas found Rose on her stool by the stage, eyes closed, head in hands as the chaos raged around her. Mercy was still embroiled in an argument with Diamond Neil, an argument that could be ended at any moment with a flash of her fists. And Tommy, well, he had swapped the stool for a fire extinguisher. Lucas did a double take. Where the hell had Tommy got a fire extinguisher from?

Unsure of his next move, Lucas switched his attention from the other three to the opposite end of the room. Dropping a shoulder, he pushed his way through the bustling crowd until he had made it to the bar. 'Where's the landlord?'

'Here,' replied the only man of the three bar staff. His arms were outstretched as he tried in vain to protect his optics. 'This is my pub. I'm calling the police.'

'Good idea,' nodded Lucas.

'I'm calling the police because of *you*!' the landlord yelled.

'Coming in here … causing trouble. You and your pals need locking up.'

Not so good, thought Lucas. He spun away from the bar, crashing straight into Mercy in the process. She had finally left the pub singer behind and was now engaged in a full on altercation with at least six other people. Lucas felt a pint glass bounce off his shoulder as he pushed between them.

'Come on,' he said, grabbing Mercy by the arm, 'we need to—'

He was cut short by a scream. A long, ear-splitting scream that reverberated around the pub. It was followed by another. And another. And another.

Lucas turned in slow motion, fearful of what he might find.

It was Tommy.

He had a gun.

It was raised above his head, pointing at the ceiling. The first person to spot it must have screamed and then others had caught on. Now they were streaming towards the exit, desperate to break out of there, the panic etched across their faces.

'What the hell do you think you're doing?' spluttered Lucas.

'Don't wet your knickers; I'm not going to fire it.' Tommy lowered the gun. 'Not like earlier—'

'I thought you chucked that gun away.'

'So did I,' shrugged Tommy. 'Turns out I didn't. Whoops. My mistake.'

Lucas looked around frantically. The Fig and Ferret was

a mess. Tables had been upturned, stools broken. The carpet barely recognisable beneath the spilt drinks and smashed glass.

'Let's go.' He guided Tommy towards the exit, glancing over his shoulder as he walked. Mercy was right behind them, Rose by her side. They passed Father Christmas on the way. He was still clutching hold of his ribs, moaning in agony.

Worst birthday ever.

They had almost made it out of there when a voice echoed around the pub.

'Hey, come back,' called out Diamond Neil. 'I won't get paid if I don't do a full set. Now, this one you might have heard before ...'

The four of them finally exited the building as the opening bars of *Sweet Caroline* burst out of the speaker. The car park was rammed with drinkers who had run for cover.

'Get in the car,' said Lucas firmly.

'Wow! That went well.' Tommy paused so he could tuck the gun down the back of his trousers. 'There was a lad in there ... ugly, little weasel ... who was begging to be pistol-whipped—'

'Just get in the car,' repeated Lucas. He climbed into the passenger seat. 'I can't sit in the back with him,' he said, scowling at Tommy. 'Just drive, Rose. Get us out of here.'

Mercy took a breath. 'I feel like we've been here before.'

'They call that de ja vu,' grinned Tommy, as he slammed the door behind him. 'Who would've thought we'd be getting into scrapes and dodging the police ... again? You lot are way more fun than I would ever have imagined.'

'Fun?' cried Lucas. 'What the hell is wrong with you? The same thing happens every time we leave the house. *You* seem to start every fight,' he said, pointing at Tommy. '*You* want to finish every fight,' he said, switching to Mercy. 'And *you* just sit there as if there's not even a fight going on,' he said to Rose. 'Am I the only one with any common sense? Don't answer that,' he added, beating Tommy to it. 'I've had it. After tomorrow, I don't want to see any of you ever again. Do you understand?'

'Fine by me, Captain Common Sense,' smirked Tommy.

'Whatever,' muttered Mercy, peering out of the window.

Only Rose remained silent. The countdown had begun. Cockleshell Farm was only a few minutes away now. She was desperate to get back in her room. Lock the door. Stick her head under the pillow and escape the world.

She could never escape her thoughts, though. Not today. Not tomorrow.

Not until it was over. Over and out.

For good.

DAY THREE

CHAPTER FORTY-SEVEN

Mercy stopped at the door to Rose's room and knocked.

She waited, but there was no reply. It was gone nine, morning had broken. Maybe Rose was still fast asleep. Anything to forget about the previous evening's entertainment.

No, not entertainment. That was the wrong word. Completely inappropriate.

Mercy knocked again. Then she tried the handle. The door was locked.

'Is there something wrong, dear?'

Mercy turned to see Proud Mary stood beside her on the landing. 'Yes … no … probably not … perhaps,' she stumbled. 'Sorry. None of that makes any sense. It's just … Rose. She's not answering.'

'You did get home quite late last night,' Proud Mary frowned. 'I heard you, just before I put my ear plugs in. It wasn't far off your curfew if I'm being honest. If you'd been any later I'd have had to send out the search party.' She paused. 'You were arguing.'

'Not arguing,' said Mercy hastily. 'Just talking. Loudly.

Whilst … erm … not really agreeing on much.'

Proud Mary raised an eyebrow. 'That sounds a lot like arguing to me.'

'And me,' Mercy had to admit. 'It was Tommy's fault.'

'Thomas?' Proud Mary shook her head. 'I don't believe that for one moment. Thomas is a lovely young man. A little mischievous perhaps, but his heart is in the right place. He's the only one of you who's mucked out the pigs so far. I didn't even have to ask him. He just did it of his own accord. Such a sweet soul—'

'I don't suppose you've got another key, have you?' asked Mercy, interrupting Proud Mary before she went as far as to form a Tommy O'Strife Appreciation Society. 'For Rose's room. Maybe it's nothing, but I'm worried about her. What if she's had an accident? Fallen over? Banged her head? She might have passed out. Or worse.'

'Take a breath, dear.' Proud Mary rested a hand on Mercy's arm. 'There's a drawer in the kitchen. It's overflowing with odds and ends. There might be a spare key in there.'

Mercy waited for the landlady to disappear down the stairs before pressing her lips to the keyhole. 'I'm not joking, Rose. You better open the door this minute or I'm going to smash it down. That's if you're awake, of course. And alive. Shit, you better be alive. Right, I've warned you—'

Shoulder or shoe? Mercy was still to decide when she heard a *click*. She tried the handle again. This time the door opened.

Walking into the room, she found Rose sat on the bed, facing away from her, fully dressed.

'Thank you.' Mercy closed the door behind her. 'That wasn't so hard, was it?'

Silence.

Mercy hesitated, unsure whether or not to enter any further. 'What's wrong? You're not still worried about last night, are you?'

Rose gently shook her head. At least it was something, thought Mercy. Some kind of response.

'Tommy's a bit of a prick at times ... a lot of times ... practically *all* the time ... but I don't think he meant any harm,' Mercy continued. 'He's just one of those. You know the type. Overbearing. If he's having a good time he wants everyone to know it.' Mercy stopped. 'I'm willing to punch him,' she laughed. 'Hard. If it makes you feel better.'

'It's not Tommy,' mumbled Rose. 'It's ... it's ...'

Mercy waited, but that was one particular sentence that wasn't about to be completed anytime soon. 'It's what?'

'It's ...' Rose drew breath. Why were words so difficult to find sometimes? Difficult to find and impossible to say. 'It's ... it's ... me.'

'You?' repeated Mercy. 'You're what? Ill? Unhappy?'

'The problem,' said Rose. 'I'm the problem. I always have been. I probably always will be.'

Mercy walked around the bed. Knelt down by Rose's side. 'You know we're meeting Benji this morning, don't you? If we can convince him to speak to his parents it'll be job done. Agatha will have no reason to keep us here. Then it's bye bye Stainmouth. Hello home.'

'Who says I want to go home?' muttered Rose.

Mercy faltered. 'Why wouldn't you?'

'There's nothing for me in Norwich. There's nothing for me anywhere. No friends. No family. Nothing.'

'I'm sure that's not true.'

'Why would you say that?' Rose finally looked up. Her eyes were bloodshot with huge rings underneath. A combination of tears and a lack of sleep. 'You don't know a thing about me.'

'I know a bit about you,' replied Mercy, enunciating the *bit* for arguments sake. 'You seem ... nice. Yeah, you're a nice person.'

'Wow! A double nice.' Rose snorted as she threw back her head. 'Nobody wants to be a nice person, do they? They want to be interesting. Exciting. Sexy. What am I? Boring. Plain. Oh, but I'm nice. In an un-threatening, easy to ignore kind of way. Nobody notices me, Mercy. I bet nobody's even realised that I died a week ago.'

Rant over, Rose dropped her head into her hands. It was only then that Mercy spotted something. A fierce red line that ran all the way around Rose's neck. Like a burn.

Mercy's couldn't just leave it. 'That looks painful. Did you do it when you strangled yourself? By accident,' she added.

Sitting up straight, Rose lifted her sweater until it almost touched her chin. 'I didn't strangle myself.'

'Then how did you die?' asked Mercy. 'I got knocked out. Tommy was shot. Lucas crashed his car. And you ...?'

Rose hesitated. A second. Or two. Or three. Too long. 'I was ... erm ... hit by a car.'

'Really? Which bones did you break?' pressed Mercy. 'Where are all your cuts and bruises?'

Rose looked towards the door. 'I'd like you to leave now.'

'Not yet.' Mercy rested a hand on Rose's knee. 'Is there something you'd like to tell me? You can trust me. I promise. I won't tell a soul.'

'No.' Rose stood up, but there was nowhere to go. 'Please. Just leave. So I can get ready.'

Mercy was about to speak again when a knock at the door beat her to it. A moment later it opened.

'I've found the spare key,' said Proud Mary, poking her head inside. 'Not that you need it anymore. Still, thanks for taking the time to look …'

'Thanks for taking the time to look,' echoed Mercy. 'Honestly. I was worried.'

'Is that why you two were arguing?' asked Proud Mary. 'I could hear you downstairs. What was it? A lover's tiff?'

'We're not gay,' said Mercy. She glanced at Rose. 'I mean, I'm not. She might be.'

'I'm not,' insisted Rose.

'No need to get defensive, ladies,' smiled Proud Mary. 'Each to their own and all that. Who am I to judge? Right, if there's nothing else to say I think I'll leave you both—'

'She's leaving too.' As if to emphasize her point, Rose nodded at Mercy and then nodded towards the door.

'Yeah, I guess I'm leaving too.' Without another word, Mercy followed Proud Mary out onto the landing and closed the door behind them 'You didn't waste your time searching for that key,' she whispered, creeping up behind the landlady. 'I'll look after it from now on if that's okay with you.'

'Will you now?' Proud Mary seemed to weigh it up before eventually handing over the key. 'Just so you know, I have a no intimacy rule in my house. It's nothing personal; it's just the walls are quite thin.'

'No, this is nothing like that,' said Mercy, trying not to laugh as she put the key in her pocket. 'I've a feeling, that's all. A bad feeling. And bad feelings have a nasty habit of leading down some very dark holes.'

CHAPTER FORTY-EIGHT

Lucas stamped his feet to keep warm.

He was stood beside the Fiat, waiting for the others to join him outside. The time was nine-forty. In twenty minutes they were meeting Benji Hammerton. The last thing Lucas wanted was to be late. Think about it. The sooner they met him, the sooner they could go home. Why drag it out any longer than was necessary?

Mercy was the first to appear. Head up, shoulders back, she marched over to the car and sat on the bonnet. 'Morning, grumpy. Still mad?'

Lucas nodded. 'Still mad.' Paused. 'Not with you.'

'Pleased to hear it,' said Mercy. 'I didn't do anything wrong. Well, not much anyway. I was just trying to protect Rose.'

'She's a grown woman. She can look after herself.' Lucas hadn't thought that through. 'She *should* be able to look after herself.'

Mercy slid across the bonnet. Leant in closer. 'I'm worried about her,' she whispered. 'I think she might do something silly.'

'Silly? Tommy does way worse than silly every second of the day and you're not worried about him.'

'This is different. I don't think she ... died. Not like we did. I think she might have tried to—' Mercy stopped suddenly as Rose emerged from the farm. 'Hey. You feeling okay?'

Rose smiled weakly as she shuffled towards the car. For the time being at least, that was all they were going to get. End of conversation. Followed by a painfully strained silence.

'Three down, one to go,' muttered Lucas eventually. 'Either of you seen the irritating one this morning?'

'He was out with the pigs at some point,' said Mercy.

'And I could hear singing coming from the shower,' added Rose.

Lucas sighed. 'Let's just hope he did it in that order. Otherwise he'll stink the car out.'

Right on cue, a buoyant Tommy came skipping out of Cockleshell Farm. 'Greetings, people,' he said cheerfully. 'Lovely morning for it.' Without breaking stride, he yanked open the car door and dived headfirst onto the back seat. 'What you all waiting for?' he grinned. 'We're going to be late if you don't get a shift on!'

Mercy glanced at Lucas. Shook her head. 'Don't bite.'

'As if I would,' he muttered, climbing into the driver's side.

At the same time, Tommy dropped a single sheet of paper onto Lucas's lap. 'I got directions from Proud Mary,' he said smugly. 'Always thinking on my feet, I am. Now, it's

235

your turn, big fella. Put your foot down and get us to our destination as soon as. The last thing we want to do is keep young Hammerton waiting …'

They made it with two minutes to spare.

The wasteland behind the railway station was just as secluded as Benji had proclaimed. A neglected, barren wilderness, it seemed to be used primarily as a dumping ground for junk. At least a mile long from one end to the other, a tall, wrought iron fence was the only thing separating the land from both the train tracks and any social media gossips keen to expose the crimes of fly-tipping to the rest of polite society.

'You could get up to all sorts of mischief round here,' said Tommy, studying his surroundings.

'*You* could get up to mischief in a garden shed,' remarked Mercy, settling down in her usual spot on the bonnet.

Tommy winked at her. 'That's true. Show me a shed and I'll show you what mischief looks like.'

Mercy turned away. What was this? The evolution of Tommy O'Strife? Chauvinism to sarcasm to sexual innuendos in a matter of days. Maybe he was putting on a front. A front for a problem. Erectile dysfunction or premature ejaculation? Yeah, that made sense. It was always those with most to say who had so little to offer.

'It's gone ten,' grumbled Lucas. He started to walk in circles around the Fiat. 'Benji's late.'

'Only just,' said Mercy. 'Give him a chance. And stop doing that, will you? You're making me dizzy.'

'Fine.' Lucas came to a halt. 'When he gets here, let me do the talking, though—'

'You?' Tommy snorted. 'You're the stiffest person I know. The last thing Benji needs is a lecture from mister high and mighty. No, let me do it. He'll listen to me.'

'You'll probably try and go into business with him,' said Lucas under his breath. 'Drugs 'R' Us. Buy one, get one free. Addiction guaranteed.'

'Very funny,' smirked Tommy. 'Not a bad idea, though. Maybe I've out-grown London. Maybe it's time to spread my wings. Branch out further afield. Stainmouth's not so bad when you think about it.'

'It'd be better if you weren't here,' muttered Lucas.

Stood slightly back from the others, Rose closed her eyes and let their words drift off into the atmosphere. They were bickering – they were *always* bickering – but it wasn't that which had caught her attention. Nor was it a nearby train, although it was a rumble of an engine, nevertheless. In the distance, but not for long. Edging closer. And closer. And …

Rose opened her eyes as a black transit van raced into view. The others noticed it too.

'Looks like we've got company,' said Lucas.

Rose stiffened as a wave of fear washed over her. She couldn't explain why, but everything felt wrong.

It all occurred so quickly that, when asked later on, none of them could fully explain what had happened.

It started with a screech of howling tyres on bumpy ground. Without coming to a complete standstill, the side doors to the van rolled open and a body was tossed out onto the wasteland. A wheel spin, a crunch of gears and the van was on the move again. Back the way it had just come.

The whole thing had lasted less than ten seconds from start to finish.

Seven, in fact. Rose had been counting. Now she was staring in disbelief. Staring at the body that had landed in a dishevelled heap and then stayed there, motionless.

Mercy was the first to react. Moving swiftly across the ground, she crouched down by the tangle of limbs and gently turned it over. It was a man. Dressed in black yet covered in red. His face disfigured by deep lacerations and swollen bruises.

'What the hell's going on?' asked Lucas, coming up behind her.

The breath caught in Mercy's throat when she realised who she was looking at. 'It's … it's Benji Hammerton,' she mumbled, checking for a pulse. 'We need to get him to a hospital.'

CHAPTER FORTY-NINE

Agatha Pleasant crashed through the doors of the Stainmouth General Hospital and scoured the waiting room for directions.

Intensive Care. Turn left.

She did as instructed. It was Miles who had called her. Said it was an emergency. Suggested she get there as soon as possible. That was twenty minutes ago now. A lot could happen in twenty minutes.

People could die in twenty minutes.

Lifting her head, Agatha dodged a porter at the last moment as she swept along the corridor. He was pushing a wheelchair, chatting to its elderly incumbent. He noticed Agatha's late move and smiled his appreciation. Agatha smiled back. Somewhat strained. All mouth, nothing in the eyes. How did he do it? The porter. Keep his spirits up in the face of long hours and inadequate pay. Agatha admired him. Envied him even.

Work hard. Spend your money. Go to bed exhausted. Rinse and repeat.

If only life was that simple …

Agatha's thoughts returned to the matter at hand. *It's an emergency.* She started to wonder who that could apply to. Tommy instantly sprang to mind. Rash and impulsive, if any of them was liable to wind up in trouble it was him. Then there was Rose. She had a history of emergencies. Whilst the others had all *died* by accident, her *death* was self-inflicted. What if she had tried something like that again? Agatha knew she should feel some sense of responsibility. She should … and yet she didn't. Instead, she worried about the numbers. One quarter was a big proportion to lose.

Her Nearly Dearly Departed Club were a four-piece, not a trio.

Agatha turned a corner and found them clogging up the next corridor. She did a quick head count. One … two … three … four. And Miles. All of them were either stood up or sat down. Awake and alert. And almost certainly alive.

Tommy was the first to spot her. 'Pleasant Agatha, fancy seeing you here.'

Agatha ignored him. Stupid boy. 'Emergency?' she said, shifting her attention to Miles.

Miles gestured towards a closed door. 'In there. Benji Hammerton.'

'You found him?' Agatha raised an eyebrow at the others.

'Kind of,' said Lucas.

'We never really had him in our grasp,' admitted Mercy. 'We were meeting him this morning.'

'But someone beat us to it,' Tommy added. 'In more ways than one. Benji's taken a right pounding. I've seen healthier roadkill.'

THE NEARLY DEARLY DEPARTED CLUB

Agatha looked around, on edge. There were too many people in the vicinity. Doctors and nurses. Coming and going. Listening in. 'We can't speak here.' She indicated for them to follow her as she made her way back along the corridor. She stopped at the first door she came to. A brass plaque said *Doctor Singh.*

Agatha wandered in without knocking. 'You must be Doctor Singh.'

'Indeed I am.' Singh – mid forties, rolled-up shirt and loosened tie, fashionably hairy – was seated behind a desk. Laptop open, coffee in hand, he glanced up, surprised. 'Can I help you?'

'Yes,' nodded Agatha. 'You can help me by vacating this room. Now. Please.'

'You want me to leave?' Singh pulled a face, slightly offended by such a suggestion. 'You know this is my office, right?'

'And you can have it back,' remarked Agatha. 'But for the time being at least, I'd like to use it. We need privacy. It's a matter of great importance.' Agatha reached into her coat and removed a card. She flashed it so fast it was impossible to read. 'My name is Agatha Pleasant. I'm high up in the Government. Top tier. You're welcome to run a check if you don't believe me. Check it outside though, won't you? Not in here.'

He wouldn't check. Agatha was sure of it. They never did.

Doctor Singh, however, wasn't prepared to budge without a fight. 'Get out of here. All of you. Before I fetch security and have you thrown out.'

ANTHONY GRACE

Agatha replaced the card with her phone. 'Drastic times and all that nonsense,' she said calmly. 'I'd rather it didn't have to come to this, Doctor Singh, but if you don't do as I ask and leave this room this instant I'll have you suspended with one call. Sacked with two—'

'And with three …?' Singh sneered.

Agatha didn't miss a beat. 'With three I could have you killed. That's not a threat—'

'That's a promise,' chipped in Tommy.

'No, it's a warning,' said Mercy. 'A promise sounds too cheesy.'

'Fair enough,' shrugged Tommy. 'If I was you, Doc, I'd run along and make myself useful. Better still, introduce yourself to some of those nurses. Try the hands-on approach. I've seen a right couple of crackers whilst I've been here—'

'Ten minutes.' A frustrated Doctor Singh closed his laptop and stood up. 'Then I want you gone. For good. And don't steal anything,' he said, pointing at Tommy.

'He won't,' said Agatha. 'Thank you, Doctor.' She waited for Singh to close the door behind him before she spoke again. 'We've not got much time. Tell me everything that's happened.'

So they did. Lucas, Mercy and Tommy weaved a story that was so elaborate, so utterly ridiculous, that Agatha doubted much of its credibility. Still, there was always one way to find out for sure.

'Is that true?' she asked. The question was aimed at the only person who was still yet to speak. 'You can tell me if it's not.'

Squeezed into one corner of the room, Rose lifted her head and nodded. 'It's true. All of it.'

'Wow.' Agatha put her hands on her hips. Took a breath as she processed the information. 'Things have escalated faster than I would ever have imagined.'

'What do we do now?' wondered Mercy.

'I suppose we wait for him to wake up and then we take him back home,' replied Agatha.

'A lot like us,' nodded Lucas.

Agatha turned sharply. 'Pardon?'

'We'll be going home, too,' said Lucas. 'We've done what you wanted. We've found Benji Hammerton. I'm sorry that he's had the shit kicked out of him, but that's not our fault. We've completed our side of the bargain. Now it's your turn.'

Agatha was about to speak when the door opened and a nurse burst into the office. 'Doctor, do you ... oh, sorry,' she said, clearly flustered. 'I was looking for the family of Mr Hammerton.'

'Yep, that's us,' said Tommy.

Agatha glared at him. 'That's *not* us. But if you've any information I'd like to hear it.'

'No ... I'm sorry ... that's not possible,' mumbled the nurse.

'That's *very* possible.' Agatha flashed her card. 'I demand it, in fact.'

'It's against protocol,' the nurse argued. 'News like this is for the family only. I can't tell you.'

Agatha gritted her teeth. 'I think you already have ...'

CHAPTER FIFTY

Mercy stormed out of the hospital.

She needed some fresh air. Fresh air would help her think. And if she could think then maybe, just maybe, she could make sense of what had happened.

Benji Hammerton was dead.

He had been beaten to death.

That thought alone was enough to bring a tear to her eye. Why? She didn't know him. She had only met him once and, even then, for only the briefest of moments. And yet she still felt oddly upset. Less than twenty-four hours ago they had been face-to-face. They had talked. Mercy had offered him a way out.

A day later, however, and that offer had been cruelly snatched away from him.

Benji, as a living, breathing entity, was no more. A young life snuffed out in its prime. All those years reduced to nothing. Mercy was shook by a sudden realisation that that could easily have been her. They thought she had died in the barn. Asif, Buster Blow, Heidi something or other. But they were wrong. This – whatever *this* actually was – was her second chance at life.

Benji wasn't going to get a second chance.

Mercy sensed movement behind her and spun around, desperate for some kind of confrontation. She was disappointed to see that it was only Rose.

'Are you okay?'

'Not really.' Mercy shook her head. She couldn't stop. 'I can't explain it … it just seems so wrong … so pointless. It's left me feeling … I don't know—'

'Numb,' said Rose.

'Yeah, numb. That's it exactly. How did you know?'

Rose took a breath. *Go on. Tell her.* 'I've felt that way for as long as I can remember. Life seems so empty. I've got nothing. I am nothing. It's as if I don't exist.'

'Why would you say that? It's not true.'

Rose wasn't listening. 'You think I should be more like you, don't you? Toughen up. Get over it. Stop wallowing in self-pity.'

'No, not at all,' insisted Mercy. 'I think you should be you. The person you are now. The person you've always been. Because that person is kind and thoughtful. And braver than you would ever have believed. And nowhere near as annoying as Tommy, or as pompous as Lucas. And you're my friend. There. I've said it. For fuck's sake, Rose, at this very moment you're the only woman I know who isn't over sixty. I need you. We need each other.'

Mercy started to laugh. She even detected the slightest of smiles from Rose. That was enough. Throwing open her arms, Mercy was all set to wrap them around the woman stood before her when something caught her eye.

A man. Black tracksuit and gold chains. Hood up, head down, swaggering past on his way into the hospital.

Mercy moved quickly, grabbing him by the arms before he could evade her. Without missing a beat, she dragged him away from the hospital entrance, only stopping once they were out of sight of prying eyes.

'What the hell are you doing here?' she spat, slamming the man against the wall.

The hood fell away. 'Get your hands off me, you mad bitch!' Cutz realised who he was talking to and backtracked. 'No, not bitch. I didn't mean that … I wasn't … don't hit me again.'

Mercy obliged – for now – but still refused to let go. 'Answer the question. What are you doing here?'

'I think my mate's in there,' replied Cutz, gesturing towards the hospital. 'I've come to see him.'

Mercy's eyes narrowed. 'Benji?'

'Yeah, Benji.' Cutz began to wriggle about, desperate to free himself from Mercy's grasp. 'I ain't done nothing … let me go … I just wanna see him.'

'Too late,' said Mercy bluntly. 'He's dead.'

'Dead?' Cutz's body went limp and he began to slide down the wall, leaving Mercy with little choice but to release him. 'Benji's … dead?'

'That's what I said.' Mercy pointed an accusing finger. 'Don't act all innocent. You must've known he'd been beaten up. Otherwise you wouldn't have turned up at the hospital looking for him.'

Head in hands, Cutz started to rock back and forth on

his heels. 'Shit … I can't believe it … he didn't deserve that.'

'No, he didn't,' said Mercy. 'So, tell me. How did it happen?'

'It wasn't me if that's what you're getting at.'

'Who was it then?'

Cutz lit a cigarette, his hand shaking as he flicked at the lighter. 'Vernon Gold. He completely lost his mind. Accused Benji of stealing from him.'

'And did he?'

'Course not,' said Cutz, as if the question barely deserved an answer. 'Benji's not … *wasn't* a thief. But shit went missing from the house. Coke. Cash. And a gun.'

A gun. Mercy recalled the events of last night in the Fig and Ferret. She knew the gun well. 'You're talking about the house on Eastern Avenue?'

Cutz looked up at her. 'Yeah. How did you know?'

'I was there yesterday,' Mercy admitted. 'I came in late. You were spark out at the time.'

'Your man was there, too,' said Cutz. 'The black guy. The fake cop. He was with some lunatic. His boyfriend or something. It was him who knocked me out.'

There was a lot there for Mercy to unpack. *Fake cop. Lunatic. Boyfriend.* It would have to wait, though. 'We all left when the police arrived,' she said. 'Maybe they took the drugs and money. As evidence.'

'Not possible. They didn't even get in the house for a start. Yeah, they came knocking, but Benji soon cleared them off. He put on a posh voice and pleaded innocence. He's good like that. He … *was* good.' Cutz stopped to think.

'How do I know it wasn't you who stole from Gold?'

Mercy shook her head. 'It wasn't.'

'What about the black guy? Or the lunatic?'

Mercy hesitated. It could've been. She didn't know for sure. 'No.'

'Well, someone did,' snarled Cutz. 'And that's why Benji's dead.'

'Were you there when Gold beat him up?' asked Mercy, keen to put the other thoughts from her mind.

Cutz took a drag on the cigarette. 'It wasn't Gold. It was Doberman. His bodyguard. He ripped Benji to pieces. There was nothing I could do. He's out of control. An animal.'

'And now he's a murderer,' stated Mercy. 'You should go to the police. Tell them everything you know.'

'Yeah, right,' sneered Cutz. 'I ain't telling no one nothing. 'Cept you. And that's only because you'll hit me if I don't.'

Cutz flinched as Mercy leant over him. Instead of throwing a punch, however, she simply held out her hand and helped him to his feet.

'Benji was my boy. We were tight. I'm going to miss him.' Cutz tried to look away, embarrassed by his emotions. 'It could be me next.'

'It could be any of us,' said Mercy. 'Difference is, I'd give Gold a taste of his own medicine.'

Cutz was about to speak again when a buzzing in his pocket distracted him.

'You should get that,' insisted Mercy. 'You never know who might be calling.'

Cutz removed his phone from his tracksuit. His eyes widened as he studied the screen. 'It's Gold. He won't be happy if I ignore him.'

'You don't have to.' Mercy held out her hand. 'Pass me your phone,' she demanded. 'Let me talk to him.'

CHAPTER FIFTY-ONE

Cutz handed his phone to Mercy.

It was either that or potentially suffer another fatal blow from the wild woman with her even wilder fists. He'd already been knocked out twice in the last few days. People would start to talk if he wasn't careful. Call him soft. Weak. A pussy.

Yeah, here, have the phone. Just keep it to yourself, will you?

Mercy answered immediately. 'Hello.'

A flicker of hesitation. 'Who is this?'

'Your worst nightmare.' Mercy began to pace up and down. 'The kind where you wake up crying in a pool of your own piss. You must be Vernon Gold.'

'Indeed I am,' said the caller, evidently confused. 'Where's Cutz?'

'He's here,' revealed Mercy. 'With me now. He wants it put on record that he didn't willingly give me his phone. He had no choice. I made him.'

'Is that so?' Gold snorted. 'Who are you? His girlfriend? Mother? Cutz is a big boy. He wouldn't—'

'Just shut up and listen!' spat Mercy, growing

increasingly irritated. 'Benji Hammerton is dead. And it's all because of you!'

'Benji's dead?' Gold took a moment. 'That's unfortunate. I had a lot of time for—'

'You killed him!' cried Mercy.

'Prove it,' said Gold, keeping his cool. 'I'm a respectable businessman. A Stainmouth success story. I could have you arrested for slander.'

'Go ahead,' said Mercy. 'And I'll tell the police everything I know whilst they're at it. You got your bodyguard to beat Benji to a pulp—'

'Did Cutz tell you that?' asked Gold, clearly unsettled.

Mercy side-eyed the man beside her. Correction. He was little more than a boy, nibbling on his fingernails, fearful of what might be coming his way. 'He didn't need to,' said Mercy, choosing her words wisely. 'I already knew. Don't shit yourself though, Gold. I'm not going to grass you up. Not yet, anyway. But I do want something in return.'

Vernon Gold started to laugh. 'Of course you do. Why am I not surprised? Now, let me guess … money.'

'Guess again, dickhead,' hissed Mercy. 'I'm not trying to blackmail you. No, Benji had a daughter. Amelia. Do you know where she is?'

Now it was Gold's turn to choose his words wisely. 'Possibly. Put Cutz on for a moment and then we might be able to do business.'

Mercy passed the phone to Cutz, who pressed it to his ear, listened carefully. He gave only blunt one word answers and little else. Without warning, he covered the mouthpiece.

'Gold wants to know if it was you who stole from the house on Eastern Avenue. What should I tell him?'

'Tell him the truth. It wasn't—' Mercy stopped mid-sentence. 'No,' she said, shaking her head. 'Tell him it *was* me.'

Rose raised an eyebrow. She had remained both mute and motionless for some time now, but Mercy's revelation was enough to induce a response, however small.

'I thought … you said … it wasn't …' mumbled Cutz, struggling to make sense of things.

'Don't think.' Mercy clenched her fists. A visible warning. 'Just do as I say. Tell him it was me. Or else.'

Cutz returned the phone to his ear. Without pausing for breath, he recited everything he had been told. As soon as he had finished he handed the phone back to Mercy.

'It seems we both have something the other desires,' said Gold. 'You have my product and my money, and I have the child. Maybe we could come to a … compromise.'

Mercy nodded. 'Go on.'

'Come to my home,' said Gold unexpectedly. 'Golden Slumbers. It's a large country house set in The Acres private estate on the outskirts of Stainmouth. We can do the swap there and this can all end peacefully. I have no interest in the child and I'm sure you don't want me as an enemy.' Gold paused. 'I know how this may sound—'

'Like a trap,' said Mercy.

'And yet it's nothing of the sort,' Gold insisted. 'I'm willing to trust you, but you must pay me the same respect. Do not contact the police or invite anybody else. I, in turn, will be alone except for the child. There'll be no trouble. I promise.'

Mercy didn't need to weigh it up. 'When do you want to do this? Tonight?'

'Tomorrow,' said Gold. 'Midday preferably. I'm a little busy until then. Would that be to your liking?'

'It'll have to be.' Mercy ended the call without another word. Handed the phone back to Cutz. 'You can go now.'

Cutz lingered a little too long.

'What?' shrugged Mercy. 'You won't be allowed to see Benji so there's no point sticking around.'

'I wasn't sticking around,' said Cutz defensively. 'It's just … I'm not sure what to do.'

'If I was you I'd start running and not stop,' suggested Mercy. 'You saw what happened to Benji. That could be you next. Just get out of here whilst you still can.'

Mercy watched as the youth skulked away. She waited until he was out of sight before she turned to Rose. 'Did you catch most of that?'

Rose nodded. 'Why would you lie about stealing? And do you really think you can trust a man like Vernon Gold?'

'You'll see and not on your life,' replied Mercy, answering both questions at once as the two of them wandered back into the hospital. 'There's something else that's bothering me more, though. No, *somebody* else. Somebody closer to home.' Mercy came to a halt. Placed a hand on Rose's arm. 'I think we've got a thief in our midst. Now it's time to flush him out.'

CHAPTER FIFTY-TWO

'For all we know this place may have been bugged.'

A dogged Lucas worked his way around the sitting room at Cockleshell Farm, staring up at the ceiling, scanning the mantelpiece, checking behind the pictures on the wall.

'Bugged?' Stretched out on the sofa, Tommy opened his mouth and yawned. 'You're insane.'

'No, you're just naive,' argued Lucas. 'Think about it. Proud Mary works for Agatha. Agatha works for some dodgy secret service. Who's to say they're not all listening in? Monitoring our every move? Having a good laugh at our expense? I mean, where's Proud Mary now? She could be crouching down by the keyhole.'

'She's outside with the pigs,' said Mercy. 'Do you think they're in on it, too?'

'You can never be too careful,' replied Lucas, barely listening as he dropped down onto his hands and knees so he could lift up the rug. 'Don't stop on my account, Mercy. Tommy needs to know—'

'Tommy needs to know *what*?' The man himself sat up, suddenly interested. 'I'm just waiting for the call to go home.

Run along now, Thomas. It's been nice knowing you, but you're no longer required to save the world.'

'That's not going to happen,' said Mercy, bursting his bubble with a single sentence. 'No one's going anywhere. Not until we've found Benji's daughter.'

Tommy groaned. 'Seriously? And where do you think we're going to find some random kid? I'm not hanging around sweet shops and play parks—'

'Vernon Gold's got her,' revealed Mercy. 'He told me that himself.'

'Did he now?' Tommy wagged a disapproving finger. 'You been cuddling up to the enemy? Secret dates behind my back?'

Mercy ignored that. 'Me and Rose bumped into Cutz outside the hospital. He was there to see Benji, but he was too late. Gold rang him, but I took the call. Now he wants to meet me. Tomorrow at midday. He even gave me his address. Golden Slumbers. It's on the outskirts of Stainmouth.'

'Oh, this is hilarious,' laughed Tommy. 'No offence, Mercy, but that's a trap. Clear as fuckin' mustard.'

'Of course it's a trap,' said Mercy, shaking her head. 'And that's why we're not going there tomorrow like Gold wants – we'll go there tonight. After midnight. We'll attack when he's least expecting it. If nothing else, we owe it to Benji. It was my idea, but the others are all in. So, that just leaves you. Any objections?'

Tommy pulled a face. 'None whatsoever. I mean, it's not as if I have a choice, is it?'

'Not really,' said Mercy. 'Agatha doesn't know – or Miles

– and that's how it's going to stay. Problem is, Gold wants to do a swap. Coke and cash both went missing from the house on Eastern Avenue when we were there. Gold wants them back before we can have the girl.' Mercy paused. 'Is that something you can help us with?'

Tommy snapped back immediately. 'What's that supposed to mean?'

'All clear.' Lucas stood up. Brushed himself down. 'There's nothing in here. We're free to talk.'

'Bit late for that,' sighed Mercy. 'Still, at least we now know that we can trust Proud Mary.'

'If only the same could be said for everyone in the room,' added Lucas, shifting his gaze to Tommy. Mercy soon followed suit. As did Rose.

It didn't take Tommy long to cotton on. 'What you all looking at? I didn't bug the bloody room!'

'No, but you've done something else,' chipped in Lucas. 'Something worse. You were lively in the pub last night. Some might say as high as a kite.'

'Can't blame a man for feeling happy,' said Tommy. 'I thought we were going home. Turns out I was wrong.'

'Do you know why Benji died?' asked Mercy out of the blue.

Tommy rubbed his eyes. 'Death by association, I guess. Mix with criminals long enough and, sooner rather than later, you're bound to end up six feet under. An unfortunate yet inevitable outcome of the job. Everybody's luck has to run out eventually. Even mine. That's why I'm stuck here with you losers.'

'This isn't a laughing matter,' said Lucas.

Tommy kept a straight face. 'Who says I'm joking?'

'Vernon Gold accused Benji of stealing from him,' Mercy began. 'Cutz told me that. That's why Gold ordered the beating. A beating that went too far.'

'Shit.' Tommy started to twitch. 'Okay, so that's bad … really bad … but what's it got to do with me?'

'Gold got it wrong,' continued Mercy. 'It wasn't Benji who stole from him at all. It was someone else.'

The sitting room fell silent.

'You can own up if you want,' said Lucas eventually. 'Any time you like. Take responsibility.'

Tommy frowned. 'What for?'

'Where are you hiding the money?' pressed Lucas. 'Upstairs? In your room? With the pigs? And don't tell me you've snorted all the coke—'

Tommy threw up his hands. 'What the hell is this? I haven't stolen anything.'

'What about the gun?' asked Mercy. 'The one you used to shoot Jumbo. The one you flashed in the pub.'

Tommy reached inside his waistband. Removed the weapon from his trousers. 'I didn't steal this; I just took it by accident. There's a big difference. I don't even want it. Here …'

Rose flinched as Tommy tossed the gun towards her. By some kind of miracle, she caught it … and then instantly squeezed it down the side of Proud Mary's armchair for fear of holding on to it for too long.

'Is this what you've all been doing, ever since we left the

hospital?' muttered Tommy, glaring at the others. 'Talking about me behind my back?'

Lucas took his own advice and owned up. 'Me and Mercy have. You know Rose. She doesn't really say much at the best of times. She did nod once or twice, though—'

'So, you *have* all been talking about me.' Tommy stood up and then sat back down again. 'Bad mouthing me. Slagging me off. Thanks for that. I thought we were ... I don't know ... friends or something ...'

'Or something,' repeated Lucas.

'Nah, I'm not having this.' Tommy stood up again. This time he stomped towards the exit. 'It's bullshit. You've no proof I've done anything. Remember that.'

The walls shook as he slammed the front door to Cockleshell Farm behind him.

'A man died because of you,' called out Lucas angrily.

'Keep it down,' said Mercy. 'Proud Mary will hear you.'

'Let her.' Lucas collapsed onto the sofa and breathed. 'Tommy's clearly got something to hide. We've shamed him and his only response was to run.'

'I guess,' nodded Mercy. She had started to wonder, though. What if they were wrong? What if Tommy hadn't stolen anything? She was about to raise it with Lucas when the sound of a revving engine outside on the driveway grabbed her attention. 'Who's got the car keys?'

'Rose,' replied Lucas automatically.

Rose shook her head. 'Not me. I wasn't the last one to drive.'

'No, that was you,' said Mercy, nodding at Lucas as she

hurried over to the window. 'You drove us back from the hospital.'

'So I did.' Lucas rummaged about in his pockets. 'The thing is … I can't … I don't seem to have them anymore.'

'No, Tommy has!'

The other two joined Mercy at the window, just in time to see the car disappearing through the gates.

Lucas waved him away. 'So long. I guess that's the last we'll ever see of Tommy O'Strife.'

'I'm not so sure,' said Mercy, mulling it over. 'We can't leave because we've got nowhere to go to. It was Agatha who told us that. If Tommy thinks she'll just let him drive off into the future in a Fiat 500 then he's in for a nasty surprise.'

CHAPTER FIFTY-THREE

Fuck 'em.

Tommy stamped down on the accelerator. The Fiat began to shudder as it hit forty … fifty … sixty miles-per-hour along the winding Croplington roads. He had no idea where he was going, but so what? All he wanted to do was get away from Cockleshell Farm. Away from Lucas. Mercy. Even Rose. How dare they accuse him like that? Whispering about him behind his back? Talking shit? Snakes. Every last one of them.

Well, go screw yourselves. He didn't need them. He didn't even like them. And they obviously didn't like him. That was as clear as crystal. You don't treat people like that. Not without anything to back it up. Lucas should've known that. What was the old saying? Innocent until proven guilty. They'd be in his room as soon as he had left the farm. Rooting through his drawers, looking under his bed, pulling up the floorboards. Well, they wouldn't find a thing. That was a fact. If only they'd bothered to ask …

Tommy wiped a single tear from his eye. Fuck's sake, get a grip, man. Pull yourself together. Why was he blubbing like a big baby? Have a bit of self-respect.

Another tear, another wipe. What was wrong with him? These people, these strangers, they didn't deserve that. He was better than them. Smarter and sharper. Clued up. Let's see how they coped without him.

Tommy gritted his teeth to stem the flow of tears. What now? Back to London, of course. Return to the fold. Ducking and dealing on a daily basis. First things first, he would get even with that prick Kamil Milik. No one puts a bullet in Tommy O'Strife and gets away with it. After that, he'd turn his attention to the Marquis brothers. They had probably set him up to begin with. Shit, why had he tossed that stolen gun to Rose? It still had a few bullets left in it. Three would've done the job nicely.

One for Kamil, one for each Marquis.

There. He had a plan. As easy as that. Then he'd be back. Riding the wave. At the top of the fuckin' tree.

Tommy felt the bravado slip away as quickly as it had arrived.

Who was he trying to kid?

He was never at the top. Nowhere near, in fact. He wasn't even a player; he was barely in the game. Just a lackey. A stooge. A fall guy for the bigger boys. Nobody feared him. Nobody respected him. Nobody gave him a second glance.

He meant nothing to no one.

And yet …

Tommy's thoughts drifted to Rose. She was so quiet, so unassuming, and yet she had pulled him out of Everything's Electric singlehandedly. Practically saved his life. Why would somebody do that? No, wrong question.

Why would somebody do that *for him*?

Tommy was still searching for answers when a buzzing in his pocket brought him out of his trance. Someone was calling. Which made perfect sense, of course. Who could it be? Lucas? No, Mercy. She'd be the first to apologise. Desperate for him to come back.

The buzzing stopped.

And then started again a moment later.

Stuffing a hand inside his pocket, Tommy found his phone and removed it. Stared at the screen.

Miles.

Oh. That was unexpected.

Like before, the phone stopped buzzing before starting again soon after.

This time, however, Tommy answered. 'Yeah, yeah, I know what you're going to say—'

'Stop the car!' demanded Miles.

Tommy winced as the other man's voice pulsated in his ear. 'No, it wasn't that—'

'Stop the car!' Miles echoed. 'Do it! Now!'

'Or else what?' Tommy increased the pressure on the accelerator. Sixty-five … seventy … seventy-five. Far too fast for winding country lanes. 'The thing is, I don't want to stop. I'm checking out. I've had enough. No disrespect, Miles, but you're a massive bellend, and the rest of them are just a bunch of pricks. So, if it's alright with you … and I don't really care if it's not … I think I'll—'

'Do not hang up!' warned Miles. 'Stop the car and we can talk.'

'Bit late for that now, mate,' Tommy snorted. 'I'm long gone.'

'That's not strictly true, is it?' said Miles. 'I can see you. You're on your way out of Croplington. Heading into Stainmouth. I know exactly where you are.'

Tommy scanned the interior of the Fiat for any visible cameras or trackers. He followed that up by glancing in his wing mirrors. The road was clear and there wasn't a car in sight. 'I'm going home,' he muttered to himself as much as anyone.

'Home? What home?' sighed Miles. 'You never listen, do you? You no longer exist. All of you. You have no home to go back to.'

'That's not true,' cried Tommy. 'I've done what you wanted. It's not my fault Benji Hammerton died. And I didn't steal anything from Vernon Gold.'

Miles hesitated. 'I don't know what you're talking about. Honestly. Like I said, just stop the car and we can talk. Trust me. It's your only option.'

'Is it now?' Tommy ended the call without another word. Fuck them and fuck you, Miles. What could that stiff upper shit do anyway? He perked up a little when he saw the road sign. He'd be in and out of Stainmouth in a matter of minutes. There was nothing to stop him now.

What could possibly go wrong?

The pain was so sudden, so sharp, so fiercely intense that Tommy had little choice but to let go of the steering wheel so he could grab his head with both hands. It was like a knife piercing his skull, stabbing at his senses, burrowing into his brain. He started to scream as he lifted his foot off the accelerator and padded blindly for the brake.

The car was slowing, but it was too little too late.

Lurching to one side, Tommy cracked the side of his head against the window as the Fiat began to spin. He didn't care. He just wanted the pain to end.

His wish came true when the car skidded off the road, mounted the grass verge and crashed straight into a tree.

Pain gone. Problem sorted.

Lights out.

DAY FOUR

CHAPTER FIFTY-FOUR

Midnight.

A new day. Same old shit.

A bewildered Mercy had given up banging her head repeatedly against the wall. Too loud, too painful. Now she had taken to watching the clock in the kitchen at Cockleshell Farm as she paced the floor instead. The *ticking* was oddly addictive. As were the whistles and rumbles that came from a snoring Lucas as he struggled to stay awake at the table.

Mercy turned to her other companion and sighed. 'Remind me again, Rose. How long has Tommy been gone for?'

'Eight hours and thirty-six minutes,' replied Rose without missing a beat. She was stood in one corner of the room, completely still barring the occasional blink. 'To be precise.'

'That *is* precise,' muttered Lucas. 'You're weird.' He opened one eye. That was harsh. Unnecessarily so. 'Weird … in a good way,' he added quickly.

'I like to remember things,' said Rose. 'Times … dates … events. Random pieces of information, however useless …'

Lucas lifted his head up off the table. Stifled a yawn. 'Whatever floats your boat. Rather you than me, though—'

'Keep it down, you two. We don't want to wake Proud Mary.' Mercy glanced up at the clock for the umpteenth time that evening. The landlady had been in bed for an hour now. Lucky her. 'This is such a ball ache,' Mercy moaned. 'I hate waiting around, especially if it's all for nothing. What if he never comes back?'

'I think we can safely assume that's no longer a *what if,*' replied Lucas. 'The four of us have just become a three. Still, I'm sure I'll get over it. Wait … there you go. I've got over it.' Lucas drummed his fingers on the table, deep in thought. 'Thing is, if Tommy can just speed off into the wild blue yonder, never to be seen again, then why can't we? If we pooled all our money together we would easily have enough to get home. We could get a train or a bus. Not a taxi, mind you. Far too expensive. I suppose hitchhiking wouldn't be so—'

Mercy stopped him mid-sentence with a fierce scowl. 'Store that thought for later. We're not going anywhere. Not until we find the girl. We owe Benji that much if nothing else.'

Lucas wanted to say that they didn't actually owe anything to anyone, that none of this was their fault, but somehow fought the urge. It would only stir up an argument. Verbal at a guess but, knowing Mercy like he did, the words could easily turn to fists. No, just go along with the plan and keep everyone out of harm's way. That was the smart thing to do. Besides, another day or two in Stainmouth was hardly the end of the world, was it? After that he could move on with the rest of his life. 'Fair enough,' said Lucas. 'There is one slight problem, though.'

'Feel free to share it with us,' smirked Mercy. 'Have you got a nasty rash? Cracked nipples? Some kind of toenail fungus?'

Lucas shook his head, confused. 'Tommy took the car. How are we expected to get all the way to Vernon Gold's house with no means of transport, barring our own two feet?'

Mercy waved away that particular problem with a flick of her wrist. 'Don't fret. I've got it covered.'

'Really?' said Lucas. 'You do surprise me. Still, as long as we don't rock up to Golden Slumbers in a taxi then I'm easy ...'

They *rocked up* to Golden Slumbers in a taxi.

Despite Lucas's protestations, Mercy dug her heels in and got her own way. After all, how else were they going to get across town at short notice? What she hadn't bargained on, however, was the price.

'Forty-seven pounds!' grumbled Lucas, careful to keep his voice down as the three of them gathered on the pavement, their eyes trained on the departing taxi as it disappeared into the darkness. 'World's gone mad. We only travelled a few miles. Ten at most. Ten miles for forty-seven pounds! That's daylight robbery in anybody's book.'

'Fifty,' muttered Rose, as they huddled together under the nearest streetlight.

Lucas bit his lip. Don't encourage her. You don't need to

know. 'What's fifty?' he asked, unable to help himself.

'Fifty pounds,' Rose explained. 'You gave the driver fifty pounds and let him keep the change.'

'Jeez, it gets worse,' sighed Lucas. 'Fifty pounds for a shit ride in a sweaty cab with a monosyllabic driver and his wandering hands.'

'Wandering hands?' Mercy raised an eyebrow. 'He never laid a finger on me. Not once. Or Rose.'

'You two weren't sat in the front,' said Lucas. 'He stroked my knee and tickled my thigh. Twice.'

'Some people pay good money for that,' said Mercy.

'I *did* pay good money for it,' frowned Lucas. 'Fifty whole pounds. Maybe he would've given me a refund if I'd touched him back.'

'Yeah, well, park those sexy thoughts and concentrate.' Mercy took a moment to scan her surroundings. Her plush, glamorous surroundings. *The Acres.* Five huge dwellings at the end of an exclusive cul-de-sac. Only for the select few. No riff-raff guarantee. 'Any idea which of these is Golden Slumbers?'

'That one.' Rose pointed towards an impressive mock Tudor country house with a long, gravel driveway and electric fence. 'The one with the Golden Slumbers house sign,' she added, straight-faced.

'Nice,' said Mercy, when what she really meant was *nice with bells on. Posh bells at that. None of your cheap rubbish.* 'If anything it seems a little understated for a tacky nightclub owner-cum-dodgy geezer. Where's the gold-plated Porsche? The dragon statues?'

'Swinging disco balls and naked super-models?' chipped-in Lucas. At the same time he ushered them towards an over-hanging tree away from the streetlights. Best not be seen lurking about in the middle of the night if they could help it. Especially not somewhere as top end as this. 'Someone's home,' he said, pointing up at one of the top floor windows. 'There's a light on.'

As if to be awkward, the light went out a moment later.

'Now you see it, now you don't,' said Mercy, rubbing her hands together. 'I was hoping that Vernon Gold would be out, but not to worry. We'll give him half-an-hour or so to drop off and then we'll get down to business.'

'And what business would that be?' wondered Lucas.

Mercy gestured beyond the house. 'There's woodland out the back. I saw it in the taxi on the way here. We'll come in that way. Through the garden. See if they've left a door open by mistake.'

'They still call that breaking and entering,' remarked Lucas, his serious head on. 'Also known as ten years behind bars.'

'Well, I call it finding Benji's daughter and getting her out of there in one piece,' replied Mercy. 'Also known as saving a life. I think that's a fair enough compromise, don't you?'

CHAPTER FIFTY-FIVE

Tommy opened his eyes and then closed them just as quickly.

There was a bright light shining straight at him. So bright, in fact, it made his head begin to throb and his whole body ache.

Or maybe he had been throbbing and aching before that. Ever since the crash.

Tommy flinched at the memory. That pain, that unbearable pounding in his skull had completely disabled him. What the fuck was it? No headache had ever paralyzed him in such a way. No migraine or hangover. This was something else entirely. Something terrifying. Something he never wanted to experience again.

Tommy kept his eyes shut whilst he tried to get a handle on things. Start with the facts. He was sat up straight. A chair at a guess. Cold and hard. Wood, metal or plastic. Take your pick. He slumped forward, but his arms stayed where they were, secured behind his back. Okay, so he was tied up.

Shit.

He opened his eyes just a little. The first thing he saw were his bare legs and genitals.

He was naked.

Double shit.

'Hello, sleepyhead.'

Tommy recognised the voice in the darkness. It was the last one he had heard before the crash. 'Miles ... what's going on?'

'At least there's nothing wrong with your hearing.' Stood somewhere behind the light, Miles seemed to be moving from side to side, causing a breeze as he paced the floor. 'You might still have brain damage, though. That's the price you pay for hitting a tree at top speed I'm afraid. The Fiat's a write off in case you're interested.'

'I'm not.' Tommy opened his eyes fully, but kept his head down. 'Where am I?'

'Nowhere.'

'Ah, come on. What time is it?'

'Late. Or early. Depends which way you look at it.'

Tommy nodded. After midnight then. One ... two ... three o'clock in the morning. If that was true, almost twelve hours since the accident. 'Where are my clothes?'

'I removed them,' replied Miles matter-of-factly. 'I thought it was for the best.'

'Really? Why?'

'Good question.' Miles took a moment. 'Would you like the truth, or something a little less ... let me see ... disturbing?'

'The truth.'

'I didn't want your clothes to get covered in blood. It's impossible to get out. Trust me, I've tried. Especially when there's a lot of it.'

Tommy felt his stomach turn. 'Give me the other version. The less disturbing one.'

'I just thought it'd be a laugh,' confessed Miles. 'You know, strip you naked, tie you to a chair and then threaten to kill you. Who wouldn't find the humour in that?'

Tommy faltered. 'Who said anything about killing me?'

'I haven't got to that bit yet,' said Miles. 'I seem to have jumped the gun. No pun intended.'

Tommy tried to breathe, but it caught in his chest. 'Why do you want to kill me? Surely you don't hate me that much.'

'Hate you?' Miles paused. 'I mean, you are a cocky little prick … but … no, I definitely don't hate you. Listen, let's not shift the blame onto me. This is all your doing. You have to live and die by your choices.'

'What choices?'

'Your refusal to toe the line for one. To be part of the team. We gave you a second chance. How many times have I said that? The thing is, if you're not prepared to do as we ask, then maybe you don't deserve such an opportunity.'

Tommy started to shiver. For the first time he could feel the cold against his bare skin. 'I just wanted to go home.'

'Of course,' said Miles. 'I get that. I really do. But that's not to say I'm about to let it happen. I'm not a monster – honestly, I'm not – but there are orders I have to follow. Agatha says it's for the good of the country. National security. So, what would you prefer? A bullet to the brain? Blink and you'll miss it. An overdose? A bit drawn out, but not impossible. Strangulation? I've done it in the past, but I'm not a huge fan—'

Tommy strained against his binds. 'What the fuck are you talking about?'

'Your death,' replied Miles, stepping in front of the light for the first time. 'I'm letting you choose how you want to go. I told you I wasn't a monster, didn't I?'

CHAPTER FIFTY-SIX

The woodland at the back of The Acres was everything Lucas had expected and worse.

Wet and muddy underfoot. Thick and impenetrable. And tree-y. So very, very tree-y. They were everywhere he looked and most places he didn't need to. He wasn't used to that, living in London. Concrete and pollution he could handle, but trees were something of an unknown commodity.

Wary of stumbling over any protruding roots in the darkness, he pushed a branch to one side, swearing when it whipped back and struck him sharply across the cheek. 'Do you know where we are?' he grumbled.

'Hopefully.' Mercy came to a halt by a small wooden fence. 'That's the rear of Golden Slumbers,' she said, pointing up a slight slope at a large, elegant property. 'It was the only white house on the estate.'

'Are you sure?'

'Positive.' Without another word, Mercy climbed over the fence. She kept moving, a few steps at most, but then froze when the entire garden was illuminated by a powerful searchlight.

'Too bright,' moaned Lucas, shielding his eyes. When he dared to look again he realised the full extent of what they were faced with. 'Nice garden,' he had to begrudgingly admit. About the size of a football pitch, the grass had been trimmed to absolute perfection, the bushes were immaculately pruned, and swathes of wild flowers offered a vibrant blast of colour amongst all the glorious greenery on display.

'At least we can see where we're going now,' said Mercy. 'So, are you two planning on standing there all night, looking gormless, or are you going to join me on the dark side?'

Lucas didn't need telling twice. Vaulting over the fence, he was surprised at how soft and bouncy the grass felt underfoot. Like nature's trampoline. 'Where's Rose?'

'Here.'

Lucas turned, surprised to find that she was stood beside him. 'You need to stop sneaking up on people. It's unnerving.'

'I don't sneak,' replied Rose.

'Okay, hover. You hover about. Like a human hovercraft. Just above the ground. No footsteps necessary.'

'Have you finished?' frowned Mercy. 'Let's not drag this out any longer than needs be.'

They started to run. Mercy had planned to stick to the shadows, but what was the sense in that? It would only slow them down and, besides, if Gold did happen to look out the window he'd be sure to see them regardless, whether it be in the middle of the lawn or trampling all over the flowerbeds.

They had almost made it across the length of the garden

when a thought pricked at Lucas's conscience. 'What about the dogs?'

Mercy slowed. Not to a complete stop, but close enough. 'What dogs?'

'The dogs that Gold might have,' said Lucas.

Mercy's eyes shifted from left to right. 'He's got dogs? How do you know that?'

'I don't,' Lucas shrugged. 'The clue was in the sentence. *Might*. But what if he has?'

'Dickhead.' Mercy sped back up again. 'Just keep it shut if you've nothing useful to say.'

'How am I supposed to know if it's useful or not?' argued Lucas, his words falling on deaf ears the moment they left his mouth.

Running at full pelt, it was Mercy who reached the house first. Pressing her back against the wall, she waited for the other two to join her before she sized up their options. 'There's a door over there—'

'It'll be locked,' said Lucas, interrupting her. 'That's not a problem, though. You don't need much to crack a lock. I learnt that in the force. A credit card ... screwdriver ... coat hanger—'

'And you've got all those things, have you?' Mercy didn't give Lucas a chance to answer. 'No, of course you haven't. So stop talking shit and let me do my thing.'

'You're very grizzly tonight,' remarked Lucas, not so loud that Mercy might actually hear him. He watched as she wandered over to the door and tried the handle. To his immense satisfaction, it held firm. 'Oh, how unexpected,' he said, barely able to resist shouting *told you so* in her face.

Mercy turned nevertheless, shooting him the kind of glare that could burn a hole in any forehead. Wary of making things worse than they already were, Lucas chose that exact moment to study the ground by his feet. He had a feeling. A feeling that if he looked hard enough he might eventually stumble upon it.

It being a key.

So, where would he hide it if he was Vernon Gold? Not under the barbecue. Way too obvious. Ditto the watering can. His eyes fell upon a small stone frog. Yes, that was more like it. Compact and heavy and left largely to its own devices. People – even dodgy gangsters – were so predictable sometimes.

Crouching down, Lucas lifted the garden ornament and removed the key from its resting place. 'Do you forgive me now?'

Mercy ignored him the best she could as she snatched the key from his fingers and stuck it in the keyhole.

'Stop!' Lucas, his voice little more than a whisper, raised a hand in warning. 'It might be alarmed.'

The door was already ajar by the time his words had sunk in to Mercy's brain. Rooted to the spot, she waited for the inevitable ear-splitting racket.

Thankfully, that was one inevitable ear-splitting racket that never came.

'Lucky,' muttered Lucas, as he followed both Mercy and Rose inside. They were in the kitchen. White units with marble work surfaces. Sleek and shiny. Very classy. 'Did you bring a torch?'

'Did *I* bring a torch?' scowled Mercy. 'Where would I get a torch from? Don't tell me. That magical torch shop we've never been to. For crying out loud …'

'Definitely grizzly,' said Lucas under his breath.

There was a door straight in front of them and then another to their right. Mercy edged towards the latter, opening it wide. The room was home to a small antique desk and leather-bound chair. Bookshelves galore on each and every wall. Less an office, more of a study.

Creeping over to the desk, Mercy switched on a lamp. It was a low light, not too powerful, perfect for rummaging about without drawing attention. She started by rifling through any stray papers, desperate for the slightest of clues as to the whereabouts of Benji's daughter.

She was still searching when Lucas poked his head around the door. 'Have you seen Rose? She seems to have vanished.'

'Well, she can't have vanished far,' snapped Mercy. 'You should go look for her. Now preferably. No pressure.'

'Okay, I can take a hint.' Lucas moved slowly through the kitchen and into the hallway. It was a polished wooden floor so he lifted himself up onto his tiptoes, careful not to tread too loudly. He spotted Rose at once. She was stood beside the staircase, statuesque, staring into space. Almost … ghost-like.

'What are you looking at?' Lucas followed Rose's gaze as he crept up behind her. There was at least a dozen certificates, each of them in identical frames, arranged on the wall. He leant forward for a closer look. No, not certificates. 'I've seen them before,' he said quietly. 'They're commendations. Police commendations.'

Rose nodded. 'Why would Vernon Gold have police commendations on display?'

Lucas reached out to remove one. He lifted the frame off its hook, but then mis-judged its weight and let it slip through his fingers. It crashed against the floorboards before he could react, the resulting noise echoing around the huge house like a gunshot in a tunnel.

It didn't take long for a furious Mercy to come creeping through. 'What's going on?'

'Accident,' mouthed Lucas.

They held their collective breaths and waited. Seconds passed before Lucas gave in and exhaled. Nothing had happened. No voices. No movement. No worries.

'I think we got away with one there,' he whispered.

'We?' Mercy raised an eyebrow. '*You* got away with one. Now keep your hands to yourself and—'

A sudden commotion cut her off mid-sentence. It was coming from upstairs. In one of the bedrooms. Stamping feet on creaking floorboards. A grunt. A growl. A grumble.

And then a figure. An angry silhouette at the top of the stairs.

Lucas was wrong.

They hadn't got away with it at all.

CHAPTER FIFTY-SEVEN

'No ... this can't be happening ... I'm not ... I won't do it ... forget it ...'

A frantic Tommy stumbled breathlessly over his words. How was he supposed to answer a question like that?

How would you like to die?'

Not today, thank you. See you in fifty years, you mad bastard.

'Dragging it out will only make things worse,' said Miles, disappearing somewhere behind him. 'We both know it's going to happen so we might as well get it over with. I could always cut your throat. It's harder than it looks in the films, though. You have to get a good, deep slice or you won't sever the arteries. And it's messy. Blood spurts out everywhere. Maybe I should take my own clothes off too, just in case ...'

Tommy screamed out loud as something cold pressed against his neck.

'Do that again and I'll have to gag you,' warned Miles. 'And it's not a knife if that's what you're thinking. It's just my finger. I'm trying to find the right place. X marks the spot.'

'Why are you doing this?' spluttered Tommy.

'I'm not,' Miles insisted. 'You are. You set the wheels in motion the moment you tried to leave Stainmouth.'

'I just wanted to go home.'

'So you keep on saying. And I keep telling you that your old life is no longer an option. This is a restart. You're a vital cog in Agatha's project. The Nearly Dearly Departed Club. Her name, not mine. If you don't want to be a part of it, however, then we've got a difficult decision to make. We can't just let you wander round at will when you don't exist. People will talk. So will you. That's why I've been instructed to put a stop to things once and for all. Agatha called it immediate termination.'

'I never said I didn't want to be part of that fuckin' club,' blurted out Tommy.

'Actions speak louder than words,' said Miles. 'You were driving back to London—'

'I was angry. The others … they accused me of stealing. I've calmed down now, though. I want to go back to Cockleshell Farm. I want to help.'

'That's only because I'm going to kill you,' remarked Miles. 'Besides, I'm not sure they need you. You're a bad influence. A rotten apple. I think we both know what has to be done—'

'Whoa! Hold on!' *Think, Tommy. Think.* 'What can I say that'll make you stop?'

'You've said enough. I'll make it quick. You have my word.'

Tommy felt something cold press against the side of his

head. This time it wasn't a finger. 'Fuck's sake, man, don't ... I'll do what you want ... anything ... just let me go and I'll help them find the kid. I swear.'

Miles hesitated. Lowered his gun. 'What kid?'

'Benji's kid,' said Tommy hastily. 'His daughter. The others have gone looking for her.'

Miles snatched a breath. He could hear them now. Alarm bells. Not ringing. Booming. Perforating his eardrums. 'It's the middle of the night. Where have they gone?'

'Vernon Gold's house,' said Tommy, seizing upon the chance to keep Miles talking. 'He told Mercy to meet him there midday tomorrow, but you know Mercy, she doesn't like being bossed about. They're going there tonight, instead. After midnight.'

'Any time now,' muttered Miles to himself. 'So, where does Gold live?'

'Somewhere on the outskirts of Stainmouth. Ah, Mercy told me. Golden something or other. Golden ... Golden Slumbers.'

'Golden Slumbers?' repeated Miles. The name stirred something in his brain. And for all the wrong reasons. 'I know who lives at Golden Slumbers,' he said, hurrying across the room so he could switch on the light. 'And it isn't Vernon Gold.'

CHAPTER FIFTY-EIGHT

Lucas ducked out of sight, but not before he'd given the man at the top of the stairs a quick once over.

Mid-fifties. Brown hair, side parting, with a thick moustache. Glasses perched on the edge of his nose. Small and plump in size and stature, but to call him short and fat would've been unjust. Dressed in red silk pyjamas and a white dressing gown. Matching slippers. A cricket bat in his left hand and a golf club in his right.

'Who's there?' he bellowed. 'Don't make me come downstairs and slap you silly.'

A confused Lucas glanced at Mercy, who was knelt down beside him. 'Is that Vernon Gold?'

'I guess so,' Mercy whispered, peering between the gaps in the stair rail. 'Tommy's the only one who's seen him. I have spoken to him, though … and he didn't sound like that.'

'Great,' frowned Lucas. 'So, either Vernon Gold has got other men staying in his bedroom, or else—'

'This isn't his house,' piped up Rose.

'I can hear you,' cried the man, holding his ground on

the top step. 'Listen, I couldn't give a shiny shit how many of you there are down there. Two or two hundred, I'm not scared either way. Do you know who you're dealing with? Do you? Would you like me to tell you?'

'Just our luck to stumble across the local egomaniac,' sighed Lucas. 'I wouldn't be surprised if he rips open his pyjamas and then slides down the banister. Still, rather that then he calls—'

'The police,' hollered the man. 'That's me. I'm Clifford Goose. Ah, your bum's twitching now, isn't it? You've dropped a massive clanger breaking into the home of the Chief Constable.'

'Chief Constable?' mouthed Lucas. 'Did he say Chief Constable?'

'Listen up,' continued Goose. 'I'm not coming down to beat the living daylights out of you … but that's only because I don't have to. Not when reinforcements are less than two minutes away. And not just my local bobbies neither. Nah, I'm talking about the heavy mob. Armed to the teeth. Shoot on sight and ask questions later. How does that grab you? Go on. Tell me. How … does that … chuffin' … grab you?'

Lucas had heard enough. Dropping down onto his hands and knees, he started to crawl back towards the kitchen without another word.

Of the other two, only one followed his lead. That was Mercy. Rose, however, stayed exactly where she was. Crouched down behind the banister. Rooted to the spot.

Mercy peered over her shoulder. 'What are you doing?'

'I'm not coming,' said Rose.

Mercy did a quick U-turn. Crept back towards the stairs. 'What do you mean you're not coming?'

'Exactly that,' Rose insisted. 'If the three of us try and leave now they'll come after us. If I stay and take the blame then maybe you two can escape unnoticed.'

'No way.' Mercy could hear sirens in the distance as she spoke. 'That's one hell of a bad idea.'

Rose responded with a shrug. 'Perhaps … but it's our only option.'

The sirens were increasing in volume. Mercy could picture the police pulling up at the gates. Running up the driveway. Storming the barricades.

'They're here,' laughed Goose.

Without missing a beat, Mercy turned and set off after Lucas. It was now or never. No time for arguing. Pleading. Begging. If Rose wanted to stay then so be it.

And she did. Want to stay. Rose waited until the other two were out of sight before she stood up straight and stepped out of the shadows.

Goose was still at the top of the stairs. He hadn't moved an inch. 'One bloody woman! Is that it? Bugger me, I could've tackled you myself. Still, maybe it's not too late to call off the—'

Goose was halfway down the stairs when the front door crashed open. He missed the next step and stumbled forward. He tried to regain his balance, but it was too late. By the time he had stopped falling he was sprawled out by Rose's feet, the golf club lodged under one armpit, the cricket bat stuck somewhere between his legs.

Rose, meanwhile, had found solace behind her hands. When she looked again the police had burst into the hallway. Five of them in total. Black from head-to-toe. Masks and bulletproof vests. Men or women, it was impossible to tell.

Clifford Goose had been right about one thing, though. They were armed. And that undoubtedly made them dangerous.

The five had spread out without Rose even noticing. They had her surrounded. Every angle covered. All escape routes blocked.

Then the shouting started.

'Don't move! Get down on the ground! Keep your hands where we can see them! Arms behind your back!'

Rose's head was spinning. There were too many voices fighting for attention. She couldn't do everything at once – it was physically impossible – so she did something else entirely.

Legs buckling beneath her, Rose walked slowly towards the five.

'Stop right there!'

No.

'Last warning! Do not take another step or we'll be forced to open fire!'

Rose closed her eyes. They were still shouting, but it was just a noise. A monotonous threat that barked and howled like a rabid beast.

Do it then. Go on. Stop making promises you can't keep.

And then her wish came true. A single gunshot cut through everything.

A single gunshot that could end things once and for all.

CHAPTER FIFTY-NINE

Lucas clambered over the fence that separated Golden Slumbers from the acres of woodland that surrounded it.

Mercy had edged some way ahead of him. She hadn't said a word since they had made their escape. Left the house.

Left Rose.

'Hold on,' moaned Lucas, mindful of where he stepped. 'I'm struggling to keep up.'

Mercy ignored him as she pressed on through the undergrowth, muttering to herself as she went. 'You don't run out on people … friends … not Rose … she didn't deserve that.'

Lucas reached over. Tried to rest a hand on Mercy's shoulder, but she was moving too fast. 'Okay, I get it,' he said, stumbling slightly. 'And I agree with you. We shouldn't have left her. But what choice did we have? She gave herself up so we could get out of there. It was a brave, selfless thing to do. Like … I don't know … a sacrificial lamb or something.'

'Don't say that.' Mercy could feel her heart pounding against her chest. 'Rose is one of us … part of the team … and we let her down.'

Lucas was about to argue when something distracted him. The cracking of a twig. The rustle of leaves. Footsteps in the dark perhaps. He came to a halt and listened. Gave it a few seconds, but the woods were momentarily silent. Just an animal then. At the same time he looked back towards the house. He was checking for movement in the garden.

There was none.

'I think we're okay,' said Lucas, weaving his way between the trees so he could catch up with Mercy. 'There doesn't seem to be—'

A gunshot stopped him mid-sentence. It was coming from somewhere behind him.

From Golden Slumbers.

Lucas was still staring, open-mouthed in disbelief, when Mercy rushed past him. His instincts kicked in and he grabbed her by the arm. Not enough to hurt, but enough to slow her down.

'Get off me!' She let fly with her free hand. Less a punch and more of a slap, it struck Lucas weakly on the shoulder. 'They're going to kill her! We need to go back!'

'We're not going anywhere.' Lucas tightened his grip. 'Just calm down, will you? If we do anything stupid now we'll—'

Mercy lashed out again. This time she caught him on the jaw with a clenched fist. Staggering backwards, Lucas had little choice but to let go of her as he lifted his hands up to his face.

Free at last, Mercy turned towards the house, ready to run. Something held her back, though. A feeling. Regret perhaps. Guilt. It was hard to tell. 'I'm sorry.'

'Don't be,' mumbled Lucas. 'It's fine.'

'It's not,' said Mercy. 'I shouldn't have done that. None of this is your fault. It's just … Rose. She could've been shot. Or worse. What if she's—?'

Lucas cut her off. 'She won't be. The police don't just shoot people in cold blood. And it's not like Rose is much of a threat, is it? No, I'm guessing that the gun went off by accident. It does happen from time to time.' Lucas looked towards the night sky. Stretched his neck muscles. His face, somehow, was still in working order. 'Good punch. Next time save it for some other chump.'

'Like Vernon Gold?' Mercy tried to draw breath. She could feel a stirring in the pit of her stomach. It was starting to rise again. The overpowering rage. The uncontrollable fury. 'Gold set us up,' she said through gritted teeth. 'He knew we'd do something stupid and he was right. First Benji and now this. If anything's happened to Rose I'll …' Mercy let her sentence fade to nothing. 'We can't just let him get away with it.'

'You're right,' agreed Lucas. 'This isn't over. I promise. We'll track down Benji's kid and then we'll find a way to get Gold.'

'We don't *need* to find a way.' With that, Mercy was back on the move. Away from the house. Through the woodland.

'What do you mean?' asked Lucas, hurrying after her. 'Let's not do anything rash. We should head back to Cockleshell Farm first and take stock. Talk to Miles. And Agatha. She'll need to know.' Lucas could sense he was clutching at straws. 'I'm … erm … tired. It's really late.'

'No, it's early,' argued Mercy. 'Early morning. And we both know what closes early morning, don't we?'

Lucas just shrugged. 'Is that a cryptic clue? Am I supposed to say my eyes or—?'

'Nightclubs,' revealed Mercy.

'Of course. Why didn't *I* think of that?' Lucas knew where this was heading. Or, to be precise, where *they* were heading to. 'And is there one nightclub in particular you've got in mind?'

The silence seemed to speak for itself.

Lucas shrugged again. 'Fine. Have it your way. Just promise me one thing, won't you? Whatever happens, however desperate we become, we won't get another taxi, will we?'

CHAPTER SIXTY

Tommy waited for his eyes to adjust to the light.

He recognised the room immediately. It was the same room he had stormed out of in the not-so-distant past.

Also known as the sitting room in Cockleshell Farm.

That was the trigger. 'You're a sneaky fucker, Miles, bringing me here of all places. Proud Mary would've gone berserk if you had stained the carpets, though. Probably explains why you didn't blow my brains out.'

'Don't tempt me,' muttered Miles. At the same time he wandered in front of Tommy's chair, his phone pressed firmly to his ear. 'Come on … answer.'

'Where are the others?' asked Tommy, looking around.

'Not here, that's for sure,' said Miles. 'We arrived just before one and they were nowhere to be seen. I thought they might be out drinking, drowning their sorrows after what happened to Benji. Not according to you, though.' A furious Miles ended the call before stabbing at the screen. 'I don't believe this. I think they've turned their phones off. There's no way of reaching them.'

'Chill out. I've told you already. They're busy.'

'And that's precisely what I'm worried about. If they get caught breaking into Golden Slumbers there'll be all hell to pay.'

Tommy snorted. 'You can't be *that* scared of Vernon Gold.'

'I'm not scared of Vernon Gold in the slightest,' shot back Miles. 'Clifford Goose, however …'

'Clifford *what?*' Confused, Tommy waited for an explanation.

'Goose,' repeated Mils. 'He's the Chief Constable of Stainmouth police force. Golden Slumbers is the name of his house.'

'Shit.' Tommy burst out laughing. Then he stopped. Just like that. As quickly as he had started. Because it wasn't funny, was it? Not one bit. 'You need to warn the others.'

'What do you think I've been trying to do?' Miles glared at his phone as if it had personally insulted him. 'I'm going to have to call Agatha.'

Tommy shifted awkwardly in the chair. He was desperate to uncross his legs, but knew he couldn't. Not unless he wanted to fully expose himself to the other man. 'Please, Miles, untie me. I won't try anything. I just want to get dressed before my balls get so cold they drop off.'

Without another word, Miles removed a small knife from his pocket and set to work on the binds around Tommy's wrists. Once he had finished, he reached behind the sofa and returned with a bundle of clothes.

'Don't worry, I'll not peek,' he said, tossing them across the sitting room.

'How did you know Proud Mary wouldn't come in?' asked

Tommy, glancing at the door as he pulled on his underwear.

'I didn't,' admitted Miles. 'Not for certain. But I do know she goes to bed with ear plugs in. Better that than be woken up by bumps in the night. Or, worse still, grown men begging for forgiveness.'

Tommy swore under his breath as he buttoned up his shirt. 'What now? What we gonna do about the others?'

'Oh, keen to help now, aren't you?' sneered Miles. He regretted it instantly. Wrong time, wrong place. 'I've got the car outside. We can track them—'

'Is that the same way you tracked me?' wondered Tommy. 'Care to explain how you did that? The pain in my head was unbearable. Have you put something in there?'

'Like a brain,' muttered Miles. Again, neither the time nor the place. 'We can't do anything until I tell Agatha. She needs to know all the details. No one told you to go searching for the child,' he felt inclined to add.

'It was Mercy's idea,' said Tommy. 'She reckoned we owed it to Benji.'

'Well, that was just plain stupid,' remarked Miles.

Tommy started to nod as he stepped into his shoes. 'Yeah, that's what I thought at first, but now I'm not so sure. Mercy just wants to make things better. You can't blame her for that, can you? If nothing else, I should be there too.'

'How noble of you. Bit late, but at least you're—' Miles switched his attention from Tommy to his phone when Agatha answered the call. 'Hello … yes … there's something I need to … okay … no … you're joking! Right … will do … bye.'

'That was short and sweet,' said Tommy, as he finished tying his shoelaces.

Miles corrected him. 'Short … but in no way sweet. Agatha's at the police station. We've got a situation.'

CHAPTER SIXTY-ONE

Agatha looked the Chief Constable up and down and up again.

He was dressed in red silk pyjamas and a white dressing gown. Not the usual attire for somebody so senior in the police force. Then again, it was the middle of the night and he had just been rudely interrupted. Give the poor guy a break.

'Don't you bloody dare,' warned Clifford Goose, reading her mind. 'I was in a rush. It's not often you find an intruder roaming about your property.'

An intruder. Singular. Just the one person then. 'We need to talk,' said Agatha. 'In private.'

'Damn right we need to talk,' barked Goose. 'Starting with you telling me what any of this has got to do with you.'

'And I will,' Agatha insisted. 'In private.'

'No, I think I'd rather talk here,' said Goose stubbornly. They were stood in the entrance to the Stainmouth police station. Located in the dead centre of town, it was packed to the rafters with stumbling drunks and rowdy teenagers. The Saturday night, Sunday morning crowd. 'The intruder we arrested – a woman – named you directly,' continued Goose. 'Told me to contact you. Said you could explain everything—' Goose broke off to burp. 'I'm waiting.'

Agatha was in no rush to fill in the gaps. She had a number of options. Two sides of the coin. Tell the truth or formulate a fabrication? Maybe a bit of both. Enough facts to make it seem plausible, mixed with a handful of lies to keep the dogs at bay. 'She's one of mine,' Agatha revealed. 'Part of my … elite squad. Her name is Rose Carrington-Finch, but you won't find her on any database. She's deep undercover. Beyond deep. Practically buried up to her eyeballs.'

Goose scrunched up his face. 'That much I can believe. What I can't get my head around, though, is why she was creeping around my house?'

'Do I really need to spell it out to you?' replied Agatha waspishly. *Please say no. Go on. Don't let me down.*

'Yeah, spell it out to me,' said Goose, biting back. ''Cos I'm strugglin' here. Perplexed would be the understatement of the bleedin' century. If you've not got a rock solid reason why Carrington-whatsit was in my house then I'll be chargin' her with—'

'I sent her.' Agatha paused. That wasn't enough. She would have to elaborate. 'I sent her to spy on you.'

'You what?' A weary Goose let that sink in. 'Why would you do that?'

'It was an order from above,' said Agatha. It wasn't. 'The powers that be have had their suspicions about you for ages. Your card is marked. That's why they called for me. And I, in turn, called for Rose.'

'Bullshit,' spat Goose. That was a gut reaction. The next time he spoke it came from the head. 'Did she find anything?' he asked warily.

Strange question, thought Agatha. Especially when you've got nothing to hide. 'Not as far as I'm aware—'

'Well, she wouldn't have, would she?' boomed Goose, his bluster back intact. 'I'm as straight as a die. Respectable from the arse up. You and your poncey mates down in London can't lay a glove on me. I'm practically a saint round these parts.'

'Pleased to hear it,' smiled Agatha. 'Now, if you can just fetch my agent I'll be on my—'

Goose stopped her with a shake of his head. 'Hold your horses, lady. I've had a rough evening. I had to call for back-up. A shot was fired—'

Agatha stirred. 'You shot my agent?'

'No. I said a shot was fired. Took a bloody chunk clean out of my floorboards. Trigger happy work experience. Can't trust anyone. That's serious shit, though, that is. Reports need to be filed. I'll have to talk to your woman before I let you see her—'

'Let me stop you there,' frowned Agatha. 'I don't just want to see her – I'm going to *take* her. Take her now. Rose is coming with me. End of conversation.'

'In your dreams,' Goose snorted. 'She's about to be charged. Breakin' and enterin' any old house is bad enough. Breakin' and enterin' *my* house is about one hundred times worse. You can visit her, of course, when she's banged up.

Once a week for an hour, like every other poor sucker. I'll get you a pass if you ask politely.'

'I don't need a pass,' snapped Agatha. 'I can go where I like.'

'Not on my watch, missus.' Goose puffed out his dressing gown. 'You seem to be forgetting who I am. I'm a very powerful man.'

'No, you're not,' Agatha laughed. 'You're a small fish in a small pond. Take one step out of Stainmouth and you're nothing. I, however, am the exact opposite. I've marched in here and laid down the law. I control you.'

'Do you fuck?' snarled Goose.

'Yes, I do. And I'll prove it. Just one word and you'll do everything I ask …' Agatha paused for effect. Let the tension build. 'Blackcurrant.'

'Blackcurrant? What's that supposed to—' Now it was Goose's turn to pause. His brain ticked over as a dark memory reared its ugly head. Another time, another place. Long forgotten. Until now. 'Who told you about that?'

'That's none of your concern.' Agatha smiled inwardly. Miles had done his homework on the Chief Constable and passed with flying colours. 'Now, take me to Rose before I accidentally spill the beans. I'm sure your nearest and dearest – not to mention the entire Stainmouth constabulary – would be interested to hear about—'

'Alright, keep it down.' An impish Goose peered around the police station. 'If you're goin' to be like that, all snidey, proper devious, then I've got no choice, have I? Come on.'

Turning away from the entrance, Goose waddled over to

the front counter before being buzzed through into a narrow corridor. Agatha stayed close at all times. There was a row of cells to their left. Goose pressed on, stopping at the furthest one away. He nodded at the officer stood outside, who proceeded to unlock it without another word. Goose, ever the gentleman, grunted something unintelligible as he squeezed into the cell.

Agatha followed him inside.

She found Rose curled up in a corner. Knees up to her chin. Rocking back and forth on her heels.

'Funny sort of agent,' snorted Goose. 'She's bloody crackers if you ask me.'

'I didn't.' Agatha marched across the cell and crouched down. Leant in close. 'This is important, Rose,' she whispered. 'What have you told them?'

'Nothing,' Rose mumbled.

'Look at me.' Agatha placed her thumb on Rose's chin and lifted her head. Tears were running down the younger woman's cheeks. She was clearly upset by what had happened. Or fearful of what was to come perhaps. 'I need to be sure,' stressed Agatha. 'What have you told them?'

'Nothing,' repeated Rose. 'I wouldn't. I promise.'

Right answer, thought Agatha. Because if she *had* said something – anything – about being *dead* then the consequences could have been fatal.

'We're going now.' Standing up, Agatha took Rose by the hand and helped her to her feet. 'Please don't try and stop us.'

'As if I'd dare,' grumbled Goose, moving to one side.

'Maybe you'd like me to hold the doors open for you. Kiss your arse on the way out …'

'That won't be necessary,' said Agatha, guiding Rose across the cell. 'Thank you for your cooperation, Chief Constable. I hope the next time we meet it won't be so … strained. Nice pyjamas by the way. Very stylish.'

'Ah, just bugger off,' Goose muttered. 'You can see yourselves out. And if I find you anywhere near my house again, young lady …'

With Goose's threats echoing around the police station, Agatha swept along the corridor before waiting to be buzzed back into the lobby. Rose was by her side at all times. A shuffling, shaking mess.

'Catch your breath and calm down,' said Agatha, as they exited the building. She scanned the car park, relieved to see that Olaf and the Audi were just where she had left them. 'I hope it's good,' she added, opening the car door.

'Good?' Rose wiped the tears from her cheeks as she climbed onto the back seat. 'What's good?'

'Your story,' Agatha explained. 'A day in the life of the world's stupidest cat burglar. It sounds absolutely fascinating.'

CHAPTER SIXTY-TWO

Olaf eased the Audi to a gentle halt outside Cockleshell Farm.

Agatha climbed out of the car first and walked towards the door. Rose had filled her in on their journey there. How Vernon Gold had spoken to Mercy over the phone at the hospital. Tricked them into going to the home of Clifford Goose in search of Benji's daughter. Agatha understood why they had done that. She didn't condone it, but she understood. Unfortunately, they had also crossed the line. And if you crossed the line there had to be some kind of payback.

'I hope they're still up,' said Agatha, pressing down on the handle once Rose had joined her on the doorstep. The door opened and the two of them stepped inside. A short hallway led into the sitting room. That was where they found two men on opposite sofas, sitting in silence.

'Rose.' Tommy jumped to his feet. 'Thank fuck you're alright.'

Rose tensed up as he rushed over and threw his arms around her. That was her usual reaction to being touched.

To human contact of any kind, in fact. But this … this felt different. Almost tolerable. Quite comforting actually.

'Put her down,' said Agatha, taking a seat beside Miles. She waited for Tommy to do just that before she spoke again. 'So, Mr O'Strife, how did that escape plan of yours go this afternoon?'

Tommy shook his head as he sat back down. 'Not great. I didn't get far before my brain nearly exploded.'

'I think that ship sailed a long time ago,' remarked Miles. 'The Fiat's beyond repair by the way. We'll have to scrap it.'

'It was a shit car anyway,' Tommy shrugged. 'Get us a better one next time, won't you?'

'Next time?' Agatha raised an eyebrow. 'I didn't think there was going to be a next time. I thought you'd had enough. That's why you tried to run out on us.'

'Miles convinced me otherwise,' said Tommy sheepishly. 'He can be very persuasive. Especially when I'm stark bollock naked and he's got a gun in his hand.'

'Indeed,' nodded Agatha, not entirely sure what he was talking about. 'So, no more silly games then?'

Tommy stroked his chin as if contemplating his options. 'There's nothing on the itinerary, Pleasant Agatha, but one can never be too certain.'

Agatha ignored the tone – smug, condescending – and switched her attention to Miles. Hunched over a laptop, he was stabbing frantically at the keys like a man possessed.

'Where are we at?' asked Agatha, peering over his shoulder.

'Two down,' he said, gesturing towards Tommy and

Rose, 'two to go. I've been tracking the others. They made a call to a taxi rank about an hour ago. They got picked up half-an-hour later and now they've arrived.'

Agatha frowned. 'Arrived?'

'They're at Everything's Electric,' said Miles. 'It's a nightclub. One of Vernon Gold's.'

'I know it well.' Tommy turned to Rose. Winked. '*We* know it well.'

Agatha tried to blank him out. Concentrate. 'Why would they go there at this time of night?'

'Why do you think?' Tommy was up and off the sofa before the words had left his lips. 'They want to give Gold a good pasting, don't they? Slap him about a bit. We should get over there before it's too late. Don't want to miss out on all the fun, do we?'

'Sit down,' said Agatha sternly. 'We're not going anywhere. Not until we know the full extent of what's going on.'

Tommy held his ground. 'We can't just leave them to fend for themselves.'

'She said sit down.' Miles placed his laptop on the coffee table and stood up. Opened his jacket just enough to give everybody a flash of metal. 'Do you remember that gun you were worried about earlier? It's still here. Ready and waiting.'

'Oh, come on,' groaned Tommy. 'Gold's a psycho. He got Doberman to murder Benji for pity's sake. He would've killed me too if it wasn't for Rose …'

'You're just rambling now,' said Agatha. 'I understand your concerns—'

'Do you?' Tommy searched for support. He found it

stood in the corner of the room. Arms folded. Head down. Practically asleep for all intents and purposes. 'Tell them, Rose. They'll listen to you.'

Rose visibly shrank as all eyes rested on her. She knew what she had to say, though. As long as she could get it out. 'Tommy's right. We have to help them.'

'And we will,' insisted Agatha. 'But not before we've assessed the situation.'

'No.' Rose felt oddly alive as the word tripped from her tongue with neither thought nor consideration. 'That's not enough. We have to help them *now*.'

Agatha sat forward. 'Not before we've assessed the situation,' she repeated. 'Now sit down and try to control your emotions. I'm starting to think I preferred it when you never spoke.'

A seemingly crestfallen Rose slumped back into her shell as she shuffled over to Tommy. She was all set to sit down beside him when, without warning, she slipped her fingers down the gap in the sofa. When her hand reappeared she was carrying the gun she had squeezed down there the previous day. The gun Tommy had stolen from Cutz. That he had waved about in the pub.

Rose swung around, aiming it at Agatha and Miles.

'Bloody hellfire!' laughed Tommy, eyes wide in amazement. 'I wasn't expecting that.'

'No, neither was I.' Agatha went to stand, but then thought better of it when both Rose and the gun began to tremble. 'I'm not sure you've thought this through, have you?'

'I have.' Rose watched as Miles's hand moved slowly across his body. Inside his jacket. Towards his own weapon. 'Don't,' she said. 'Believe me, I will shoot.'

'You go, girl,' cheered Tommy, clapping his hands together like an excitable seal. 'I always knew you had a big set of balls tucked away somewhere.' Tommy hesitated. 'No offence.'

'I think we should all take a moment,' said Agatha calmly. 'This is a very drastic course of action, Miss Carrington-Finch. You don't have to do this.'

'Mercy's my friend,' Rose replied. 'I can't just sit here as if everything's fine. As for Lucas—'

'Lucas is a dick,' chipped in Tommy.

'No, Lucas is a good man,' said Rose, correcting him. 'Neither of them deserve to suffer.'

'Fair enough.' Tommy moved towards the opposite sofa. Reaching inside Miles's jacket, he removed his gun and tossed it across the sitting room floor until it was safely out of reach. 'Don't look so nervous. I'm not going to strip you naked like you did to me. You can keep that kinky stuff to yourself. Maybe it's a public school thing.'

Tommy walked back to Rose and leant in close. She was shaking so much that they almost banged heads.

'Keep that gun steady whilst I find something to tie them up with,' he said, resting a hand on her back to reassure her. 'After that we're out of here. We're going to a nightclub, Rose. We're going to have a party.'

CHAPTER SIXTY-THREE

'That'll be thirty-six pounds please.'

Lucas's mouth fell open and refused to close. Shocked didn't do his reaction justice. He was horrified. 'Pardon?'

The taxi driver pointed at a small electronic screen to the left of the steering wheel. 'Thirty-six pounds, mate. I'll take thirty-five if it's a problem.'

'A problem?' Lucas blurted out. 'Oh, it's a problem alright—'

'Just pay him,' piped up Mercy from the back seat.

'I would if I could but I can't. I'm skint. Completely. I spent all my money earlier on when we got ripped off by that other—'

Lucas shut up suddenly as Mercy thrust a handful of notes in front of his face. He grabbed them and passed them to the driver in one smooth motion. 'Worth every penny,' he muttered.

'You want the change?' the driver asked.

'Damn right I do,' shot back Lucas. 'I'm not made of money.'

He collected the coins before climbing out of the car.

Mercy was already waiting for him on the pavement, shaking her head. It was still shaking as the taxi drove away.

'Did you have to do that? Embarrass us? Make us look stupid?'

'It's the principle of the thing,' replied Lucas. 'Four pounds is four pounds. And that's four pounds I didn't have a few moments ago.'

'It's not even yours,' snapped Mercy. 'You can keep it if it makes you happy, though. Wouldn't want to set you off again, would I?'

Tensions were fraught as the two of them crossed the road and wandered towards the nightclub. It was closing time. Clubbers were spewing out of the exit. Laughing and stumbling. High on life and whatever else they had managed to lay their sweaty palms on.

'Try and blend in,' instructed Mercy under her breath. 'We'll see if we can sneak in unnoticed whilst the rest of the crowd are coming the other way.'

So that was what they did, all the while following a simple set of unspoken rules. Stay to one side. Don't push and shove. Keep your head down. No eye contact.

There were doormen scattered about, side-eyeing the rowdiest of the men, smiling at the women. Not one of them gave Lucas or Mercy a second glance as they disappeared into the nightclub.

Too easy.

They made their way past the empty pay booth into the main room of the nightclub. The lights were on, illuminating every corner of the huge circular space. Dark walls worked hand in hand with an even darker carpet to soak up the spilt beer and disguise any blood stains. There was no one around, barring several members of bar staff and a DJ on a separate raised platform. His music was still playing. Not at full blast, but loud enough to distract those with revenge in mind.

Mercy attempted to blank out the noise. Focus.

Impossible.

'How are we going to play this?' shouted Lucas, struggling to make himself heard.

'No messing about,' replied Mercy. 'We find Gold and make him tell us where the girl is.'

'And if he won't?'

'He will. He has to. Otherwise I'll … oh, seriously.' Stomping across the dance floor, Mercy came to a halt by the DJ. Lifting a fist, she smashed it against the Perspex screen that separated him from the general public. 'Turn that shit off,' she demanded.

The DJ peered down at Mercy in disgust. He was older than he should've been. Forty going on twenty-five. Muscle vest without the muscles; just big, flabby arms that wobbled when he moved. Over-sized sunglasses perched on top of a glistening forehead. 'Night's over, darling,' he said, dismissing her.

'Good,' nodded Mercy. 'Now turn that music off before I turn it off myself.'

The DJ smirked. Bad move. For a split-second Mercy considered picking up the mixing desk and launching it across the room. Bit much if she was being honest. Instead, she took a detour and wandered all the way around the platform until she found what she was looking for.

A plug socket, hidden away from prying eyes and stray feet.

Mercy pulled out the plug without a second thought.

Silence.

The DJ leapt down onto the dance floor, fists clenched.

'I wouldn't if I was you,' warned Lucas. He pointed at his face where Mercy had struck him earlier. He hadn't studied it yet, but he could tell that his jaw had swollen and a huge bruise had formed. 'This is what she did to me ... and I'm supposed to be her friend.'

'Slight exaggeration,' muttered Mercy.

It took a moment, but the DJ eventually saw sense. The fists dropped first before he turned back towards his decks, pretending to sort through his records.

Mercy turned her attention to the bar staff. One young boy in particular, barely out of his teens, drying pint glasses. 'Get Gold,' she said firmly.

'Please,' Lucas added.

The boy faltered. Glanced at his work colleagues. 'I can't really ... I'm not supposed to ... Mr Gold doesn't like to be disturbed.'

'Maybe he'd prefer it if I went and found him myself,' replied Mercy. 'Barged in on him uninvited—'

'I'll go,' decided the boy, hurrying along the length of the bar towards a door marked *Staff Only*.

Lucas tried to compose himself. He had no idea what was going to happen next. There was a strong possibility things could end very badly for them. Was this it from now on? His new life? Getting into a never-ending series of scraps and scrapes. Mixing with criminals. Dodging the police. Yes, it got the adrenaline pumping alright, but how long would that novelty last? A week or two? A month at best? Soon he would get bored, though. Restless. Then what? Maybe he could do a Tommy. Sneak back home to London and lie low for a while. Grow his hair. A beard. Get some glasses.

His eyes drifted towards the exit. Maybe he could vanish now and never come back. No one would ever find him. He could be in a different town or city in a matter of minutes. So long Stainmouth, you massive shithole.

The future was calling out, practically pleading. What was stopping him? No, not what. Who.

Mercy.

He couldn't leave her. Not here. All by herself. He was better than that. He had morals. Principles. Besides, how far would he get with only four measly pounds to his name?

Lucas stood his ground as the door marked *Staff Only* swung open and in marched two men. The one on the left was of average height and build with a jet-black ponytail, dark eyes and an incredibly tanned face. He was flashily dressed in a black shirt, unbuttoned to the chest, white trousers and suede loafers. Any accessories were all gold. And there were lots of them. Rings. Bracelets. Chains. Enough to make you sink if you were pushed into deep water.

The other man – bald head, handlebar moustache – was massive in both height and width. Muscle on top of muscle on top of muscle. Straight off the cover of a body building magazine.

'I'm Vernon Gold,' announced Ponytail, casting an eye over the new arrivals. 'Is there a problem?'

'Yeah, you're looking at it,' replied Mercy, rubbing her hands together. 'A big, big problem.'

CHAPTER SIXTY-FOUR

Tommy strolled out of Cockleshell Farm with a wicked grin etched across his face.

He had struck the jackpot in the form of a black Audi A8 parked up right outside the door. A lovely motor, make no mistake. Agatha's at a guess.

The grin vanished when the driver's door opened and a stocky, fair-haired Scandinavian appeared in the darkness. 'Miss Pleasant?' he said, eyeing Tommy with suspicion.

'Not the last time I looked.' Tommy cursed himself. This wasn't the time for smart arse wisecracks. 'She's still inside.'

Olaf stepped forward. As did Tommy, resting a hand on the driver's chest. 'Whoa there, tiger! You really don't want to go in—'

Olaf's reactions were lightning fast. Grabbing Tommy by the wrist, he twisted it around his back until he squealed out in agony and dropped to his knees. Olaf was all set to increase the pressure when something firm stabbed against the side of his head.

'Let go of him,' said Rose, her hand trembling as much as her voice as she held the gun at arm's length.

Olaf did as he was told. Safety first. He was no good to anybody dead.

'Where are the car keys?' asked Rose.

Olaf pointed at the Audi.

Rose kept the gun trained on the driver as she glanced down at Tommy. 'Are you okay?'

'Not particularly,' he moaned, clambering unsteadily to his feet. 'I don't know why everybody keeps trying to hurt me. I can't be that dislikeable.' Tommy waited. 'I'm not, am I?'

Rose chose to ignore that. 'What shall we do with him?'

'Kill him,' spat Tommy, his anger fuelled by the pain that was coursing through his body.

Rose started to shake. Not as much as Olaf, though.

'Okay, don't kill him,' frowned Tommy. 'Just put one in his kneecap if you like.'

Olaf leant forward, covering his legs the best he could.

'That's not ... no ... no, I won't do that,' stuttered Rose. 'We could ... I don't know ... tie him up or something.'

Tommy shook his head. Too much effort, not enough time. Instead, he held out his hand. 'Give me that.'

Rose hesitated. He wanted the gun.

'Trust me,' said Tommy.

She didn't. Not in the slightest. But she also knew that she was completely out of her depth.

Rose released her grip so Tommy could take the gun. 'That way, you big Danish lump,' he said, gesturing towards the barns behind the farmhouse.

Olaf started to walk. 'Norwegian.'

'My apologies.' Tommy slipped into step behind the

313

driver, pressing the gun into the small of his back. 'Me getting your nationality wrong, however, is probably the least of your worries at this moment in time.'

Rose watched as they disappeared into the darkness. As soon as they were out of sight she jumped into the Audi and covered her ears. Tommy was going to shoot him. Shoot him dead. That much was obvious. She should have stopped him when she had the chance. Talked him out of it. Refused to give him the gun.

She should've. She could've. And yet she didn't.

Rose was still fretting over her actions when the door beside her swung open and then slammed shut in quick succession. It was Tommy.

'Did you …?' Rose tailed off.

'Did I …?'

'Is he …?'

'Is he what?'

Rose tried to breathe. 'Dead?'

'Dead?' Tommy screwed up his face as he dropped the gun in Rose's lap. 'Why would he be dead?'

'Why *wouldn't* he be dead?' No, wrong question. 'Where is he then?' asked Rose.

'I locked him in with the pigs,' revealed Tommy. 'Told them to watch over him. They're good like that. Very obedient.'

The breath came easier now. 'I thought—'

'Yeah, I know what you thought,' said Tommy, wagging a finger at her. 'Now, put your foot down and get us to Stainmouth quick sharpish. None of that twenty-miles-per-hour shit neither. This motor deserves better than that.'

CHAPTER SIXTY-FIVE

Agatha used her tongue to push the gag out of her mouth.

She was sat in the middle of the sitting room carpet, back to back with Miles. Tommy had used some plastic ties he had found in the kitchen to secure their wrists together. Yes, it hurt when she tried to move, but nothing serious. Not enough to anger or upset her. And certainly not enough to hold a grudge against Tommy when they met again.

If they met again.

'They must've taken the Audi,' she said between breaths. 'That wasn't Olaf driving. He's more ... graceful than that. The thing is, if that wasn't him, then where is he?' Agatha frowned as dark thoughts permeated her brain. 'They wouldn't have killed him, would they? I hope not. Good drivers are so hard to find these days. They're normally so chatty. Olaf's barely spoken to me all the time I've known him. You are listening to me, aren't you, Miles?'

Miles only reply was to mumble something completely unintelligible to the human ear.

'Move your gag,' said Agatha. 'It's not that tricky. I managed to do it.' She waited for Miles to stop huffing and puffing before she spoke again. 'You made hard work of that.'

'O'Strife forced it down the back of my throat,' Miles panted. 'I bet he didn't do that to you.' He took a moment to study what he had spat out on the floor. 'Are they ... tights?'

'Proud Mary's tights,' Agatha guessed. 'Probably the same ones she wears when farming. Covered in mud and manure.'

'You're enjoying this, aren't you?' Miles twisted his neck until he could see one side of Agatha's face. 'I mean ... you're smiling ...'

'I'm not.'

'You are. God knows why. It's the middle of the night ... we've had a gun pointed at us ... been tied up ... by your own team ... who have then stolen your car ... maybe killed your driver ... and you're still smiling! That's a tricky one to get my head around.'

Agatha straightened her face. Fair point. Nevertheless, there was always a counter argument. 'Try and see the bigger picture, Miles. Yes, some of their actions may have been a little ill-advised, but at least the four of them are working together now. Even Tommy. They care about something. The child perhaps. Maybe each other. It doesn't matter. With a bit of fine tuning they'll be a well-oiled machine.'

'They'll be dead before that,' muttered Miles.

'So negative,' said Agatha, shaking her head. 'Right, do you think you can stand? Maybe we can make our way into the kitchen. Find something sharp.'

That was more like it, thought Miles. 'Yes, I can stand. We should be able to stay upright if we keep our backs pressed together. Shall we give it a go? On three?'

'On three,' agreed Agatha tentatively. She wasn't as young as she used to be and feared her knees may struggle to support her weight without her hands to aid and assist. Still, it was too late to pull out now. 'One ... two ...'

The *three* caught in her throat when the door to the sitting room at Cockleshell Farm burst open and in stomped Olaf.

'That answers that particular question,' said Miles, glancing over his shoulder.

'I never had a doubt,' lied Agatha.

Crouching down beside them, Olaf produced a knife from somewhere about his person and silently set to work on the binds around their wrists and ankles, starting, naturally, with Agatha.

'They stole my car,' he grumbled under his breath.

'I'll get you a new one.' Agatha stopped and sniffed. Turned up her nose. 'What's that smell?'

'Pigs,' grunted Olaf.

'I'll take your word for it.' Agatha held her breath until her driver had finished. By the time she had stood up and brushed herself down, Miles was already on his feet.

'The Saab's still here,' he said, gesturing towards the rear of the farm. 'I parked it around the back.'

'Fine.' Agatha removed her phone from inside her jacket before turning her back on the two men.

'We should probably think about leaving,' urged Miles,

itching to get out of there. 'You can talk in the car on the way to the nightclub.'

Agatha raised her free hand. 'Patience. Have you learnt nothing? You don't just rush head first into the lion's den.'

'Don't you?' Miles ground his teeth, frustrated. 'What *do* you do then?'

A smiling Agatha placed the phone to her ear. 'You get another lion.'

CHAPTER SIXTY-SIX

Vernon Gold lifted a finger and wagged it in Mercy's direction.

'I know you. I recognise your voice. We spoke on the phone, didn't we?'

Mercy nodded. There was no point lying. 'We've come for the swap. Benji's child for the cash and drugs. Just like you wanted.'

'Please … a little decorum,' winced Gold. 'I want you all to leave,' he said, addressing the bar staff. 'Don't worry about the mess. You can sort it out later. And you,' he added, turning towards the DJ. 'You can fetch your equipment another day.'

The DJ was quick to reply. 'That might not be possible, Mr Gold, I'm—'

'You can fetch it another day,' repeated Gold. 'Or don't fetch it at all. The choice is yours.'

End of conversation.

'Yes … of course … sorry,' spluttered the DJ, hurrying towards the exit.

Gold waited for the last of them to leave before he spoke

again. 'I thought we had an agreement. We were supposed to meet at my house—'

'That wasn't your house,' said Mercy.

Gold began to laugh. A sneering cackle that bounced off the ceiling and reverberated around the huge room. 'Looks like I've been rumbled. Have you been there? Oh, you have, haven't you? I bet the Chief Constable was overjoyed to see you.'

Mercy tensed up. 'One of our friends is dead because of you. The police shot her—'

'We don't know that for sure,' chipped in Lucas.

Mercy wasn't listening. 'She wasn't part of this world. She was innocent. She didn't deserve to die.'

'So sad,' said Gold, sticking out his bottom lip. 'Maybe I can contribute to the funeral costs. Doberman, grab me the loose change out of the nearest till. I don't mind stumping up twenty … thirty pounds even …'

Doberman made a curious snorting sound. A laugh perhaps, from a man who didn't know how to.

'Cut the bullshit, Gold,' said Lucas, growing increasingly frustrated by the second. 'Let's get this swap done and then we can all go home.'

'Yes … well … that might not be possible,' said Gold slowly. He walked behind the bar. Poured himself a drink. 'There's no easy way to tell you this,' he began, swilling the contents around his glass. 'That swap deal I mentioned … it's off the table. My fault predominantly. I jumped to conclusions. You're not entirely blame-free, though. You lied to me. You're lying now.'

'What do you mean?' growled Mercy.

'I know you didn't steal from me,' said Gold. 'So, why do you keep pretending you did?'

Mercy tried to remain impassive. It was hard, though. Especially when the bottom had just tumbled out of her plan.

'Don't get me wrong,' continued Gold. 'Cocaine and a large amount of money were stolen. Just not by you. It was someone you know, though. That's what I was dealing with when you turned up uninvited. Maybe you'd like to see what happens to those who dare to steal from me.'

Gold nodded at Doberman, who promptly disappeared through the door behind him. He returned a few seconds later, dragging something across the ground. Something big and heavy. A body.

It was Cutz.

'Naughty boy.' Gold gently shook his head. 'He should've known better than to take what wasn't his. Still, rest in peace.'

Mercy swallowed. 'He's dead?'

'Not quite,' replied Gold. 'Like I said, you rudely interrupted us. No time like the present, though ...'

Without missing his cue, Doberman lifted a boot and pressed it down on Cutz's throat. A harsh rasping sound rose up from the youth's prostrate body, as if the last gasps of air were escaping from his chest.

'Stop!' Mercy lunged forward. She had almost made up the distance between them when Doberman swung, his forearm chopping her at the neck. She dropped like a stone, curling up into a ball. Over and, for now at least, out.

'That was a bit silly,' said Gold, coming out from behind the bar. 'She actually thought she had a chance.'

Lucas rushed to Mercy's side. At the same time Doberman lifted his foot off Cutz and prepared himself for the prospect of a new challenger.

'Relax,' said Gold, coming to a halt beside his henchman. 'There's no need for you to raise a sweat. Not when we've got others who are willing to get their hands dirty at the click of my fingers.'

Gold did just that. At once, they emerged from the shadows. From every crack and every crevice. A dark and imposing presence. The stench of violence seeping from their pores.

'The Gold Squad,' grinned Gold. 'My boys on the street. My distributors. They do what I ask without question—'

'Like peddling drugs to the daft and desperate?' muttered Lucas. 'Giving out beatings to those who dare to cross you? I'm sure their mothers would be proud.'

'So judgmental,' laughed Gold. 'If I was you I'd be careful what I say. The odds on you getting out of here alive are decreasing with every passing second. Any one of these men would willingly stick a knife in your back if I gave the word.'

Lucas tried to sit Mercy up, wary that she might collapse at any moment. Her body had gone worryingly limp and she was struggling to breathe. 'Okay, so we lied,' Lucas admitted. 'But that's only because we were desperate. We're not here to cause trouble; we're here for Benji's child. That's all. After that we'll go. You'll never see us again. I mean, what can you possibly want with a little girl?'

'Nothing,' replied Gold, unable to stop himself from smiling. 'Especially when the little girl in question doesn't even exist.'

CHAPTER SIXTY-SEVEN

Rose parked the Audi around the corner from the nightclub.

'Wait here.' Tommy opened the passenger-side door. Stuck a leg out. 'Give me half an hour. If I'm not back—'

Rose moved quickly to grab his arm. 'No. Not again. You're not leaving me. Not on my own.'

Tommy tried to shrug her off. 'Don't be like that. I'm better flying solo.'

'What makes you think that?' argued Rose, holding on tight. 'You'd have been killed at least three times in the past few days if it wasn't for other people.'

'That's not true.' Tommy stopped struggling. 'Okay, so it's *partly* true. There have been occasions when I might have needed a minuscule amount of assistance.'

'And this will definitely be another of those occasions.' With that, Rose released her grip and climbed out of the car. She waited for Tommy to get out too before locking it. She felt the dull tap of the gun against her hip as they made their way towards the nightclub. What was she still doing with it? How had she even ended up with it in the first place?

Closing time had been and gone. The clubbers had

largely dispersed, but there were still three or four doormen hanging around in the entrance, idly chatting before they called it a night and headed for home.

'I know another way in,' said Tommy. He steered Rose onto the opposite side of the road so the two of them could walk straight past the nightclub without being noticed. Once they were out of sight they crossed back over again. At Tommy's behest, they kept moving. Down a side street. To the rear of the building.

Tommy raised himself up onto his tiptoes when he reached the wall and peeked over the top.

There was nobody there. The yard was all clear.

'Follow me,' he said, scrambling over the best he could. It was only when he had dropped down onto the other side that he realised that particular request may have been easier said than done.

'It's too high,' grumbled Rose. 'My feet keep slipping. I can't get a purchase.'

Tommy looked around. Spotted a bucket hidden behind one of the industrial waste bins.

'Here,' he said, passing it over the wall. 'You can use it to stand on.'

'Really?' sighed Rose. 'I was thinking about taking a shower.'

Tommy smiled. 'You've changed. You never used to be so sarcastic.'

'Not until I met you.' With that, Rose's head and shoulders appeared over the top of the wall. 'Nearly there ... can't quite ... can you help me please?'

'Certainly, ma'am,' grinned Tommy, reaching up. 'Let me take you by the hand and lead you to paradise.'

He grabbed her by the armpits instead. It wasn't particularly ladylike, but at least it did the job. A few seconds later and he had hauled her over the wall without too much difficulty.

With both of them back on two feet, Tommy turned his attention to the fire exit.

He stopped suddenly. Cursed himself.

The yard wasn't quite as clear as he had first imagined.

There was someone there. Hunched over by the door. Listen hard enough and Tommy could even hear them breathing. No, not breathing. Panting. Like a panic attack turned up a notch.

Tommy raised a hand before Rose could walk straight past him. Pointed at the figure. Placed a finger to his lips.

Rose nodded her understanding, the message loud and clear.

Do not make a sound.

Tommy strode forward, eating up the ground in a matter of seconds. He was close now. Close enough to touch.

No, don't do that. He didn't want to startle them. Something more subtle would do the trick.

Tommy coughed loudly and the figure jumped out of their skin.

It was Jumbo. The third youth from the house on Eastern Avenue. He tried to stand up straight, but failed tragically when his leg gave way beneath him. It was the same leg that Tommy had put a bullet in. Now it was bandaged up.

'I see you took my advice and changed out of that white tracksuit,' remarked Tommy. He studied the youth's hands for any potential weapons. There were none. 'What you doing out here?'

Jumbo wiped his sleeve across his face. His cheeks were wet, his eyes stained with tears. 'This is fucked up, man. So fucked up.'

Rose kept her distance. 'What is?'

'They killed Benji and now they're going to kill Cutz. I'll be next. I know it. I don't want to die.'

'Then go.' Tommy gestured towards the wall. 'Up and over and don't come back. Nobody will ever know.'

Jumbo shook his head. 'Gold will know. He'll find me. And then Doberman will make me suffer.'

'Gold's over, mate,' Tommy insisted. 'One way or another, he's going down. Now you need to get gone before that particular shit hits the fan. Trust me, you don't want to get caught in the crossfire.' Tommy rested a hand on Jumbo's arm. 'I shouldn't have shot you,' he said sincerely. 'That was a dick-ish move. I was just showing off. Trying to prove how tough I am. Sorry.'

Jumbo nodded. He tried to stand again, struggling for a moment before Tommy supported his weight. Once he was steady on his feet, Tommy led him over to the wall. Found another bucket.

It took longer than either of them would've wanted or expected – coupled with an infinite amount of grunting and groaning – but, finally, Jumbo was over.

'I'm not the only one who's changed,' said Rose, as

Tommy made his way back towards her. 'You have too.'

'Nah, that was all an act,' he argued. 'I had to get rid of him somehow. He was ruining our date night.'

Tommy opened the fire exit door and looked along the narrow corridor. It was dark in there, but he could still make out something up ahead. Laid out in the doorway to the Manager's Office. It looked like clothes, discarded in a heap.

Then it shifted slightly. Moaned in agony.

Yes, it was clothes. But it was clothes with a body still inside.

Tommy shut the door gently behind them as they stepped into the corridor. He was all set to creep towards the body when the door to the nightclub opened and Doberman appeared in the entrance. Slipping into the shadows, Tommy pressed his back against the wall, relieved to see that Rose had followed suit. They watched as Doberman headed straight for the Manager's Office. Bending over, he grabbed the body by the arms and started to drag it back towards the nightclub. He kept his head down at all times, concentrating on the job in hand. He hadn't seen them. Tommy was sure of it. They were safe.

For now.

Doberman hauled the body over the threshold and slammed the door shut, plunging the corridor once more into darkness.

Tommy moved swiftly. Taking Rose by the hand, he hurried towards the Manager's Office and practically threw her inside.

'Shit. That was close,' he whispered, closing the door behind them.

'The body,' said Rose, breathing heavily. Her stomach turned over when she noticed a fresh patch of blood by her feet. 'Was it ... Mercy?'

Tommy hesitated. 'I don't think so—'

'Lucas?'

'It's hard to tell. Maybe it was Cutz. You heard what Jumbo said.' Without thinking, Tommy veered towards the Cognac he has sampled the last time he was in there. He needed a drink. Badly. 'Do you want one?' he asked, waving a glass at Rose.

'No ... I'm not really a drinker.' Rose shifted awkwardly by the door. 'Besides, I don't think we should be—'

'Cheers.' Tommy lifted the glass to his lips and swallowed its contents. He could feel it going down, burning his throat, settling in his empty stomach. It tasted delicious.

Exactly how your last ever drink should taste.

CHAPTER SIXTY-EIGHT

Lucas replayed the sentence several times in his head.

Especially when the little girl in question doesn't even exist.

'Oh, you look so confused,' said Gold, trying not to smile. 'Maybe Cutz would like to fill you in on the details. I mean, he was as guilty as me of leading you astray.'

Doberman walked casually over to Cutz and hauled him to his feet, holding him there with one hand. His eyes were closed and his body was limp. There was blood running down his face.

Lucas had seen some sights in his life and Cutz was up there with the worst of them. He doubted the boy could speak at all, let alone speak the truth.

'Go on,' urged Gold. 'You're not usually so shy.'

Doberman took Cutz by the jaw, squeezing it until the youth's mouth flopped open. 'No ... child,' he spluttered, before coughing uncontrollably.

'A little more please,' insisted Gold. 'Just the facts. No need to embellish.'

Doberman squeezed again, hard enough for Cutz to cry out in agony. He knew the way to make it stop, though.

'There was … no child,' he sobbed. 'There … never was.'

'That's not what Gina said,' argued Lucas. 'She told us Benji took her.'

'She lied.' Cutz gasped, the pain clearly too much for him to take. 'She had a … miscarriage. That's why … her and Benji … split up. They never … got over it.'

Lucas could feel the colour draining from his face. A wild goose chase. That's what this was. A wild goose chase without the wild goose. Just a chase then.

A chase that could ultimately lead to their deaths. Again.

'I think we've heard enough.' Gold put a hand to his mouth. Yawned. 'It's late. My bed is calling and yet … perhaps there's time for a little more fun. Doberman, release that snivelling thief and go to my office. There's a baseball bat behind my desk. Bring it to me please.'

Doberman let go of Cutz, the youth crumpling to the floor in an ugly heap. As an afterthought, the big man lashed out with his foot, striking Cutz cleanly in the face. The resulting *crunch* was enough to make Lucas turn away in disgust. When he looked again, Cutz was still.

Doberman, meanwhile, had gone.

Tommy put the glass back down on the desk.

He was half-wondering whether or not to have another drink when something caught his eye. It was leant against Gold's armchair.

A baseball bat.

He picked it up, testing its weight. It was made of wood. Good quality. Solid. Smash someone in the mouth with that and there'd be shitting out teeth for the next few weeks.

Tommy walked back towards the door with an extra spring in his step. At least he had a weapon now. Which reminded him ...

'Have you still got that gun?' he asked Rose.

She nodded. A reluctant nod. Like she didn't want to admit it, but she felt obliged to tell the truth.

'Maybe I should have it,' Tommy suggested. It was partly for Rose's peace of mind. Mostly, though, because he liked the idea of walking out there with a gun in one hand and a baseball bat in the other. How cool was that? Jaws would drop. Bottoms would wobble. People would run for cover.

'No,' replied Rose.

Tommy stared at her, dumbstruck. His mind had strayed so far he had forgotten the question.

'I'm keeping it.' Rose pulled the gun out of her pocket, gripping it in both hands as if to emphasize the point. 'It's all I've got.'

Tommy screwed up his face. 'Fine. Just make sure you use it if and when the need arises. Don't go all ... *mousey* on me. If I give the word you've got to start firing. Comprende?'

This time Rose chose to neither nod nor shake her head. She simply trembled.

Tommy rested his fingers on the door handle. 'I haven't got a clue what we're going to find out there,' he began. 'It could be calm and serene. It could be mayhem and chaos. Either way, you and me have got to stick together, right? If it's all kicking off we've got to watch each other's backs. I don't mind if it's a fuckin' blood bath as long as it's not our fuckin' blood we're bathing in. Got it?'

'I think I'm going to be sick,' mumbled Rose.

'Relax,' said Tommy, regretting the tone of his team talk. 'We're dead already, remember. How bad can it actually be?'

He opened the door, took one step forward and stumbled to a halt. There was something there. At one with the darkness of the corridor. Snarling instead of breathing. Inhuman.

Vernon Gold's pet pooch.

Doberman.

'*That* bad,' muttered Tommy under his breath.

CHAPTER SIXTY-NINE

Mercy could feel herself growing stronger by the second.

The breath came more freely now. Her head had stopped spinning and her neck no longer throbbed. She stayed down, though, waiting for the opportunity. Any opportunity.

Take your eye off the ball, Vernon Gold, and I'll whip your head off your shoulders.

He was a cockroach. A small man with a loud mouth and a fat wallet. She had fought bigger, stronger, faster. She had nothing to fear.

Doberman, on the other hand, was a different proposition entirely.

Mercy tensed up. She could feel someone pulling at her. Grabbing her by the arms. Trying to lift her up. It was Lucas. What was he doing?

Gold had the same thought. 'What are you doing?'

'What does it look like?' said Lucas.

'Don't get all cocky,' Gold sneered. 'Doberman may have gone, but I've still got the rest of my boys at hand.'

Doberman had gone. Mercy let that sink in. Any opportunity.

'On your knees.' Gold was enjoying himself. Mercy could tell that by his voice. 'I want you to beg for forgiveness. Plead with me. Try and appeal to my better nature.'

Lucas lowered Mercy gently to the ground before kneeling beside her. Mercy kept her head down. Don't give anything away. Not yet. It was hard to resist, though. To fight the anger. Not when Gold was goading them.

'If you want to leave here alive then you'd better start—' Gold stopped without warning. Mercy knew why. She had heard it, too. A disturbance in another part of the building. Crashing and banging.

'What's going on back there?' Gold called out.

Mercy lifted her head. Gold had turned away from them. He was looking in the other direction.

Any opportunity.

This opportunity.

Tommy slammed the door shut in Doberman's face.

That wouldn't hold him. Not a chance. And it didn't.

Tommy had barely hopped out of the way when the door flew open. Rose wasn't so lucky, though. The door hit her and she fell. Tommy kept an eye on her as she rolled over, relieved when she clambered, albeit slowly, to her feet.

He kept his other eye on Doberman.

For a big lump, he moved surprisingly quickly. Striding into the office, he ignored Rose completely and focussed his full attention on Tommy.

Tommy's response was to leap up onto the desk. He had no idea why. This wasn't some shit action film – this was real life. All Doberman had to do was charge at him and it would be game over. He could take him out at the ankles. Legs. Waist. Torso. Neck. Whichever he preferred. Maybe all at the same time.

As expected, Doberman turned his strides into a sprint. He left the ground a moment later, arms outstretched as he flew through the air.

Tommy tried to think. He had two choices. Dive out of the way or—

Doberman slammed into him before he could think of the second.

Wrapping his arms around Tommy's waist, there were two of them flying now. Not for long, though.

Tommy landed first, his back taking the brunt of it as he crashed into the wall behind him. He yelped out loud and then screamed even louder as Doberman landed on top of him. The big man's weight was enough to knock the air clean out of his lungs. He couldn't breathe. And if you can't breathe …

Tommy watched helplessly as Doberman began to stir. Placing both hands on the carpet, Gold's henchman was preparing to push himself up, ready for round two.

Finally the breath came. It was enough to jerk Tommy into life. Wriggling furiously, he tried to squirm out from under Doberman's body and sit up. To his astonishment, the baseball bat was still in his hand. That was more than a stroke of luck; that was a bloody miracle. Doberman was too close, though. Tommy couldn't swing. He could barely move his arms at all.

There was another way, though. There was always another way.

Clutching the bat in both hands, Tommy waited for Doberman to raise his head just a fraction off his chest before he jabbed him under the chin with as much force as he could muster. It made a peculiar *clunking* sound. Bat on bone. Followed by the ugly rattle of *crumbling* teeth.

Doberman's face fell forward, coming to a rest in Tommy's crotch. A frantic Tommy pushed it to one side before crawling out from under the man mountain's limp body. He carried on moving. Around the desk. Out into the open.

'Rose.' He looked around the office, but his eyes had glazed over. 'Rose ... where are—?'

The sentence died as Tommy was rolled onto his back. Before he knew it, Doberman had clambered on top of him, pinning him to the ground. There was blood pouring from his mouth, fuelling his rage. Tommy didn't have the strength to push him off, but at least he had the bat.

Had the bat.

Tommy was already swinging it at Doberman's head when he realised his hands were empty. A second later the bat was being pressed against Tommy's throat. A second after that the pressure increased and Tommy couldn't breathe. A second after that and ...

Wait.

No more seconds.

Rose held the gun at arm's length as she shuffled across the office.

What was wrong with her hands? Stop shaking. Please, stop shaking.

She came to a halt. She was right behind Doberman. He was leaning over Tommy. He hadn't seen her coming. She had a clear shot.

No, that wasn't her. She couldn't shoot a man in the back. Not in cold blood. She wasn't a murderer.

The counter argument. He was evil. A savage. He would kill Tommy and then he would kill her. Taking a life meant nothing to him.

'Rose,' croaked Tommy. She stared at him in horror. His eyes were popping out of their sockets. Doberman was choking the life out of him. Tommy was going to die.

Rose pulled the trigger.

She was aiming for the back of Doberman's head.

She missed.

CHAPTER SEVENTY

Mercy was up and on her feet.

She was almost within touching distance of Vernon Gold when the gunshot rang out around the nightclub. It was too late to stop now. Whilst everybody else froze, Mercy made her move. She grabbed Gold by the neck. Kicked out at his kneecap. Dragged him to the ground.

He squealed like a stuck pig and the whole room came alive again.

The Gold Squad emerged from the shadows, surrounding Mercy in a matter of seconds.

'Come any nearer and I'll break his neck,' she shouted, securing Gold in a headlock. She increased the pressure and he squealed again. Could she do it? Break someone's neck? It was a horrible thought. Sickening. Her mind swerved and a different perspective entered the fray. Revenge for those that had fallen. Benji. And Rose. Poor Rose.

Mercy had no doubts now.

More than anyone she had ever met, Vernon Gold deserved to die.

The gun recoiled in Rose's hand the moment she pulled the trigger.

She dropped it, panic-stricken. It would've landed by her toes if she hadn't stumbled backwards.

She had shot him …

Tommy was laid out on the carpet, flat on his back. He was still breathing, though. Short, gasping breaths. Drawing strength from a draining reserve, he pushed the baseball bat off his throat and lifted his head. He was fine. Well, almost. Close enough to fine as he was ever going to get.

Unlike Doberman …

Rose had been aiming for the back of his head. In one end, out the other. A kill shot, make no mistake. Unfortunately – or as luck would have it – she had missed that particular target and hit another instead.

Doberman's left buttock.

Now he was on his knees, clutching at the wounded area. Blood was gushing between his fingertips, staining his trousers, running down his legs.

Tommy stood up slowly. He was holding the baseball bat. 'I should cave his skull in.'

'Don't,' said Rose hastily.

'I should … but I won't.' Tommy lowered the bat. 'Thanks by the way. You saved my life.'

'Again.' Rose stepped around Doberman, who was making a strange whimpering sound. 'You don't think he'll bleed to death, do you?'

'Oh, because that would be a massive shame, wouldn't it?' Tommy picked up the gun. Made his way towards the exit. 'Come on. We need to find Mercy and Lucas. I'll pull the bullet out of that big goon's arse when we've finished. I promise. I'm looking forward to it already.'

Tommy opened the door more cautiously this time. The corridor was empty, but he could hear noises coming from the nightclub. Shouts and screams. Chaos and commotion. He tried to swallow, his throat drier than ever. He was desperate for another drink, but that would have to wait.

He held out the gun. 'Do you want this?'

Rose shook her head.

Tommy understood. He set off along the corridor, baseball bat in one hand, gun in the other. The all action hero he had always dreamt of.

Once perhaps. Not anymore.

The *Staff Only* door swung open to reveal two, not one.

Mercy tried to focus. There was a man, but it wasn't Doberman. Too small. Too thin. Too normal.

Too Tommy.

And behind him. Smaller still. Female. How could that even be?

'Rose,' she cried. 'You're still alive.'

Rose nodded, keen to provide extra confirmation.

'Say hello to the fuckin' cavalry,' roared Tommy. He looked around the nightclub. Counted the heads that surrounded them. 'Shit. Probably gonna' need more horses.'

'Where have you been?' snapped Lucas. '*Both* of you,' he added, half-smiling at Rose.

As if drawn by a magnetic force, the four merged

together. Gold was somewhere in between, struggling to stand, Mercy's forearm a constant reminder of everything that had gone wrong.

'There is no kid,' whispered Lucas. 'They lied to us. All of them. Gina. Gold. Cutz ...'

'Talking of which ...' Tommy pointed the bat at the crumpled body on the ground.

Lucas nodded. 'Doberman's handiwork.' He stopped to glance over his shoulder.

'Don't worry about that meathead,' grinned Tommy. 'Rose dealt with him.'

'Rose?' Lucas opened his mouth and then shut it just as quickly. How Rose had managed that was a question for another day. *If* they ever saw another day. 'Any ideas how we get out of this mess alive?'

'You need to watch more films,' said Tommy. 'The good guys always win.'

'Who says we're the good guys?' muttered Lucas.

'There's always one character that has to die, though,' Tommy continued. 'It's normally the most boring one. The one the viewers haven't really warmed to.' Tommy patted Lucas on the shoulder. 'Bad luck. Don't take it personally.'

Mercy had heard enough. 'Cut it out, you two. This isn't some kind of last stand. They're just teenagers. Nothing more. We can walk out of here any time we like.'

Vernon Gold began to laugh. It was strained, nothing more than a staccato gasp, but it was still a laugh. 'Silly bitch,' he croaked. 'You have no idea what they're capable of.'

As if a switch had been flicked, powering them into life, the Gold Squad drew their weapons. Tommy grimaced at the vast array. Knives of all shapes and sizes. Wooden clubs and batons. Metal chains, steel poles. And a taser. *A fucking taser.*

Not a gun in sight, though. Well, only one …

Tommy raised his arm and fired a warning shot into the ceiling.

Except he didn't. And neither did the gun. He had pulled the trigger, but nothing had happened.

'Bollocks.' Disheartened, Tommy tossed the gun across the dancefloor.

It was only when it hit the ground that a *crack* echoed around the nightclub.

Everybody ducked, dived, dodged. Took cover. Crawled to safety. Everybody except Tommy. He was still trying to figure it out. That wasn't possible. The gun was empty. Unless … maybe it had jammed. Stalled. Let him down like everything else in his life.

Or maybe it wasn't his gun at all.

He was still none the wiser when a voice snapped him out of his thoughts. Clear and concise, it was the kind of voice that demanded immediate attention.

'Good morning, ladies and gentlemen. Would anybody like to explain what the hell is going on here?'

CHAPTER SEVENTY-ONE

All eyes shifted towards the exit.

Towards the three people stood in the doorway.

Mercy smiled. Lucas frowned. Tommy screwed up his face. And Rose … Rose remained largely impassive. Neither happy nor sad. Scared, yes. Permanently scared. But that was nothing out of the ordinary.

On the face of it, the three new arrivals were hardly that impressive to those who knew no better. Two women and a man, one of the women much older than the other. A mother and her children then. At first glance perhaps.

A second glance, however, would have suggested otherwise.

All three were armed, although two had nothing on show, discretion a priority. The message was still clear, though. Not shouted from the rooftops perhaps, but quietly effective, nonetheless.

Miles was the only one with his weapon on display. His trusty Sig Sauer P365, he still had it raised above his head, arm locked, hand steady. That explained the gunshot, thought Tommy. And the hole in the ceiling. Tommy had seen him do that before, of course. Back when nobody knew each other and it was all a blur. A lifetime ago. Or just a week. Same difference really.

Tommy worked his way along the line. To Miles's left was Agatha. She seemed calm enough. Maybe she was used to these kinds of situations. Fair play to her.

'As tempting as it may be, Miss Mee, please try and refrain from killing that man,' she called out. 'Especially with your bare hands. You don't know where he's been.' She gave Mercy less than three seconds to do as she asked. 'You did hear me, didn't you,' she said impatiently. 'Under no circumstances are you to kill that man. There are far too many witnesses for a start. We can't silence them all.' Agatha paused. 'Can we?' She paused again. 'That was a joke. Nobody will be silenced. Not if you all do as you're told.'

'He killed Benji,' shouted Mercy, increasing the pressure on Gold's neck. 'Maybe not with his own hands, but on his orders. He deserves to die.'

'That's as may be, but not like this,' replied Agatha. 'Justice will prevail. Trust me. But for now, let him go.'

Mercy huffed and puffed, stamped and swallowed. Without warning, she released her grip on Gold and let him fall to the floor. He was up quickly, though. On his knees. Waving his arms about. Screaming at all those who usually obeyed him.

'Stand your ground … fight back … don't run away.'

'Oh, we don't want anyone to run away,' said Agatha. There was a twinkle in her eye. Rose had spotted it, even if no one else had. What did she mean? *We don't want anyone to run away.* The uneasy feeling in the pit of Rose's stomach switched suddenly to a gruesome image. Picture the scene. A bloody mess where everybody in sight had been riddled with bullets, wiped out on the dance floor in a violent massacre. Not just Gold and his Gold Squad either, but the whole lot of them. Her Nearly Dearly Departed Club included. After all, it wasn't as if Agatha needed them anymore. They were surplus to requirements. And what better way to dispose of them than with an assortment of other bodies. The more the merrier. Pile 'em up high. Toss a match on top and stand well back.

Or maybe Agatha meant nothing of the kind. She probably just disliked running. All exercise perhaps.

Stop. Take a breath, Rose. Relax.

'This is Zara Carmichael,' said Agatha, introducing the third new arrival. The lion she had insisted on calling back at Cockleshell Farm. 'She has a proposition for you.'

Tommy's interest piqued as the woman beside Agatha stepped forward. This was more like it. Ooh la la. Very nice. Right up his street. If he had a street. Unfortunately, his natural habitat was loitering down dark alleys where they had carelessly neglected to install any security cameras. A woman like that, however, deserved to be in full sight at all times. Up close and personal.

An elbow in the ribs brought Tommy back to reality.

'Put your tongue away, dickhead,' whispered Mercy. 'Carry on drooling and we'll all drown.'

Back in the doorway, Zara Carmichael cast an eye over the assembled throng. 'You can lower your weapons,' she said calmly. 'All of you. I'm here to talk business; not get embroiled in gang warfare.' She waited for a handful of the Gold Squad to do as she asked before she spoke again. 'Many of you will know – or at least heard – of my father, Jackie Carmichael. He's run Stainmouth for years. Controlled the town with a firm hand and an iron rule. And yet now … now things have changed. He's ill. Dying. My father won't be around forever—'

'What is this? Some kind of eulogy?' Vernon Gold tried to stand, but didn't get far before Mercy swiped his legs out from under him, sending him sprawling to the ground with a satisfying *splat*.

'I am not Jackie Carmichael,' continued Zara. 'Yes, I'm his daughter, but we come from different worlds. I'm not such a … blunt instrument. I'm a little more sophisticated in my ways. But, like my father, the one thing I can spot is an opportunity. If I'm going to continue to run Stainmouth then I need my own people. Men and women who are willing to work for me.' Zara paused, keen to lift the anticipation levels before she delivered the punchline. 'Whatever Vernon Gold pays you I am prepared to double,' she announced. 'If any of you are interested, talk to me on your way out. If not, well, that's your choice I suppose. The wrong choice, of course, but who am I to judge?'

Armed with only her phone and an empty contact list, Zara Carmichael moved away from the door, readying herself for any new recruits. She didn't have to wait for long as, one by one, the Gold Squad formed an orderly queue. They lowered their hoods, straightened their hair. Zara took their details accordingly. It was a win-win for everyone involved.

'That's the strangest job interview I've ever seen,' muttered Lucas. 'Half of that lot probably can't even write their own name.'

'I don't think she wants them for their spelling ability,' said Mercy.

'I'd join her,' Tommy grinned. 'She wouldn't have to pay me double either. I'd work for free. Given half a chance I'd—'

'Do no such thing.'

Tommy jumped. His eyes fixed on the delectable vision that was Zara Carmichael, he hadn't noticed Agatha stroll up beside him.

'You work for me, Mr O'Strife,' she said, forcing a smile. 'All of you do. That is not up for debate. Now, what should we do with … with …?'

Agatha stopped. Vernon Gold had gone. Vanished before their very eyes. She looked around, finally locating him by the exit. He was being carried by three youths. Three youths who only a few short minutes ago had been part of his Gold Squad. Not anymore.

'You do not have to worry about our Mr Gold,' said Zara casually. 'I'll take care of him.'

'Will it be painful?' wondered Agatha.

'Do you need to ask?' On that note, Zara Carmichael departed the Everything's Electric nightclub. She had entered alone; now she was leaving with an army. The lion had found her pride.

'And then there were six,' said Agatha, as the five of them joined Miles in the entrance.

'Seven.' Mercy gestured over her shoulder at Cutz who, against all the odds, had inched his way across the dance floor.

'I'll call an ambulance,' said Agatha. She didn't remove her phone. 'Is that it?'

'Not quite,' said Tommy. 'Doberman's still out the back, feeling sorry for himself.'

'How sorry?' Agatha asked. 'He's not dead, is he?'

'Not the last time I looked,' shrugged Tommy. 'He's nursing a nasty wound, though. Rose shot him in the arse.'

'Of course she did.' Agatha rolled her eyes as she led them out into the early morning gloom. The streets had cleared, a peaceful harmony descending upon the town. 'Because that's what you do, isn't it? You four. You take a perfectly normal situation and twist it into something unexpected. Nothing's ever simple. Straight forward. It's a miracle you're all still alive if I'm being honest.'

'I didn't think we were,' said Lucas, slamming the door shut as the last one out. '*You* told us that yourself, Miss Pleasant. We've been dead from the moment you first met us.'

THE AFTERMATH

CHAPTER SEVENTY-TWO

Agatha waited on the sidelines, alone but for her thoughts.

The funeral of Benjamin Daniel Hammerton was drawing to an end. A burial. Peculiar in this day and age when so many preferred to be cremated. Maybe it was one of those fancy ones. Bio-degradable cardboard coffins. A clear conscience for the Eco-friendly amongst us. Thinking of the future at a time when it no longer matters to you. Very noble. Agatha herself was woefully ignorant to the endless possibilities available to her. That would have to change, of course. At some point she would have to do her research, especially in her line of work. Prepare for the inevitable. And sooner rather than later if the last few weeks were anything to go by.

Agatha, stood beside a bench, not sat, far too wet, looked on as the mourners started to disperse. Grim-faced and sombre, the occasional passer-by glanced at her, but saw nothing to hold their gaze. Not to worry. There was only one person's eye Agatha wanted to catch. The father of the deceased. The man she had promised to help.

Roger Hammerton, his arm around his wife's waist, was chatting to an elderly couple. Friends, guessed Agatha. Neighbours. Close, but not that close. A stiff handshake, no awkward hugs. There through obligation, not love. Fair enough. No need to give your reasons.

Agatha shifted slightly, disturbed to note that the damp grass had soaked through her shoes. She was growing impatient. With herself, more than anything. It shouldn't have been this difficult. How to grab a man's attention at a funeral when you've not been invited? There was probably a book out there somewhere. Step by step instructions. Don't wave. Don't jump up and down. And definitely do not shout.

Hiya. It's me. Aggie. Have you got a minute, Rog?

Chance took the lead and Roger looked over regardless. Did a double take. He had seen her. He returned to the couple and, just for a moment, Agatha thought that that was it. He had ignored her. Pretended she wasn't there. Then he turned again. Released his grip on Cynthia, made his excuses. He was coming over.

Agatha readied herself for a potentially volatile conversation.

'You don't have to stand in the shadows,' began Roger, forcing a smile.

'Old habits are hard to break,' Agatha replied. 'Besides, I didn't like to intrude. I'm not naive, Roger. Not everyone would welcome me with open arms. Cynthia for instance ...'

'Cynthia?' Roger probed his shirt collar, loosened his tie.

'Well, I wouldn't say … she's not … yes, you're probably right. Best to keep out of her way when emotions are running high.'

'I don't blame her for holding a grudge,' said Agatha. 'My team were the last ones to see Benji. To speak to him.'

'How did he seem?' asked Roger, his question snapping at her heels.

Agatha hesitated. 'Honestly?'

'You were never anything but.'

'He was scared,' Agatha admitted. 'He'd had enough. He wasn't a villain; he just got sucked in by the lifestyle.' She stopped. Drew breath. 'He wanted to come home. Back to you and Cynthia. And we were so close to getting him out of there. I'm sorry, Roger. We did everything we could, but the wheels were already in motion.'

'I know. Thanks for trying.' Roger seemed to drift off momentarily. He had something else to say, but couldn't quite spit it out. 'Amelia,' he mumbled eventually. 'Our granddaughter. Did you …?'

Agatha gently shook her head. 'That was never going to happen. We only found out after Benji's death, but Gina had a miscarriage days before her due date. Gina's a mess now. Drugs. I'm sorry nobody told you.' Agatha paused. 'I'm sorry it's had to come from me.'

Roger ran a hand over his face. He looked exhausted. Drained by the last few days … weeks … months. Time had taken its toll. But then time tends to do that.

'What's done is done,' he said, louder than Agatha would've expected. He puffed out his chest, lifted his chin.

New man, new start. No point crying over spilt milk. Best make the most of what we've got. Agatha wasn't fooled, though. He had lost a son and a granddaughter in the blink of an eye. Yes, they had been elsewhere, living different lives, not even living at all, but, to Roger, they were still there. An apology away. A phone call from forgiveness. A motorway from a reunion.

Now they were gone. Gone for good. No coming back from that.

Roger gestured over his shoulder. 'Cynthia will be wondering where I am. I shouldn't leave her with Terry and Fiona for too long. No bloody tact those two. Listen, we're going back to the Beggar's Arms if you fancy it. Just sandwiches. Nothing too fancy …' The look on Agatha's face was enough for him to break off. 'No, of course not. Well, I guess that's that. Thanks for coming. Be seeing you.'

Agatha smiled weakly. 'If there's anything you ever need, you know how to reach me.'

'Let's hope not,' muttered Roger, turning to leave.

Agatha held her ground whilst he wandered back towards both the funeral and his future. Then she left herself. Head down, she walked swiftly across the length of the graveyard towards the Audi. Olaf was waiting for her there. Honest, dependable Olaf. He could take her back to Stainmouth, back to the hotel where her bags were already packed. The room had been paid for in advance. No extras. She had even tidied up after herself. As far as she was aware there was nothing to keep her in Stainmouth a minute longer than was necessary.

There was nothing to keep any of them in Stainmouth.

Miles would be pleased. He could get back to his family. His wife. His child or children. Agatha wasn't sure how many. Maybe she should ask some time. Show an interest, even if it was all just a pretence. As for the others, her Nearly Dearly Departed Club, she would have to keep them on a short leash. They couldn't just go back home, resurrect their old lives, that much was obvious. She had already planned to set them up in another town, another city, maybe another country. The possibilities were endless. She would have to choose wisely, though.

The funeral had brought closure. That was it. She had drawn a line in the sand. Tied a ribbon around the box. Washed her hands of the entire situation.

It was over.

The end.

CHAPTER SEVENTY-THREE

At least, it should have been the end.

Agatha had almost made it to Olaf and the Saab when one of her phones began to vibrate. She found the offending article and removed it from her handbag. Studied the screen.

No caller ID.

That made sense. Not many people had that number.

Not many people … with one added extra. Clifford Goose. The Chief Constable. He had called her several days ago. Maybe a week. Time flies when you're busy clearing up loose ends.

The phone was still vibrating.

Surely it wasn't Goose. As far as Agatha was concerned they had nothing left to say to one another. Cross fingers, she would never have to see him again.

No, it couldn't be Goose. It wouldn't be Goose. It wasn't Goose.

Agatha took the call.

'About bloody time, woman. No one takes that long to answer the ruddy phone.'

Goose.

Agatha moved the phone away from her ear. She wanted to toss it in the bushes and drive off. Dare she do that? Would it come back to haunt her?

Two very different answers. Categorically no. Most certainly yes.

'You still there?' barked Goose.

Deep breath. Clear voice. 'Yes, I'm still here.'

'Thank the sweet lord for that,' said Goose, breathing far too heavily into the speaker. 'I want a word with you.'

'Clearly. Otherwise you wouldn't have called.'

'Hey? What's that? Well, yeah, quite. Listen, let's not fanny about with the fishes. There's been a change of plan.'

Agatha closed her eyes. She had formed a mental picture of Goose sat at his desk, legs spread, drink in hand. Stained tie and dirty collar, proud as punch. *I am what I am ... I say it how it is ... if you don't like it then tough titties.* He was a relic from the past. A dinosaur from a different age. Not a T-Rex or Triceratops either. One of the shit ones that nobody ever remembers. Agatha didn't need to speak to him. She was better than that. And yet ...

'What plan?' she asked.

'*Your* bloody plan!' cried Goose. 'You've pleasantly surprised me, Miss Pleasant, no pun intended. I thought you and your elite squad were going to be nothing but an inconvenience. And I was right. At first. But now ... well, now I'm prepared to admit that I was wrong. Seems like you've come up trumps, after all.'

'Go on,' said Agatha.

'Vernon Gold has vanished,' revealed Goose. 'There's

been no sign of him in days. And his big brute ... I don't know ... Bulldog or something—'

'Doberman.'

'Yeah, that's the laddie. Nasty piece of work, he is. Proper villain. Well, they both are. Always popping up on the radar. Drugs. Intimidation and violence. You can even trace a few deaths back to those two.'

Agatha watched as Roger and Cynthia Hammerton guided the last of the mourners away from Benji's grave. 'I can imagine.'

'Well, now he's scarpered, too,' Goose continued. 'Both of them ... Gold and his gorilla ... gone. Just like that. In a puff of smoke. As if by magic. Now, I'm no intellectual, Miss Pleasant, but I'm thinking that might have something to do with you.'

'Me?' Agatha feigned surprise. 'What makes you think that?'

'Intuition,' said Goose smugly. 'I've been in this game a long time, love. I can feel it in my water. Listen, I'm not complaining. You've done me a favour. A huge favour. Stainmouth is a much better place without lowlife like Vernon Gold polluting the atmosphere. And that's why I've had a word. I've spoken to those at the top. The powers that be. Even your superior, Lady Jane herself. And they all agree with me.'

Agatha sighed. This could all have been avoided if she had just ignored the call.

'You're staying,' announced Goose. 'In Stainmouth. You and your band of merry men. And ... erm ... women. Your wonderful women. Even that one that broke into my bloody house. That's all forgotten now by the way. No hard feelings. So, if you hang around here for the foreseeable and help out whenever the chance arises then everybody's happy, right?'

'Everybody?' hissed Agatha.

'Don't be such a sourpuss,' Goose shot back. 'It's not that bad in Stainmouth. Admittedly, we've not got the glitz and glamour of London.'

'More spit and sawdust.'

'Exactly. Honest folk leading honest lives. Mostly. You're here to clear up the minority. The rogue element. Those undesirables who choose to operate outside the law. Police can't do it all, you know. Our hands are tied. Yours, however, appear to be unburdened by rules and regulations and all that other shite.'

'I don't know what to say,' muttered Agatha.

'There's not much you can,' laughed Goose. 'It's a done deal. I'll be in touch, Miss Pleasant. When I need you.'

Goose ended the call abruptly. No long goodbyes or stumbling exchanges. It left Agatha gazing at her phone. Pondering her future. Wondering how her life had just taken an enormous swerve in little more than a few minutes.

Opening the door, she slid onto the backseat of the Audi and fastened her seatbelt. Olaf was staring straight ahead with his hands on the steering wheel. There was no doubt that he had heard the entire phone conversation, but you would never have guessed. He was good like that. Discreet.

Agatha cleared her throat. 'The Nightingale Hotel please, Olaf. I need to unpack my things.'

Olaf turned slightly. Unusual for him. 'I thought we were leaving.'

'Leaving?' Agatha forced a smile. 'No, there's been a change of plan, I'm afraid. If anything, we've only just arrived.'

CHAPTER SEVENTY-FOUR

They found Tommy outside in one of the barns, sat on the edge of the pen.

He was talking to the pigs. It was relentless. A constant stream of blabbering rhetoric. Chatter for chatter's sake. No commas or full stops. And certainly no breaths. Breathing was for wimps. Besides, if you paused for even a second you might forget where you were, lose momentum, drift off topic. No, it was better to just keep going. Let the pigs decide if it was interesting or not. They could always walk away if they didn't like it.

And yet, curiously, they *did* like it. They seemed to be hanging on his every word. Taking it all in between snorts and snuffles.

One heavy footstep, however, was enough to knock Tommy off his stride. 'Oh, here they are,' he pretended to whisper. 'The boring ones. Best not talk about them anymore, my little porkers. Wouldn't want to get on their wrong side now, would we?' Tommy leapt to his feet, instantly regretting it when the pain awoke from its slumber. Suddenly, everywhere hurt. His bones. His organs. Even his brain. Not that surprising really. It wasn't that long ago that Doberman had almost choked the life out of him.

It wasn't that long ago, in fact, that he had died …

Tommy tried not to think. Thinking just dragged him down. Anyway, there were more important things to focus on than the past. Starting with the present. 'When we leaving?'

'We're not.' Like his sentence, Lucas came to an abrupt halt, the others falling into line beside him.

Tommy responded with a simple nod. Then he sat back down on the edge of the pen, the pigs, once again, the centre of his attention.

Mercy left a suitable gap, just to be sure. 'Well, that was unexpected. We thought you'd lose your head. Kick off.'

'Lots of shouting and swearing,' added Lucas. 'And yet … you don't seem that bothered.'

Tommy shrugged. 'Don't I? Who knows? What's happened to change your minds?'

'This isn't our doing,' said Mercy. 'Miles called. He's spoken to Agatha. Apparently, Stainmouth needs us.'

'We did such a good job with Vernon Gold they want us to hang around a bit longer,' said Lucas. 'We can't go even if we wanted to. Unless …' He paused. 'We've been talking—'

'And now you're going to tell me what you've already decided,' finished Tommy.

'No, now we're going to ask you what happened that afternoon,' said Mercy, correcting him. 'When you stormed off in the Fiat. We thought you'd gone, got out of here for good. You've never really spoken about it. We know you crashed the car—'

'I didn't crash.' Tommy checked himself. 'Okay, I *did* crash, but it had nothing to do with me.'

'It was an accident,' said Mercy.

'No, not an accident.' Tommy stewed over his words. 'There's something in my head. In all our heads probably. I was driving away ... I had gone so far ... and then *bang*!' Tommy winced at the memory. 'It was like an explosion in my skull. Almost as if someone was drilling a hole into my brain.'

'Must've been one hell of a small drill,' smirked Lucas.

Tommy ignored him. 'I never want to experience that pain again. I can't. And if that means I have to stay here, at Cockleshell Farm, a little longer than I hoped, then so be it.' He studied the others. Their faces. Expressions. They seemed to be listening. Appeared to understand. There was one, however, that gave nothing away. That he couldn't read, whatever the circumstances. 'What do you reckon, Rose?'

Rose stiffened at the sound of her name. She wasn't expecting that. Her opinion of all things. She could always just shake her head. Stare at her shoes. Pretend it wasn't happening.

No, not this time. This time she had something to say.

'We've no choice but to do as they ask,' she began, her voice increasing in volume with every word. 'Things have already been decided so there's no point trying to fight it. Our only option is to toe the line.'

Mercy turned to look at her. Frowned. 'Tell me there's a *but*. There's got to be. Because, if there's not, well, that's got to be the most depressing motivational speech I've ever heard.'

'There's not a *but*,' said Rose. 'There's an *until*. Until the moment comes. Until the opportunity arises. And then we make our move. We're not dead. And I don't want to die. That's what I've learnt during my time here. Yes, we should all be grateful we're still alive, but that's not to say that one day we can't live the life we want to live. Not the one that's been forced upon us.'

Tommy started to clap. 'Well said. Now, would anyone mind shortening it into one easy to understand sentence?'

'This is all a bit shit, but it won't last forever,' said Mercy.

'That'll do me.' Tommy opened his arms. Beckoned the others towards him. 'Bring it in, people. Group hug.'

Seconds trickled past as time seemed to grind to an uncomfortably awkward halt. And then it happened. Mercy moved in first. Rose followed. And Lucas ... well, he could hardly say no, could he? They already thought he was a cold fish. Stiffly serious. Maybe it was time to loosen up a little. Throw off the shackles.

Wrapping his arms around the other three, Tommy drew them close and, for a moment, felt something that he had never felt before. A stirring sensation. What was it? Pride? Joy? Love?

Or just somebody else's phone vibrating against his leg?

Mercy broke away first so she could answer. She listened. She nodded. And then she spoke. Just a single word before ending the call.

Okay.

'Who was that?' asked Lucas, unravelling himself from Tommy's grip.

'Miles,' replied Mercy. 'He's coming over. Says it's urgent.'

And that was that. Without another word, they set off back towards the farmhouse. Mercy, Lucas and Rose. Three out of four. Only Tommy remained. The feeling, the stirring sensation, had passed. Maybe one day it would return. Maybe not.

'Are you coming?' asked Mercy, poking her head back inside the barn.

'Just saying my goodbyes.' Tommy gestured towards the pigs. 'I know them all by name so it might take a while. I mean, I wouldn't want to upset them, would I? Good friends are so hard to find these days.'

'They're not your only friends.'

Tommy smiled. 'I'll remind you of that next time I piss you off.'

'Shouldn't have to wait too long for that,' said Mercy, before ducking out of sight.

Tommy stood up. Walked towards the exit. The pigs seemed disappointed, but it was nothing to get their trotters in a twist about. He'd be back soon. That was a promise. They could wait.

The Nearly Dearly Departed Club, however, would not.

THE END

THE

NEARLY DEARLY DEPARTED CLUB…

WILL RETURN …

ACKNOWLEDGEMENTS

Big thanks to …

The wondrous Sian Phillips for her eagle-eyed editing skills and glowing praise.

The incomparable Stuart Bache and all the team at Books Covered for the front cover.

The exceptional Polgarus Studio for their first-rate formatting.

Right, I can put the thesaurus away now …

Printed in Great Britain
by Amazon